HEARTS ABROAD

SKYE MCNEIL

HOT TREE PUBLISHING

For information, contact the publisher, Hot Tree Publishing.
WWW.HOTTREEPUBLISHING.COM

EDITING: HOT TREE EDITING

COVER DESIGNER: SOXSATIONAL COVER ART

FORMATTING: RMGraphX

ISBN: 978-1-925853-20-9

LIST OF BOOKS

*For Josh L. Even though you beat me at NaNoWriMo
while I was writing this story,
you consistently encourage me as a writer
and I appreciate your friendship.
P.S. Totally going to win this year.*

CHAPTER ONE

A Summer Love, by Blake Connelly. The name and title stood out boldly on the cheap piece of paper at the other end of Londyn Bellerose's nose.

Son of a bitch.

Blinking, she hoped the outcome would differ at the next flick of her gray-blue eyes. Nope. Her ex-boyfriend's name was still there and hers wasn't. *Dammit.* Now he would cast and direct the theater's summer play. It wasn't the big time, but if the play did well, Broadway bigwigs would attend. One playwright even snagged a job alongside the bright lights last year and hit it big. It was why every writer associated with the Wilder Theater participated in the competition in hopes of joining the red-carpet stars. Once upon a time, Ryan Wilder performed on Broadway. He still rubbed shoulders with the executives, though the connection wasn't the best if judged by his theater's overall condition.

"Oh, hey, Londyn, sorry about that. Better luck next time, eh?" Blake said, popping his head over her shoulder. It was an annoying habit of his. One she didn't miss when he left her for a short, cute blonde who was also his ex-girlfriend.

"Congrats, Blake," she ground out, twirling around. "I'm sure you really deserved it." A crowd of playwrights and actors milled about, making her determined escape nearly impossible.

"I'll need a good stagehand," he called after her.

Coming to a halt, Londyn took a deep breath and resisted the urge to knock him on his ass. She could do it too. They both knew she cowrote the winning play, but he took all the credit. Another one of his nasty habits.

"Or maybe a personal assistant," he added, laughing.

Ick. She cringed. That damn laugh she used to love now sounded like the mating call of a cicada. Repetitive, annoying, and shrill.

She smirked. *Not unlike his lovemaking skills.*

"But I don't have a role for you, sorry," he snorted. "You're too tall."

She clenched her jaw so tight she swore it would shatter. A chorus of snickers accompanied Blake then. No doubt his posse of assholes was standing alongside him with shit-eating grins.

Turning, she replied, "Thank God. I didn't want

to deal with another pompous, short prick anyway." She flicked her long chestnut-colored hair over one shoulder and met Blake's eyes. "They're terrible kissers and worse lovers."

Blake's mouth dropped open and his gaggle of guys roared with laughter.

Scrunching her nose in disgust as a final gesture, Londyn whirled around and disappeared through the throng of thespians. Normally she wasn't one to make a scene, but they were in a theater, dammit, and drama was necessary in such a situation. Her face burned with rage and embarrassment when she tripped over her feet as she turned the corner. She'd had enough for the day, and only one person could understand her plight.

Ducking into the wardrobe room, she exclaimed, "I hate Blake."

That received no response from the woman sitting behind a sewing machine.

"He's a dick," she said, plopping face first into the outdated orange couch.

"You've known this, doll."

Londyn propped her chin on her fist and glared at her best friend of five years, Abi Baker. Her skin was a perfect dark-caramel color and she had the brownest of eyes to emphasize her origins. She was the result when dark chocolate mixed with white chocolate. Pure perfection. "Yeah, well, I didn't think he'd steal my play."

At that, Abi's sewing machine stopped. Her alert

eyes whipped to Londyn. "He did what?"

"He changed most of it—"

"But still, Londyn." Abi adjusted the needle and positioned the shirt under it. "You should talk to the director. He'd look into it, at least."

Sinking into the cushion that smelled of cheesy puffs, Londyn listened to the hum of the sewing machine. Even if she brought it to Mr. Wilder's attention, it wouldn't matter. The director, who was also the owner of the theater, adored Blake. Short, black-haired, blue-eyed Blake and his perfect smile. Even if the man investigated, Blake would prevail.

"You can resubmit your play in the fall," Abi reminded her.

"If he didn't choose mine this time, he won't in three months." She eyed the ceiling and wondered how in the hell a basketball got wedged up in the rafters.

"Maybe you should send it to one of those Broadway directors we met last week. They seemed interested in you."

"Seeing how the old guy was checking me out and the other slipped me his number, I think they were interested in something else entirely."

"You're no fun."

"I've been at it five years, Abs." Londyn closed her eyes. "If I can't make it here, I sure can't make it anywhere else."

A moment of silence settled over the two women, and Londyn wondered if she was right. The upcoming fall would mark the start of year six since she left Ankeny, Iowa for a bigger stage to write plays. The one time her script was chosen, Mr. Wilder took over all direction since she was still finding her footing in Queens.

Well, her size eleven feet were plenty sturdy these days. The problem arose when she wouldn't sleep her way or kiss ass to the top of the stack of plays awaiting processing.

She picked at her cuticle as the memories surfaced of her fresh eyes on the New York skyline. That lasted a whole two days before she realized the NYC theaters wanted more than college experience to join their crew. She'd done plenty of dramas, comedies, and musicals, but writing was her passion. So she'd moved to another borough and tried her luck in Queens. Thus far, she was 100 percent sure she wasn't Irish by blood. The string of rejections of her plays from larger theaters reiterated that luck wasn't on her side. At least not at the moment. She held out hope that eventually, she'd hit the jackpot and would leave the Wilder Theater behind for good.

"You're brooding," her friend pointed out.

Londyn rolled to her side and watched Abi tie off a stitch. The woman was a wonder. She'd even made them matching sundresses for the upcoming summer months. There wasn't much her best friend couldn't create with thread and needle. "Yeah, so?"

"So go home, order Orange Dragon Chinese, pop in a chick flick." She paused. "Oh, and don't eat all the chocolate before I get done here."

A smile found Londyn's lips as she sat up. "This is why I love you." She stood and quickly kissed Abi's cheek. "You always know what will cheer me up." Grabbing her purse, she added, "Don't stay too long. My self-control is really lacking tonight. I'm liable to do anything. Three orders of pot stickers sound delicious right about now."

"Save me some," her friend called.

Breezing out of the room filled with enough wardrobe changes to clothe a packed theater, Londyn navigated the backstage maze to one of the exits. Once outside, she let out a sigh of relief and slipped on her sunglasses. The sunny disposition of the June day did wonders for her sulking mood.

As she walked up the street, a loud squeak from the theater door caught her attention. Looking over her shoulder, she eyed the group of stagehands loitering in front of the door, homemade cigarettes in hand. Though she was positive nicotine wasn't the ingredient in the rolled paper.

The neon sign above the exit blinked, warning that the bulbs were on their last legs. The same could be said for the whole place. The dumpster to the left smelled of food from the Indian restaurant down the street, and stray cats sunned along the cracked sidewalk. No, this wasn't Broadway. It wasn't even Off-Broadway. It was way, way, way Off-Off-Broadway's cousin once removed. As in a run-down community theater in Queens.

Hailing a cab, Londyn's journey to the one-bedroom apartment in Forest Hills went smoothly. After paying the driver, she climbed up the two flights of stairs and unlocked the front door. Abi's cat, Oreo, meowed at her entry.

"Hey, buddy," she greeted, dropping her purse.

The black-and-white cat who looked as though he wore a fancy tuxedo jumped on the counter and nudged her hand with his furry head. Absently, Londyn stroked the puffball and surveyed the tiny apartment. She and Abi met at an improv group, and she moved in the following week. They were soul mates, if those existed for best friends. Abi's love of all things fashion only helped when it came to their love for the theater.

When not at the theater, her dark-haired roommate worked at a retail-clothing store while Londyn passed her time at a café up the road. All in all, their arrangement worked, even if neither of their dreams was happening. *Yet.* Abi wanted to design for the runway, while Londyn dreamed to write and direct plays for the masses. Broadway was her end goal, even if it was a lofty one.

"Have a good day?" she asked as Oreo followed her to the bedroom. Since they couldn't afford a two-bedroom, they cut the room in half with an antique changing screen they'd found at a local flea market. After a bit of a cleanup, the divider worked like a charm. Neither had a steady boyfriend, so the cramped space suited their situation just fine. Ninety percent of the time, the screen was bunched up to allow for better communication between the roommates. Oreo's large cat tower also helped chop up the room since it was positioned between the two beds. The chubber liked to jump from bed to bed and then back to his perch as often as possible, so they left it in the middle of the room.

"Because I didn't. It sucked like a leech in Cass Lake, Minnesota." She kicked off her shoes and collapsed on the bed. Oreo hopped on her back the next instant. "Damn, even you walk all over me," she mumbled with her face in the pillow.

The cat chattered, then proceeded to knead her back before curling into a ball and purring.

"I know I should've said something, but it isn't worth it. The play is decent, but not good enough for Broadway."

Oreo licked the back of her neck and Londyn laughed. When life sucked, it helped to have a one-sided conversation with a cat who loved her to pieces. Mostly because she snuck him lo mein and chicken leftovers.

Rolling her eyes, Londyn reached for her phone and saw a new voice mail from her aunt. It'd been a month since their last chat; for the duo who usually spoke every other day, she was overdue. She listened to the short message, then dialed Glenda's number. The woman took her in at ten years old and never let go. She had to commend the then thirty-seven-year-old for putting her career on the back burner until Londyn was back to normal following the car accident that took her parents' lives.

"There's my favorite niece," Glenda greeted. "How are you, sweet girl? I've missed talking to you."

The cheerfulness in her aunt's voice instantly brought up the day's events, and tears welled in her eyes. In one rushed breath, Londyn spilled the horrid details of the script fiasco. Tears slipped down her cheeks and her nose dripped by the time she finished.

"Oh, honey, that sounds terrible. I'm so sorry," Glenda consoled. "Do you want me to come up there and kick his ass? Because I've really hit my stride in my kickboxing class."

She smirked. "No, Auntie, your ninja skills won't be necessary. I got a good jab in before I left."

"That's my girl."

Oreo nuzzled the back of her head, and she reached over and scratched his chin.

"So, I was thinking. Why don't you come back to Iowa for the summer?" Glenda suggested.

Londyn didn't even blink before responding. "I can't. I have a life here." Glenda was her mom's sister, but the two couldn't have been more different. While her mother was a quiet teacher, her aunt spoke her mind and took no prisoners. All in all, Londyn was grateful to be a combination of both ladies who had formed her life and personality.

Glenda sighed on the other end. "Oh, I know, but

Londyn, you're a waitress at a coffee shop that doesn't pay you enough, your ex just got his big break with *your* play, and I miss you. You need a little time away from New York."

While she thought it over, Londyn listened to the wail of the train outside her window. She barely heard it after all this time, but the rails still wobbled the apartment and sometimes sent items off-kilter. If she was honest, a summer away from Queens didn't sound so bad. It felt a little like running away, though. She tended to have more of a flight response instead of fight.

"But what about Abi?" she began. "She'd be all alone, and rent—"

"I'll cover the rent and your friend will be fine." Her aunt giggled. "Hell, she'd probably agree with me."

"Well—"

"Come home, find an easy job, or none. I don't care. Soak up some rays by the pool at the country club with me, and then we can take a few weekend trips. It'll be fun."

Londyn rubbed her hands over Oreo's fur until he hopped off the bed. "What about—"

"Just the summer. Three months, sweetie. You hate making coffee, or so you've said every time you call. You need a break. No, you *deserve* a break."

Fidgeting with the ring on her pinky finger, she sighed. It'd do her good to get away from the city. She'd never admit it, but she was struggling to find her place there. She thought it'd be easy once she was accepted into the theater community, but that never really happened. Time to reflect on her future may do her good.

"All right, fine. But just until the fall. I have another play I can fine-tune while I'm in Iowa. I have a feeling it'll knock the socks off the director the next time around."

"Yay! And yes, it will. I have faith in you. Now, travel plans." Glenda babbled on about what fun they'd have, then confirmed that she'd already booked a flight for her niece. It was for the very next day, leaving little time for Londyn to collect her thoughts, much less clothes.

By the time they signed off, Londyn wasn't sure what to do next. Her aunt made plans a mile a minute, and she was lost halfway through the woman's ideas.

"Pack. I should pack first." She pulled out the suitcase from beneath her bed. It was blue, dusty, and full of black-and-white cat hair. Narrowing her eyes, she asked, "Oreo, have you been sleeping under my bed again?" The chubby cat opened one green eye from his perch on the cat tower. "Great. No time to get a new bag or even do laundry." She shrugged. Knowing her aunt, Glenda would buy a whole new wardrobe for her. The woman loved to shop. Londyn planned to wear a bikini most of the time anyhow.

The clock above the door struck five in the evening and her stomach growled. Dialing their favorite

Chinese restaurant, she ordered the usual vegetarian lo mein, chicken fried rice, hot and sour soup, and of course, gobs of pot stickers. She needed food in Abi's belly before she shared her news, and Chinese was the perfect segue to a good mood.

That task done, Londyn rifled through her drawers and tossed clothes into the bag—which Oreo dubbed his own when he lay amid her bras—until it was full. After gathering toiletries, the suitcase was ready to go.

"A summer in Iowa." She grinned. *Home*. It had been too long. Sure, she visited on holidays, but she never stayed more than a couple of weeks. She wasn't excited to see her old friends and their perfectly successful lives, but Glenda was her favorite person and one she missed dearly when she'd moved.

Walking to the living room, she scanned the shelf of movies. She chose one sure to please Abi, but it was also one of her favorites. Opening the DVD tray, she placed *10 Things I Hate About You* in the slot and pushed it in. It'd been a while since they'd watched that particular movie, but chick flicks were as common as breathing in their apartment. No matter what happened or the type of day they had, a romance movie could cure it.

Grabbing the bowl of chocolate candy from the kitchen, she set it on the coffee table next to the opened bottle of wine and two wineglasses. *Chinese, chick flicks, and chocolate—all the best things start with Cs.* She nodded once as if to cement her thought.

Abi's voice filled the air and Londyn's nerves jumbled. While she'd miss her best friend, Iowa was calling.

Somehow, she just knew this summer would be different.

***

Married. Their nanny of three years was married. Apparently she'd eloped to Hawaii with her long-time girlfriend, and now he was without care for his two young daughters.

He couldn't be mad at her, though. The woman had spent most of her life caring for the Archer children, including him, so her personal happiness was long overdue.

Tapping his pen against the keyboard of his laptop, Callum Archer skimmed the ad his mother created in search of a new nanny, frowning when he reached the end. It sounded as though they were a snobby, proper family. Glancing up, he caught sight of his very British father in the painted portrait on the opposite wall, remembering that they were such a family. Well, his mother mostly, but he was sure some of it had trickled down to her only child.

"Mother, must we be so elaborate?" he asked. "This is a summer job, not a full-time career."

Mary Archer sat in the straight-backed chair across the massive desk. "Yes, Cal. These are your children—

my grandchildren—and they must have exceptional care, even if only for three months."

Callum stood to his six-foot-four height and pushed a hand through his dark-blond hair. "In that regard, I don't disagree. It's just—"

"I'll handle the interviews." She stood, her silver hair in a perfect bun at the nape of her neck. The same as it'd been his whole life. Much like other facets of her demeanor. His mother liked to take control, and he always let her.

"Sure. Seems appropriate."

"Don't you have a plane to catch?" she asked, walking to the door.

"Um, yes, I do. Thanks for the reminder." He closed the laptop and was relieved when she was gone by the time he looked up again. As much as he loved his only living parent, Mary Archer was a force to be reckoned with when it came to business. And everything with her was business.

His office phone rang, summoning him back to the present. "Yes?"

"Sir, your car is ready up front," the crisp voice of their butler said from the other end of the line.

"Thank you, Alfred. Can you have someone grab my bag? I'll be down in a minute."

Hanging up, Callum listened to the noises of the house. One gardener wrestled with rose bushes outside the window while another mowed the estate's lawns. Their aging basset hound, Sherlock, howled—at a squirrel up a tree, no doubt—while the animal caretaker begged him to return to the barn.

Those weren't the sounds he waited for, though.

Giggles drifted up from the hallway and the sweet tones washed over him, chasing all downtrodden thoughts asunder. The reasons for his existence—his girls—were playing in the games room. From the sound of it, they were having a grand time too.

A pang of remorse set in when he glanced at his watch. He didn't have time for a round of croquet or even one hand of cards before he had to leave. Again.

Sighing, Callum packed up his laptop and locked his office door. One too many times, priceless items had been broken in his haven, so a key was a necessity whenever he was gone.

Quietly he moved through the long hall until he reached the room that was once supposed to be a formal sitting room. That quickly changed when two toddlers took over the house. He could stand in the doorway forever merely watching them play, but the honk at the front door made that impossible.

"Lovelies, I'm leaving," he announced.

Four perfectly blue eyes pinned his feet to the hardwood floor. Lord, if he could only look into them without seeing *her*.

"But, Daddy, you said you'd take us horseback riding," Bailey protested with a pouty lip.

Hugging his youngest first, Callum kissed her cheek and brushed back her red braid. "I will, darling,

I promise. Right after I return from Dubai."

"That's what you said last week, except it was Tokyo," the oldest, Bethany, argued.

Callum's heart fractured a little at the pitiful expressions on their faces. Swallowing hard, he offered her a weak smile. "I know. I'm sorry." He hugged her but was met with resistance. "Work is very busy right now. I'll have more time to be with you two after I finish this new exhibit for the museum."

"When will it be done?" Bailey asked, tugging on his wrist.

He gently patted Bethany's cheek. "Not until August, I'm afraid."

Both girls grumped at his response, so he added, "But Grandmother is hiring a new nanny. She'll be here by the time I return. That I know for certain."

Bethany's freckled face beamed. "And she'll be pretty?"

"And fun?" Bailey chimed in.

"Oh, I'm sure she'll be everything you want and more." Another honk from the car. "But I'm late, girls. I'll call you tonight." He hugged them both at once. "Love you two so much."

The girls, who were two years apart, waved farewell, then returned to their tea party. It killed him to leave, but it was his job as head curator for one of London's most prestigious museums. He had no choice in the matter; he knew what the job entailed when he'd first started, and how the board desired him to take over the entire museum someday.

To his relief, his one bag was already in the waiting car when he arrived. He'd perfected simple packing over the last seven years.

"Have a pleasant trip, sir," Alfred said, closing the car door after Callum had settled.

Callum pulled out his sunglasses. "I always do."

He stared at the mountainous scenery until his phone rang from the seat beside him. He checked the caller ID and prepared himself. Taking the call from one of France's museums, he only remembered where he was when his driver opened the door at the airport. Long phone calls weren't uncommon for his job.

Before he knew it, the plane took off from Colorado Springs' airport. Firing up his handy e-reader, Callum flipped to the latest article about a newly discovered historical site in Turkey. Normally the subject of history and archaeology intrigued him, but for some reason he couldn't concentrate. After staring at the same page for five minutes, he put the device back in his bag. Focusing on work was what he did best, but today he was failing miserably.

Swiping through the photos on his smartphone, he smiled at Bailey and Bethany's cheery faces and matching blue eyes and red hair. They looked so much like their mother that it physically hurt to be around them. Pinching his septum, Callum tried not to think about his ex, Jessica.

Though they were never married, the redheaded

American beauty stole all his desire to ever love again. Thankfully she'd left their daughters when Bethany was a mere two years old, so the girls didn't remembered her at all. A fact he was grateful for on a daily basis. However, despite four years passing, Callum wouldn't allow himself a reprieve from Jessica's rejection.

Slouching in his seat, he stared out the window. She'd said she needed to find herself and chase her dreams. Evidently that meant without him or their two girls. To this day, he didn't know what he did wrong. They'd seemed happy, even if he was gone most of the time for work. She never said anything or let on that she wasn't content with their life, which made the midnight disappearance all that more painful. And of course, it was on his Christmas Eve birthday. A lovely reminder he couldn't forget as each Christmas passed.

The few times Jessica attempted to make contact with him, he'd sent her packing. Legally, he was the sole parent to Bailey and Bethany; his mother's entourage of attorneys saw to that when they terminated Jessica's parental rights. Now and then, the aspiring model would call or send him emails. Those were the times when she was sober or bored. It didn't happen much anymore, though, and he was glad.

He nodded at the flight attendant as she rolled down first class with her cart. The desire to down a glass of bourbon made him lift his finger to the brunette. He rarely drank at university, but once he met Jessica, it became second nature when she'd ignore him for days on end.

I should've seen it coming.

Jessica's abandonment hurt him more than the girls, but he could handle it. At least, he told himself that lie. Work was his mistress ever since, and he didn't see that ever changing. Those two beautiful girls were all he needed.

Love was something of the past, and nothing about the upcoming summer would change his mind.

CHAPTER TWO

Chomping on the strawberry garnish, Londyn watched her aunt fawn over the man in the shirt befitting a Hawaiian adventure. She slurped the margarita and rolled her eyes when Glenda's high-pitched laugh rang out amid the humid day. They were supposed to be relaxing at the club's pool, but instead, Londyn had been abandoned when Glenda's boyfriend showed up after his round of golf. Now she was lucky to get any attention at all.

The whole beau thing wasn't surprising. Glenda was a hottie back in the day, and she had the money to maintain her perfect appearance. Thankfully, her aunt didn't do too much dating during Londyn's youth, though it was why she'd been set on moving out as soon as she turned eighteen. Her aunt deserved a life after a child was unexpectedly dropped in her lap, and

Londyn wanted to make sure she had one.

Lathering sunscreen over her shoulders, Londyn groaned when the two sixty-year-olds kissed. Glancing around, she realized they weren't the only couple necking by the pool. She was surrounded by love. It was the summer, after all. *Isn't that a big faux pas about the summertime? A fling for three months, and then you never see them again.* She rubbed in the lotion as she pondered. *I wouldn't mind that one bit.*

Glenda and Stew—as he was introduced the other night—chatted in low tones, making Londyn glance away. Her phone chirped with a new message, so she opened it to see a text from Abi.

Abi: Hey, girl. Miss you. How's Iowa?

Londyn: Other than auntie having a new BF? Boring, but that's Iowa.

Abi: Oh, ew! You find a job?

Londyn paused her fingers and glanced to the tablet on the poolside table. She'd skimmed over the classifieds, but nothing stuck out earlier. A job was a necessity if Glenda was going to act like a teenager for the duration of her stay.

Londyn: Not yet. Still looking. How're things there?

Abi: Cool. Oreo's fat and sleeps on your bed, work's dumb, and Blake is bombing his auditions. It's so funny.

Smirking, Londyn sent a plethora of emojis to her best friend. It came as no shock that Blake wasn't doing so hot. He was a decent actor, but a director he was not.

Londyn: Good. Maybe they'll choose a good play next time.

Abi: Agreed. So, don't get mad, but I may have sent in one of your plays to a Broadway exec…

The grin slipped off Londyn's face and she hurriedly dialed her friend. This wasn't text message news. She sat up straight as the phone rang, causing an instant head rush from the frozen alcoholic drink.

"Abi, what the hell were you thinking? Are you crazy?" she asked when her friend picked up. "What play did you send? How could you?"

Her heart raced at the thought of a director scouring her script. She was planning to send one, just not until she edited more.

"Okay, calm down, Londyn," her friend said once she had the chance. "It was the play you should've entered in the competition. *Rampant Thoughts* is the title, I think."

Closing her eyes, Londyn grimaced despite it being her best work. "Abs, it's not ready."

"Oh, baloney. I read it and it's fabulous. Even Oreo thinks so."

Not taking an illiterate cat's opinion as gospel, Londyn groaned. "And you won't tell me who you sent it to, will you?"

Abi snorted. "Ha! And risk you calling and begging them to return it? No. Sorry, girl. You should've sent it a long time ago. I did you a favor."

"We'll see about that." She tightened her ponytail. "You know I'm pissed at you, right?"

"Bah, you'll forget and forgive me by the time you get back."

Londyn smirked. Abi wasn't wrong there. Forgiving and forgetting was something she did without even realizing it. Though usually not with men. They were another beast entirely.

"You're probably right." She couldn't forget the whole sending of the play bit, but she had zero control over the situation. Shrugging, she figured whatever happened couldn't be worse than losing to her ex-boyfriend.

Abi sighed. "Well, now that you're in Iowa, see any cute guys? I'll bet there are so many there."

Londyn looked around the pool area. There were a few decent-looking men, but none she would clamor for. "Nah."

"Boo, you're no fun. It's been six months since you broke up with Blake." Her friend's voice took on a sultry tone. "You need to get back out there and explore. Maybe taste a few exotic guys before—"

"Abi—"

"No excuses. You ran away from Queens—not that I blame you—so now I'm demanding you get some hanky-panky." Before Londyn could argue, Abi added, "Just a summer fling, girl. You know, the hot, sweltering sex with no commitment type. And did I mention sweaty sex?"

Londyn laughed at her best friend's antics. The woman was diabolical when it came to relationships. It was probably why they got along so well—neither could sustain a steady man.

"Yes, you mentioned it." She adjusted the towel behind her back. "I wouldn't mind a summer thing."

"Good, it's settled. You hop on the first sexy guy you see."

"Not sure about that, but I'll keep my options open, okay?" Londyn promised.

"Good enough. I gotta run. Text me later. Kisses!" Abi signed off.

Placing the iPhone on the table, Londyn settled back into the comfortable pool chair. The sun's rays melted into her skin, a tan more than likely after a week of doing nothing but that same act every day.

"Londyn, honey," her aunt called, flip-flops smacking the concrete. "Are you having a good time?"

Pushing off her shades, Londyn met her aunt's brown eyes. "It'd be more fun if it was just us."

Glenda perched on the edge of her seat. "Aw, I'm sorry. Stew and I started seeing each other not long ago." She lowered her eyes to her lap. "If you want, I can tell him to go."

"Ugh, no, I'm not a child." She couldn't resist that pout if she tried. It was Glenda's trademark move. Londyn was certain it was how she made her business as a realtor such a thriving success.

Grabbing the iPad, Londyn ignored the article

her aunt had been reading about an heiress, Ireland Leighton, who'd returned to Iowa. As enticing as the gossip blog about a local celebrity sounded, she scanned the newly published classifieds. "I've been thinking about getting a job. All this fun in the sun is draining."

Glenda grinned and snatched the tablet from her. "Ooh, then let me help." Her finger scrolled up the page. "Have you ever considered coming back to Iowa? I could show you the ropes of being a real estate agent if you wanted. Then you could slowly take it over for me."

She knew Glenda was offering her an out. She'd done it more than once since Londyn's move to New York, but this time felt different.

A part of Londyn wanted to accept the offer; she was down on her luck in Queens, and the future looked dismal. "I don't know. I've never considered it."

Her aunt nodded. "All right, well why don't you think about it? The worst that can happen is you love it."

"Yeah, I guess you're right." Londyn took a sip of her drink. "How about I get a summer job, and then we can come back to that option?"

Glenda beamed at her niece. "I can live with those conditions. Now, let me see what we have here." Her manicured nail slid up the screen. "How about this one? 'Nanny needed for two young girls for the summer.'" She paused. "Oh wait, it's in Colorado."

Stealing the iPad again, Londyn read the ad. Memories flooded through her mind of the few vacations she'd had with her parents. Colorado was one of the locations that stood out, always new sights to see and places to go. "Hmm, this doesn't sound too bad, honestly. It pays really well." She bit her bottom lip. "I wouldn't have to take as many shifts at the coffeehouse this fall if I got it."

"You know I'll help you out, darling," her aunt reminded her. "It's no trouble."

Clicking on the link, she shook her head. "It is, Auntie. You've done so much for me already. I want to make it on my own. Plus, it's a good way to put money away for a rainy day." Her aunt's bottom lip quivered again, so she added, "I'm twenty-eight, for God's sake. I should be sending you money."

"Soon enough." Glenda patted her leg. "Are you going to send your résumé?"

"You know, I think I am." She grinned. "I loved being a nanny in college, and this job has so many perks. Just listen to this: a car, room, food, unlimited credit card for activities, travel, and more. It's a dream come true."

"Well if you say so. I'm not keen on you leaving again." Glenda sipped her mai tai and sat back under the umbrella.

"Aw, don't be like that. You have Stew, remember? You don't need me around cramping your style." She uploaded her résumé and pushed Send. "Plus, I could use a little Colorado in my life. Who knows? Maybe I'll find something I love more than the theater."

She laughed, doubting it would ever happen.

***

Holy crap. I got the job.

Londyn stared out the window as the plane neared the Colorado Springs airport, gripping the armrest as the wheels touched down. *No turning back now.*

As the jet taxied to the terminal, she wondered how this all happened. One minute she was in a swimming suit, and the next she was packing for a summer job in another state. Her aunt took it well, though her retired boyfriend helped matters. It was more than obvious that everyone was uncomfortable with the third wheel, particularly when Glenda and Stew started acting like randy teens.

The pilot came across the speakers, and she pressed her forehead against the window. The woman she'd interviewed with via Skype was the grandmother of the girls she would nanny for. It concerned her a tiny bit that her employer hadn't been there, but Mrs. Archer explained that he was away a lot on business. *I wonder what he does.* The English woman mentioned he was a doctor of some kind, but she figured more the PhD route than the physician type.

She gathered her bag from the overhead bin and squeezed into the aisle. The subject of the girls' mother didn't come up, which made Londyn curious as to the story there. Maybe once she settled in and spoke to Mr. Archer, she'd figure it all out.

Before she could register what was happening, a man in a suit met her at the arrival area, collected her luggage, and popped her in the back seat of a black Cadillac SUV.

"I'm Theodore Willis, Miss Bellerose. I'll be your driver any time you need one. Should you require my services, simply call," he informed her as the city merged with a densely wooded forest. Dark aviator shades covered his eyes, but he appeared to be only a few years older than her. *Curious.*

"Theodore. Hmm, can I call you Teddy?" she asked, skirting his British accent. It seemed the grandmother wasn't the only one with it. Her intrigue level went up a notch.

"No, miss."

She frowned. "How about Ted?"

Theodore sighed and turned down a long drive. "No again."

"Tedster?" she suggested with a grin.

The driver slid his sunglasses down his nose and met her gaze. "Theodore."

Londyn shrugged and sat back in her seat as the trees slowly gave way to an expansive house. The word mansion came to mind as they pulled up to the front door on the roundabout driveway.

Not waiting for help, she opened the car door and

took in the sights. The brick exterior was one thing, but the house was easily double the size of the theater back in Queens. A barn was visible down a separate drive, and an enormous garage sat to the left of the house.

"Whoa," she breathed, awestruck. She'd never seen anything like it before.

Theodore smiled and grabbed her bags from the trunk. "This is Archer House. It's complete with everything two rambunctious girls could want. Do you approve, Miss Bellerose?"

"Um, yes. One hundred times, yes. It's incredible."

Feeling better about the family behind the house, she followed Theodore into the mansion. Vaulted ceilings with an enormous glass chandelier were the first to catch her eye, light bouncing through the crystals. The main entry was huge and opened to a massive dual staircase. *What fun it'd be to slide down!* A formal room sat to the left, but looked as though it had gone untouched for quite some time.

Before she could investigate more, a crisp voice met her ears. "Miss Bellerose, I presume?"

She turned to see an older gentleman in a suit. *Damn, must be their dress code.* His gray hair accented the black attire and made him appear regal.

"Please, it's Londyn." She held out her hand and he shook it lightly.

"A pleasure. Now, please follow me. I'll give you the condensed tour of the house. I suspect the girls will do a better job once you've settled in."

"Okay, great, thanks." He began walking, and she was amazed at the quick pace. "Wait. What do I call you?"

The man paused at the first step. "You may call me Alfred. Everyone here does."

Londyn's eyes bugged. "Oh my God. Your name's Alfred? As in Batman's Alfred?" She normally didn't spill her secret obsession with all things comics and superheroes, but this was too funny to be a coincidence.

He looked down his long, straight nose at her. "Yes, I'm sure that's precisely what my parents had in mind when they named me."

She smirked. British humor was quickly becoming one of her favorite types. "Or perhaps DC Comics based the character off you." That earned a slight lip twitch from the man old enough to be her grandfather. "Now tell me, where will I find Batman—er, Bruce Wayne?"

Alfred's fingers laced together, and his gray brow rose. "Why, the Batcave, of course, miss."

Grinning, Londyn stuffed a hand in her pocket and followed the spry man. If her new employer was anything like Alfred, they'd get along just fine.

***

Opening the door to the playroom, Callum smiled at his two daughters. Bailey was dressed as a chef, complete with a tall white hat and apron, while Bethany wore a long blue gown and sat at the miniature-sized table nearby. He stood in the doorway for a moment and watched the two chat about the latest pretend delicacies of Paris. Though they'd never been to France, both girls dreamed of eating pastries and baguettes. At least, that's what they told him they'd do if he ever took them to Paris.

Bethany giggled when Bailey set a platter of plastic fried chicken on the table. No matter how many times he saw them play, it made his heart swell with pride. They were his life, despite his frequent flights and trips abroad. He tried his damnedest to carve out time to spend with each daughter individually and together, but more often than not, there weren't enough hours in the day.

"Lovelies, I'm home," he said, stepping into the room.

Bailey paused at her pretend kitchen set and ran toward him at full speed. Crouching, Callum hugged her tight and kissed her cheek. "Somebody missed me."

Bailey nodded. "I always miss you, Daddy."

Her cute voice saying those words cut at his soul. He needed to do better for them.

"Are you quite finished with your eloquent meal, Bethany, or shall I return when you've cleaned your plate?" he teased.

The older of the two stood, careful not to catch her bedazzled dress on the table's edge. Out of the two of them, she resembled him the most. Though she was only 50 percent English, Bethany was a prim and proper lady in training. She bunched her dress and sprinted toward him. *Well, most of the time.* He laughed when she knocked him over with her hug.

"I'm glad you're home," Bethany said, sitting on his stomach. "Don't leave again, please."

Callum stared into her adorable face. "Darling, you know it's part of my job." At those words, Bailey joined her sister on top of him. He chuckled at the extra weight. "You're going to smush me."

Bethany shrugged indifference, but Bailey jumped up and down on him. He tickled Bethany's sides, then held up his hands in defeat. "All right, all right. How about I read you an extra story tonight?"

"Yay!" both girls yelled, hugging him once more before returning to their game of make-believe.

Callum sat up and rested his forearms on his knees. If he could simply spend his days with them, it'd make life so much better. But nothing was that easy.

After a few more minutes, he gave the girls one last kiss and left them to play. He still had a few things to accomplish before dinner.

He didn't bother to say hello to his mother, knowing she'd find him eventually, retreating to the serenity of his study instead. Pouring a healthy serving of bourbon in the tumbler, Callum loosened the blue pinstripe tie from his neck. Recently back from a fast and difficult flight, he more than deserved to mellow his thoughts.

First Dubai and then China to wrap up the trip. The time zone differences consistently wreaked havoc on his body even after all his years of travel. He doubted he'd ever truly get used to it all.

Sitting, he reasoned a fresh pair of clothes would get rid of the teriyaki smell lingering on his current outfit. After a quick shower, falling into bed for a day or two was next on his agenda.

Taking a sip, he leaned back in the leather office chair as the sound of running feet came from the patio. After dinner, he'd do something fun with the girls. Maybe take a hike around the grounds or watch them ride their horses.

Just as he cracked open his laptop, his peripheral caught a body lingering in the doorway.

"Alfred, do come in and get it over with," he said with an annoyed tone. "I'm quite tired and not in the mood."

"Oh, sorry, it's not Alfred," a woman said. "It's me, the nanny."

Callum's fingers paused on the keyboard and he looked up. A gust of fresh air might as well have smacked him in the face at the vision in purple before him. The sourness from his recent trip transformed into lemonade at the sweet scent she brought into the room.

"The nanny?"

"Yes." She stepped into the study and held out her hand when she reached his desk. "I'm Londyn Bellerose. You must be Mr. Archer, or is it Dr. Archer?"

A wide smile with straight teeth graced her beautiful face.

He stood and was delightfully surprised at the realization that she wore flip-flops and yet was nigh on six feet tall. It wasn't common in his experience, and he liked it.

"Either is fine. Pleased to meet you, Ms. Bellerose." He shook her hand, the calluses on her fingers another irregularity.

"I didn't mean to barge in, but Alfred said you'd want to speak with me before I met the girls. I'm excited to get started." The smile on her face only deepened with her words.

Slowly, he nodded. In reality, he didn't need to do anything of the sort, but he was glad the butler sent Londyn his way.

His eyes drifted over the woman in front of him. Her long brown hair held streaks of auburn, making him curious as to their validity. Gray-blue eyes peered at him in muted humor while the purple thing she called a shirt barely covered the dark wash jean shorts. And those legs. *Bloody hell.* Long, lean, and way too enticing.

All in all, his new nanny resembled a delicious morsel in every aspect.

"Have a seat." He motioned to the chairs in front of his desk and took his place across from her.

"Mr. Archer, I app—"

"It's Callum, please."

She blushed and his breath caught. "Okay, sure. Callum, I appreciate your willingness to open your home to me."

"You're our nanny," he pointed out, loving the way his name sounded on her lips. "Anything less would be inconsiderate and improper."

"Ah, sure." Her fingers laced over her stomach—a very flat one at that. Eyes darting around the room, she asked, "So, what did you want to talk about?"

Callum reached for the bourbon, then stopped. The urge to drink had suddenly disappeared when she set foot in his study. An odd change of events when it came to his interactions with women—generally it went the opposite direction, and he couldn't get a drink fast enough. "Well, the girls, of course."

"Okay. I'm looking forward to meeting them." Her eyes lit up and she moved to the edge of the seat. "Is there anything I should know before I start?" When he didn't immediately answer, she floundered. "I mean, unless you've decided I'm not the right person for the job. Some girl from Iowa—well New York, really— just pops up in your house and…."

She stopped and bit her bottom lip. It was cute, her worry. He chided himself for giving her any reason to doubt herself.

"Iowa or New York? Which is it?" he asked.

She smirked. "Both. I grew up in Iowa, but I moved to New York about six years ago."

The bourbon sounded better as she spoke. The move

from small-time to the big city made his insides cringe. Londyn may have been drop-dead gorgeous, but she reminded him of Jessica in that moment.

"And what do you do there?" He held the glass tighter, anticipating her reply.

"I write plays for a theater and work at a coffee shop."

Releasing the breath he hadn't realized he was holding, Callum took a sip of the dark liquor. Just as he suspected, a free spirit chasing a dream.

My luck is absolute shit.

"Lovely. Well, Bethany and Bailey will adore you, I'm sure." He stood and walked to the door. "They are my entire world, as I'm theirs." He hoped he was clear without saying the words. Discussing the girls' mother wasn't something he wanted to do in the near future.

As if reading between the lines, Londyn nodded and crossed the room. "Makes sense." She fell in step beside him.

Damn, he liked her height. *Apparently they grow them tall in Iowa.* He didn't have to crane his neck to look into the eyes resembling a stormy sky. He swallowed thickly as other perks of her stature flooded his mind. Shaking his head, he focused on walking, an act he normally didn't need to concentrate on.

"Have you lived in Colorado long?" she asked when their conversation lapsed.

"Not exactly. We summer in Colorado Springs, but we'll return to our home in England for the rest of the year." He held open the door. "My mother—you met her in the interview—insists we stay each summer with her."

"Why?"

He took a left turn toward the nursery. "Our family bought a rather large company in the Springs a few years back. Her hope is that I'll take it over someday."

Londyn matched his gait, another impressive trait since he walked as if in a race. "And will you? Take over, I mean."

Pausing at the last door, Callum shook his head. "No. My current job is my passion."

"Which is?" she led.

"I'm the curator for a London museum," he explained, swinging the double doors wide. "And these young ladies are the reason we have horses in the backyard." He stepped inside and tugged on Bethany's braids. Both girls stopped playing with their dolls and looked up. He should've snapped a photo of their faces when they saw the lanky girl in the doorway. It would've been worth more than a million words.

"Girls, this is Londyn." He watched their faces closely. Normally they weren't keen on caretakers. "She will be your nanny for the summer."

Shrill cries of delight nearly split his eardrums. They rushed toward her, dolls flying.

Londyn squatted to their level. "Hello there. Who are you?"

Bethany shoved in front of her sister. "I'm Bethany,

and I'm six. You're pretty."

Smirking, Londyn poked her side. "Well, thank you, Bethany. May I call you Beth?"

The redheaded beauty shook her head vigorously. "No. My name's Bethany."

"All right, no problem. By the way, I love your romper. I wish I could wear those still. It looks awfully comfortable."

While Bethany blushed, Bailey wedged her body between the two. "I'm Bailey."

"And how old are you?" Londyn asked.

Bailey held up her fingers. "Four."

"That's a fun age," Londyn said with a smile.

Bailey nodded and reached over to touch Londyn's hair. "Ooh, it's so soft."

Londyn chuckled. "You think so? I think I like your braids better."

Bailey pointed to her sister. "Bethany did them."

"Did she?" Londyn looked to the other girl, who preened like a cat with a dish of milk. "Think you could braid my hair next?"

Without replying, Bethany ran off toward the bathroom, no doubt to fetch the necessary items for the request.

Bailey tapped her chin. "I like your name. Are you named after London, England?"

Londyn shook her head. "Actually yes, though it's spelled a bit different."

"Why'd they name you after a city?" she asked.

"Bailey," Callum chided when he noticed Londyn's face shadow.

"No, it's fine." Londyn tucked her hair behind one shoulder. "My parents met in London and wanted a constant reminder of their love."

"Whoa, that's cool," Bailey said after a moment.

"Yeah, I think so too."

"I better go help Bethany." Bailey scampered off after her sister, a grin as wide as the Thames on her little face.

"You're a natural," he complimented.

Standing, she scratched her elbow. "Thanks. So far, your kids are great."

He nodded, still surprised at how easily his daughters had bonded with Londyn. "They usually fight having a nanny, so I'm glad they like you."

"Aw, well good. I'm glad this time is different for them. I think we'll get along just fine."

Moving to the exit, he agreed. "Yes, I believe you're right. I'm going to get some work done. I'll see you at dinner."

"Great, see you then." She flashed him a brilliant grin, then turned back to the girls heading toward her with hair accessories in hand.

Callum closed the doors behind him and smiled. Watching Londyn with his daughters soothed a sliver of his heart. They loved her already, and there was still an entire summer left.

Retiring to his bedroom, he tossed his suitcoat to

the bed. He may have approved of her for his children, but Callum resolved to steer clear of her as much as possible. There was something light, carefree, and dangerous about Londyn. *She just reminds you of Jessica,* he told himself as the shower sputtered to life. His heart tugged at the memories involved with his ex. He didn't want to compare Londyn to Jessica, but he found himself doing it regardless.

Shedding the rest of his clothes, Callum stepped into the warm waterfall and closed his eyes. Londyn had smelled perfect, like a cup of hot chocolate dotted with tiny marshmallows. Sweet, sugary, and much too addictive for him to handle.

He rolled his eyes at the description. *Seems my international jaunt muddled my brain.*

No, staying away from Londyn was in everyone's best interests.

CHAPTER THREE

"How is it?" Abi asked.

Londyn pushed back the drape across the window. Mountains stared back at her from the distance. "Abs, it's awesome. Stunning views, adorable girls, and plenty to do around here. I'm excited to travel around with them." She plopped on the queen-sized bed and sat cross-legged. "This place is huge too. Like mansion huge. I swear I'll get lost."

Abi laughed. "Glad to hear it. How's the family? Nice? Snobby?"

"Mostly nice. They're very British." Picking at a string on her shorts, she said, "I've only really met the dad. The girls' grandma hasn't been in yet today. She has her own wing of the house. Can you believe it? The staff is nice, though. They're all British, Abs. Their accents are delicious."

"Hmm, and how's the dad? Delicious too?" Abi guessed.

A smile edged its way to Londyn's lips. She couldn't deny that Callum was hot. Like Indiana Jones meets Thor hot. His professor vibe, charming eyes, and height made her mouth water. Not to mention his accent. "Well—"

"No, really? I was joking." Londyn heard Oreo meow in the background. "What's he like? Details, girl. Is he single?"

Londyn sprawled to her back and gazed up at the beige ceiling. "He's tall, dirty-blond hair, gorgeous brown eyes, and yes, single." Abi squealed, but Londyn kept going lest an interruption ensued. "He's a doctor—well PhD, anyway—and his accent." She fanned herself with her free hand. "God, it's incredible. And he smelled like Chinese food and chocolate. How much more could I want?"

Abi snorted. "Food whore."

"I like my food, what can I say?" she defended.

"How old is he?"

Londyn pictured Callum, then shrugged. "Probably somewhere in the thirties, but he doesn't look it. From what I could tell, he was perfectly in shape beneath the gray suit."

"Okay, so let me get this right. He's rich, single, hot, British, and smells like your version of heaven? How have you not locked him in a closet?" Giggling, Londyn opened her mouth to comment, but her friend asked,

"Wait, what's his name? You never said."

"Callum." The moment the word slipped from her tongue, both women sighed whimsically.

"Damn, even that's sexy."

Londyn turned to her side. "Yeah. Too bad he's out of the question."

"What? Why?"

Frowning, she sat up. "Because we have nothing in common. I'm a 'fly by the seat of my pants' type, and if his office is any indicator, he's meticulous in planning. We wouldn't get along. Plus he's my boss and the father of the girls I'm taking care of. It wouldn't be right."

Her friend groaned in frustration. "Yeah, I'm gonna stop you there. He's perfect. The situation is perfect. You said you wanted a summer fling, and hello, you just walked into his castle."

"Well, that's in England, actually," Londyn added cheekily.

"Oh. My. God. Are you serious?" Abi sounded as flabbergasted as Londyn when she'd found out. It was a shock even thinking it now. The Archer family had money to spare, it seemed.

Londyn bobbed her head. "Yeah, Bailey told me about it. It's enormous, according to her. They only live in Colorado for the summers."

"All right, then that makes it even better." Abi clucked her tongue. "A summer job and some summer loving. It has an expiration date already, so why not? You'll never see him again after August."

Slipping into a pair of red sweat pants, Londyn thought it over. On one hand, it was ideal, but on the other, it felt a little wrong. "I don't know, Abs. He didn't seem too interested in me. 'Repulsed' is the word I'd use, honestly. No chitchat or getting to know me. Just strictly business."

Abi laughed, and the jingle of a bell chimed from the other end of the call. "Oh, please. That's just a British thing. I don't believe he doesn't like you for a second. You're gorgeous, fit, and need to get banged more than a gong in a museum."

"Abi—"

"What? Just saying. Your nighttime naked nature has been lacking. Get some, girl."

Ignoring the tease, Londyn pulled off her shirt. Without a doubt, her best friend was wiggling her eyebrows like crazy in New York. "Yeah, yeah. I better head down for dinner. Talk to you later."

"Jump on that curator and make some art!" Abi called.

Rolling her eyes, she hung up. If she didn't, Abi would go into illicit detail about what exactly she should do to Callum if given a chance.

After rummaging through her bag, Londyn settled on a black hooded sweatshirt with a penguin playing hockey on the front. One look in the mirror and she was good to go.

Her long braid, courtesy of Bailey and Bethany, swished behind her back as she ambled down the hallways, passing closed doors along her way. *One of these days, I need to check these all out.* Retrieving a slip of paper from her pocket, she studied it. Alfred had been kind enough to draw her a rough map of the estate, so she followed his directions until she reached a brightly lit formal dining room.

Stepping inside, she caught sight of Callum at the head of the table. Though he'd changed into slacks, a button-up shirt, and wore a different tie, he still looked ready to give a seminar about modern art. The spread on the table looked scrumptious, and her stomach growled in response. She hadn't eaten since that morning, a mistake she wasn't used to making.

"Oh, um, I didn't know we dressed up for dinner," she said, taking a seat between the girls. "Whoops."

Bailey patted her hand. "It's all right. Daddy likes to look nice all the time."

Ouch. She smiled at the cutie in the same blue outfit as earlier. Even that looked dressy compared to her attire. "I guess I'm used to going with the flow. Abi and I never dress up for anything, much less dinner."

"And Abi is your girlfriend? Or is it life partner or wife?" Callum's accented voice asked, startling her. "I never remember which is politically correct these days."

Londyn shook her head. She hadn't thought he was paying attention. "Oh no. I mean, she's a girl who's a friend—er, I mean she's my best friend and we live together." Her face was on fire. She'd never felt like she had to explain her situation before.

"Ah, I see. That's nice. Our last nanny eloped with her girlfriend after being together for twenty years. Perhaps you and Abi are the same?" Callum's face was pinched in question, awaiting her fumbling reply.

"No, nothing like that. I like guys," she finally blurted, clearing the air.

Bailey giggled and clapped, while Bethany bit into a roll as if she was bored with the conversation.

Looking over, Londyn managed to catch a small smirk on Callum's face before he masked it.

"Good to know," he murmured, picking up a fork. "Wouldn't want there to be any confusion there."

Suddenly warm, she tore off her hoodie. It wasn't until Bethany's mouth dropped open and the roll fell out that she remembered she'd forgotten to put on a shirt underneath, too distracted with Abi's talk of sex and kissing.

Gaze swiveling to Callum, she found the hue in his brown eyes darkened, his expression suddenly undiscernible.

"My, my, I wasn't informed you were a burlesque dancer as well," a new voice clipped.

"Shit!" Londyn scrambled for the hoodie she now swore would be the death of her and yanked it on. "I, um—"

"Mary Archer," the woman said, taking her seat to Callum's left. "We spoke the other day on Skype." Her brown eyes grazed over Londyn. "You had on more clothes then."

Heat crept up Londyn's neck and face until she wanted to rip the sweatshirt in two. "Yes, glad to meet you in person."

Mary ignored her and turned her attention to the meal. "Ah, my favorite. Lamb stew. How'd you know?"

Callum took a sip of red wine. "I didn't. You made the menu, Mother."

Londyn bit back a smirk, but the girls openly giggled.

An hour later, Bailey and Bethany gave Londyn the grand tour of Archer House. She met the cook, Gloria, who happened to be Alfred's wife, learned that Alfred's name was actually Lionel Alfred, and discovered her new favorite spot in the house.

"Come on, Londyn. Let's swim," Bethany suggested, running toward the natatorium.

Stepping through the glass doors, Londyn bit her lip to keep from screaming with joy. With a retractable roof and walls, the pool could be both indoor and outdoor. She was officially in love.

"You don't have a swim suit on," she reminded the girl.

Bethany frowned. "True. How about we swim tomorrow? Daddy makes us take lessons each afternoon. I can show you what I know. I'm great at swimming underwater."

Bailey tugged on her pants. "Me too, me too!"

Nodding, she walked to the glass walls. There was

a perfect view of the mountains with enough privacy from the trees. There was no way the spot could be more serene.

"Sounds good to me." She took both their hands. "I was a swimmer in high school, so maybe I can teach you a thing or two."

Bailey jumped up and down while Bethany bobbed her head in agreement. The summer wouldn't be too bad if there was a pool to swim laps in.

"Let's go build a fort," she said, racing for the door. She desperately needed to let off a little steam after the dinner fiasco. Both girls squealed in delight and followed her.

Yeah, she would definitely enjoy her time at Archer House, with or without a summer fling.

***

She stripped.

Callum hid his smile behind his fist at the not-so-distant memory. As inadvertent as it was, Ms. Bellerose had stripped at dinner.

He looked up to see his mother drone on about the chocolate business. She'd come back around about it to him eventually, but for the time being, he'd think back to the horrified look on Londyn's face when she'd realized her mistake. Good God, but it was a welcomed mistake. He normally didn't get that far with a woman even after a month of dates, and yet she showed off her perfectly sized breasts in that adorable sunshine-yellow bra on the first day.

"Cal, are you listening?" his mother's voice broke through his thoughts.

Eyes up, he nodded. The borrowed nickname irked him. "Yes, Mother. Stock market fluctuations." He gripped the glass of water tighter as he waited to see if he'd guessed correctly.

His mother shook her head, apparently appeased, and continued on about business.

He took a sip of his water. It wasn't hard to predict where she was in their nightly chat about Archer Chocolatery. She kept on about upper management, so he switched his mind to Londyn once more. It was more enjoyable, to say the least.

Londyn. Even thinking her name brought a smile to his normally straight face. Throat dry, he finished off the water, though it did nothing for the thirst. He desired something else entirely to quench him.

He shook his head. *Just because you're in a bit of a dry spell doesn't give you an excuse to lust after the nanny.* Londyn's beet-red face swam into his mind, and he swallowed hard. She was quickly becoming a distraction. One he couldn't tangle with. She was just like Jessica. That was the problem, yet also the solution. *Perhaps a short and sweet affair would be all right.*

He let out a frustrated huff at the thought.

What he needed was a good, difficult run to clear his

mind before the trip to Spain in the morning. He'd be escorting a Picasso from a museum there to the one in London, a simple enough task. Afterward, maybe he'd stop at one of the pubs in the city and find someone cute and nameless to steady his lustful mind. Yes, that was all he needed. A quick fling.

"Great recap, Mother." He loosened his tie. "As they always are."

Mary glared at him. "I won't live forever, Callum. You'll take over the chocolatery upon that eventuality, and you need to know how it runs. It's why we meet whenever you're in town."

He sighed and undid the top button of his shirt. It felt too constricting at the moment, not unlike the conversation. His rising blood pressure probably wasn't helping things along either. They'd had this talk before, and it always ended the same.

"We've been over this. You know I'll sell it when you're gone. I've no interest in chocolates."

His mother stood and paced, her small heels clipping the hardwood floor. "Why ever not? Your father loved it and—"

"And I'm not Calvin Archer. I'm Callum," he said forcefully. Massaging his temples, Callum moved to the door. "I love what I do, and I'd appreciate it if you'd accept that." Turning the knob, he added, "Now if you'll excuse me, I'm off for a run."

He left before she could retort. Thank God she didn't follow him, as she'd done before. Space, time, and a bit of sweat were in store for his evening.

After a quick change of clothes, Callum set off down the long driveway at a sprint. Normally he took it easy and paced himself, but that night, the need to smother his excess energy overcame his usual marathon jog.

The summer sun set to his left, spreading an orange glow over the evergreens along the path. The raised altitude took some getting used to, but he preferred to push himself whenever possible.

The steady thud of feet on concrete stabilized his thoughts, and he quickly forgot why he was so uptight. Running was the best problem solver he could come up with. Some people drank to forget, but Callum exhausted his body until he couldn't remember. The drinking came later, when exercising failed to fix things.

Only once a stream of sweat slid down both cheeks and his back did he return to the house. Checking his watch that kept track of his stats, he smirked at the three-mile sprint calculated for his time. He swore to stay healthy and in shape after his father passed away from a heart attack at fifty-five years old. Ever since then, Callum pledged to daily workouts and healthy meals as often as possible.

Catching his breath, he stretched both legs and watched the windows of the house. It was rather fun to see the flickers across the huge structure. The nursery light was off, meaning both girls were on their way to dreamland. Alfred and his missus played chess in the front room, and Theodore's light was off. No shock there. His old friend was early for everything, including turning in for the night.

When he looked to Londyn's room, a frown spread over his face. Her light was off as well. He shouldn't have been disappointed, but he was anyway. For some reason, he pegged her as an evening owl who barely slept.

You don't know her, he reminded himself.

He finished stretching his legs and started in on his arms as he walked around the house. The crystal-blue water beckoned him as he neared. A refreshing swim was exactly what he needed after his run around the property.

Not bothering to check his surroundings, Callum tore off his shoes, shirt, and athletic shorts until all he wore were his boxers. Tossing the items to the floor as he entered the side door, he grinned at the still water.

Diving in, he set his arms moving. *Probably should've left the shorts on.* He didn't bother to give it another thought, though, as no one else would be in the pool house at that time of night.

He came up for air, slicing through the water with each determined stroke. Yeah, he was over his moment of weakness when it came to Londyn. A solid workout was all he'd needed.

***

Hot damn! Should I say something? Londyn ducked into the hot tub until she was sure only her eyebrows were visible. Now she felt like a creeper as she watched Callum effortlessly lap the pool with professional strokes. *I should say something.* She nodded as if encouraging herself. It wasn't her fault her boss tore off his clothes and dove into the pool before she could form a sentence. Of course, she'd been too busy staring at the muscles normally hidden beneath those suits of his to utter a single word.

He needs to not wear them so often.

When she opened her mouth, Callum stopped swimming and treaded water. He faced away from her, but his neck was slowly craning in her direction. Gasping, she slipped down until her lips skimmed the warm depths. The only sounds meeting her ears were the soft lapping from Callum's arms.

Maybe I'll just casually get up and leave. She thought it through as she swallowed the bite of chocolate in her mouth. *Yeah, no way he would believe I wasn't watching him.* But how could she not? His broad shoulders and perfectly timed breathing had her enraptured. Watching Callum swim was porn for a former swimmer, and not the raunchy stuff—the real deal.

Another minute passed, and she reviewed her wrinkly fingers beneath the water. Her idea had been to soak a little in the hot tub, lap the pool twenty-odd times, and then hit the sack after a quick shower. If she stayed there much longer, all her skin would resemble a raisin.

Yeah, if I leave now, it'll just be awkward. She cursed to herself. Normally she didn't shy away from confrontation, but after the whole incident at dinner, she wanted to give herself time to present a better face. *Clearly not happening in my lifetime.*

She let out a huff, then froze as Callum's voice bounced against the glass walls. "Miss Bellerose, are you planning on sleeping in there, or do you simply prefer to ogle me from afar? I don't mind the latter, but I believe your room has an adequate bed for the former."

Face heated, Londyn slowly straightened her torso until Callum's lightly tanned face came into view. "Oh, Callum, hey. I didn't see you there." She reached for the towel near the ladder. *How did he know?* She eyed her pile of clothes nearby. *Duh, your shit is everywhere.* Still, she asked, "How did you know I was here?"

Swimming to the side of the pool, he climbed the ladder and grabbed a towel. His slow movements were droolworthy and his green boxers… yeah, those were useless. Her head tilted on its own to get a full view of him. And it was a wondrous sight. She had to force her mouth to stay shut. Her eyes, on the other hand, shamelessly drifted along the length of his body.

"Your hair." He pointed with his left index finger, a smirk on his lips. "The bobbing bun gave you away." He chuckled and neared her. "It isn't every day that a lone head of hair floats in the hot tub. I thought we may have a ghost there for a minute."

Londyn's hands shot up to her ballerina bun. "Damn. Yeah, that'll do it." She carefully maneuvered out of the water and into the towel so he couldn't see her scanty bikini. He'd already seen more than any employer should, and she really didn't want to cause further embarrassment. "All right, well, I'll see you tomorrow."

"Actually you won't. I'll be in Spain and then London." He sat on the edge of a wicker beach chair. "I'll be back the day after next, unless something comes up." His brown eyes skimmed her despite the towel. "Try not to burn the house down in my absence."

The heavy British accent with a hint of humor sent a jolt right to her stomach. It shouldn't. Hell, it should've sent her straight to bed, but she was intrigued by him every time they interacted.

"What will you be doing?" she asked, wanting to hear him speak again. It was addictive.

He rubbed a towel over his head, the hair now sticking up every which way. It was cute.

I wonder what he looks like in the morning. Or even after—

She smothered a smile. *No! Bad, Londyn!*

"Escorting a priceless painting to the museum. A normal, mundane job." He crossed his legs at the ankles, forcing her eyes to dip there. He wasn't a body builder, but his defined muscles extended up his calves, his thighs…. Londyn felt her cheeks flare when she went higher. Skipping the next region, she noticed a flat stomach with hints of a six-pack, toned pecs, and arm muscles any girl would deem sexy.

Clearing her throat, she met his cognac-colored eyes. "Sounds like fun, I suppose."

"It has its perks." Callum smiled. "My passport is always full, and I'm quite fond of traveling."

"Mmhmm." She eyed the bright nail polish on her toes, unsure where the conversation was headed. She knew where she wanted it to go. Well, her body did, at least. Her mind wasn't convinced that shacking up with the gorgeous man in front of her was a good idea.

"Do you like art?" he asked at last.

Londyn shifted her weight. "Me? Sure, I like looking at it, but do I understand it? Not usually."

Callum ran his fingers through his hair, his gaze never once leaving her face. "In that case, I'd be glad to give you a crash course on some of the art we have around the house if you're interested."

Clearly art was important to him, so she nodded. "Sure, sounds great. Thanks."

"I like to hear myself talk, so you'll have to tell me when you've had enough," he warned.

"Oh, I could never get sick of hearing you talk. It's so sexy." Londyn slapped a hand to her mouth after the words slipped out. At her act, the towel also fell away, and she suddenly wasn't sure which part to hide.

Grinning, Callum leaned down and picked up the

towel, carefully placing the fluffy cloth around her shoulders. Any other guy would've undressed her with his eyes, but not him. His upbringing shone through. Callum wasn't your typical man—he was a gentleman. And she desperately wanted to know if he had a wild side stored away for rainy days.

Pulling it tight around her, he lowered his head. "Maybe we should talk more often, then."

Londyn found herself leaning closer to him. Neither his run nor the subsequent swim dampened the hints of nutmeg and cedar on his skin. Whoever created the cologne was a genius; he smelled better than the love child of an ancient book and a spiced candle. Good Lord, she wanted to lick his neck to see if he tasted as good as he smelled.

Callum's eyes darkened as if hearing her thoughts. "If you keep losing articles of clothing around me, I'll start to take it personally." His lips drifted closer. If she moved an inch, they'd collide.

She giggled and was relieved when he took a step backward. She wasn't ready to cross the invisible line of employee and employer yet. Determined to focus on something other than the lingering tension between them, Londyn retreated to her pile of clothes.

"I take it you travel a lot." He nodded, so she continued. "I'd think some of the art shuffling could be done by an assistant, especially with you in the States for the summer. It'd make sense if you were always in London, but all the airfares and travel must be costly."

She scratched her neck and dropped her gaze. "For both the bank and your personal life."

A muscle in Callum's cheek twitched at her slight jab. She hadn't meant it as one, of course, but surely he didn't *have* to travel as much as he did. After only knowing the girls a whole five hours, Londyn could see how much his time abroad affected them.

Studying his features, she felt her stomach bunch up. His demeanor shifted at her words. She'd crossed a line. Not the one she'd wanted to cross, but she'd crossed one nevertheless.

Callum licked his lips and with one long stride, he reached his discarded items and tossed the towels to the nearby laundry bin. Gone was the easygoing art lover; in his place was the fully British counterpart. Disconnected and curt. Even his back seemed straighter.

A chill swept over Londyn's wet hair, signifying the end of the good-natured conversation. She swore under her breath when his brown eyes narrowed toward her.

"Miss Bellerose, I suggest you do the job you were hired for." He patted down his hair, water still clinging to his long eyelashes. He looked younger despite the stern words.

I really ought to find out how old he is.

Somehow during her staring at Callum, he stood in front of her again, heat radiating off him and transferring to her exposed skin. Looking up, she gulped. His light brown eyes held warning, but also something else she couldn't decipher. His lips lowered dangerously close to hers. If she moved even slightly, they'd meet her own, and she just knew they'd be the right amount of soft and firm. Despite his sudden shift from joking to serious, the desire to be closer to him remained.

"Stay in your lane, Londyn," he directed.

Cocking one eyebrow, she tilted her chin up. "I'm doing my job, Dr. Archer." Walking around him, she paused at the door to the main house. "And this isn't driving, Callum. It's life. Lanes were meant to merge."

She didn't miss the humor light up his face or when his hand covered a smile he was attempting to smother.

"Good night." Londyn swept out of the room, not allowing even a mirror response. Heart pounding, she didn't stop until she shut the bedroom door and leaned her back against it. She'd almost given in and kissed him. The miniature Abi-devil on her shoulder would be disappointed that she hadn't made a move.

God, she wanted to do so much more than kiss him.

Shivering, Londyn stripped off her swimming suit and stepped into the en suite bathroom. Once the shower was scalding hot, she slipped under the waterfall.

It's only been a day. Lathering her hair, she was suddenly very content with Callum being away on business every week. She wouldn't—no, couldn't make a move on her boss. Even if he was her cup of tea.

***

Later that week, Londyn dragged the spade across the black soil and inhaled the earthy scent. It was the ideal day for planting, even if she had to convince the two gardeners that she wouldn't destroy their beautiful landscaping.

Glancing over her shoulder, she spotted Bailey dangling an earthworm at Bethany. The older girl jumped at first, then carefully took the worm away from her sister. It appeared the Archer girls were more than ready to get their hands dirty.

Londyn adjusted the large-rimmed blue hat and grabbed the potted flowers. The girls chose Gerbera daisies for the back side of the house where the gardeners hadn't planted yet. It was just their luck too, since they caught a ride into town with the two older gentlemen who offered advice for good flowers in that location.

While the dazzling pink, yellow, and white flowers were a tad lopsided, Bethany and Bailey raved about what fun they were having. Going back over and straightening them, Londyn couldn't help but enjoy her time in Colorado so far.

"I'm glad we picked these flowers. They're cheery," Bethany said, placing a pink one in the hole. "We never did this with our other nanny."

"Why not?" Londyn asked, patting the soil around the flower.

"She did what Grandmother wanted. Mostly boring stuff."

"Hmm, well, we'll do a ton of fun things you want to do this summer, all right?" she offered, hoping it was enough. Girls needed their dad as long as he was available. It was one of the truths she'd learned once her parents were gone.

Both girls nodded excitedly. The hum of bees caught her attention, and she grinned. Being outside was the best, in her opinion. She'd always been a sun bunny, and living with her aunt had only intensified the attraction.

"Do you think Daddy will like these?" Bailey asked, digging a new hole.

Londyn handed them a yellow plant. "Of course he will. You'll have to get his attention after we're done so he can see them."

"If he has time," Bethany said with a glum expression.

"Yeah, he may be on the phone," her sister added.

Rocking on her heels, Londyn frowned. The fact that these gorgeous girls were positive their own father wouldn't have five minutes for them disappointed her. He'd come and gone from one business trip thus far, and his one-on-one time with his daughters was limited to meals.

We'll have to fix that.

Londyn sprinkled plant food around the flowers. "Is he busy a lot?"

The Archer girls exchanged an eye roll. "Yeah, but it's his job," Bethany said matter-of-factly.

"Mmhmm, well maybe he should come outside with us." Londyn pointed to the clouds. "After this, we should watch the clouds and see if there are any animals hiding in them."

Bailey nodded enthusiastically, whereas Bethany shrugged. It appeared the older girl was maturing much faster than she should.

Well, some nonstop fun will help with that.

"Bailey, why don't you start watering? I still need to finish mine." Londyn nodded to her sister. "Can you help fill up the can, Bethany?"

"Yes!" The four-year-old skipped over to the green can and brought it back to the hose where her sister stood.

"This isn't as fun," Bethany complained. She turned the nozzle for the hose, which sputtered to life and then shot out of the watering can, spraying them both.

Londyn laughed and quickly wrangled the out-of-control hose. "There. Does that spice things up enough for you?" she teased.

Bethany wiped water from her freckled arms. "The water is so cold." She shivered when the sun ducked behind a cloud.

"Run inside and grab a couple towels," Londyn suggested, helping Bailey with the can. Bethany nodded, then ran toward the back door.

While Londyn held the majority of the can, Bailey gently doused the newly planted flowers with water.

"I like this," the younger girl said, her face never

without a smile. "We should do it all the time."

Agreeing, Londyn steered her toward the next row of daisies. "I would be totally up for that. Flowers are really the best to have around, you know?"

"Why?" Bailey asked.

"Well, they attract bees, hummingbirds, and other useful critters for pollination," she explained.

Bailey's lips pursed together. "Then we better plant more!"

"I'll let the gardeners know." Londyn grinned and let the girl finish the rest of the water. Spending time with children was a good reminder to slow down. Ever since she could remember, she'd had to grow up faster than she'd like. Her parents' death was the main contributor, but her early growth spurt also had something to do with it. Now, as Bethany returned wearing a swimming suit and holding two beach towels, all Londyn could imagine was how much better life was when it wasn't rushed. There was plenty of time for structure and disappointment when they were older. She was determined to make this summer the best they'd ever had. After all, they deserved it.

"All right, I'm going to finish my sunflowers," she called when Bethany took the hose once more. She aimed it at her sister, who screamed in response to the chilly temperature.

"Don't you dare hit me with that."

Both girls seemed to have heard her, and Londyn hoped it'd stay that way. While she wouldn't mind a thorough drenching, she really needed to get the flowers in the ground. It was supposed to rain later in the day, and it'd do the plants good to be properly settled before then.

"Sunflowers really are the best flower." The silky petals slipped through her fingers. "So sunny and welcoming."

She sighed and listened for the girls. From the sounds of it, they were having a grand time. Focusing on the job at hand, she didn't notice anyone near her until a shadow fell across her face.

"Now that's a surprise. I had you down as a rose woman." Callum's voice startled the spade out of her hand, but she recovered quickly.

She lifted her eyes, but with the sun behind his head, she couldn't see his face. "Nah, those are so generic. Everyone likes roses." She pointed a dirt-covered finger at him. "They die in like three days. You can't enjoy them." Patting the soil, she nodded once. "But sunflowers last forever, especially when they're planted and not plucked."

"Hmm, I suppose you're right." He reviewed their work. "Long-lasting buds. Great idea, Miss Bellerose."

"Thanks, I think." Curious as to why her boss was outside, she asked, "Are the girls done spraying each other already?"

Callum shook his head. "Not exactly. Currently they're chasing Sherlock with the hose and water guns."

Londyn glanced over to see Bailey at the top of the wooden swing set with a water gun while Bethany watered the dog from the swings underneath. "Oops, I guess they found something new to do."

Callum held out his hand and helped her to her feet. When she was steady, he immediately dropped her soil-covered hand. The act seemed more awkward than anything, but she shrugged it off. He was wearing a suit probably worth twice as much as her first car. She wouldn't want it covered with dirt either.

"They doused my office window before enticing Sherlock outside with the promise of dog bones," he told her.

Chuckling, she saw Bailey dangle a treat from her spot where the dog would never be able to reach. "Ah, inventive too. You should be proud."

He sighed and narrowed his eyes. "I am proud of their achievements, when they don't drag me away from my work."

"Yes, we mustn't pull you from your beloved work." She mumbled it under her breath, but when he crossed his arms, she regretted saying it out loud at all.

"Do you let all children run amuck or just mine?" The tilt of his head gave her pause. He looked like a professor scolding his student.

She gathered the gardening tools in her arms and gave him a pointed look. "Yours mostly. They seem to enjoy the freedom I provide."

Callum's left eyebrow rose. "Excuse me? Are you

saying I don't let them do as they wish?"

Londyn walked past him and dumped the tools in the gardening box she'd found in the garage. "No, I'm sure you do." She plucked the watering can from its side and was surprised it had any water in it at all. Returning to the flowers, she sprinkled the remnants on the buds. "I'm just saying they prefer when someone is with them while they're roaming."

"You're with them," he reminded her.

She set the empty can down and studied his face. "I am, but it'd mean a whole lot more if you were out here too."

Callum batted at a mosquito, though his brown eyes never left her face. "Then what am I paying you for?"

She brushed a piece of lint from his shoulder. Meeting his hard glare, she grinned. "I believe it had something to do with summer fun."

"Miss Bellerose—"

"Now, now, don't be the fun police, Callum," she called over her shoulder, walking toward the swing set. "You really should join us." She raced to the swings and hopped on an open one. "You may enjoy yourself."

Walking slowly, he reached them in time for Sherlock to howl at Bailey. The poor dog even tried to climb the slide, which was quite funny to watch since his ears kept getting in his way. Bailey glided down and did her best to pull the dog up, but her valiant attempt only led to both falling all the way off the slide.

A smile crept across Callum's face while he watched

the comical debacle, and Londyn's body warmed at the precious scene. All that was missing was his interaction. He had it in him. She just knew it.

"Daddy, push me!" Bethany called, her hair a tangle of red. Somehow it made her look even more adorable.

After surveying the situation, he nodded. "All right, but you have to drop the hose."

His daughter did so without argument, and within seconds, he was pushing her high into the air. Bethany laughed with glee, which prompted Bailey to climb onto the swing next to her.

Londyn watched from her spot on the slow-moving swing as Callum pushed and his girls had a competition to see who could go the highest.

This is more like it.

She returned the grin Callum offered her. He appeared to be enjoying himself just as much as his daughters.

"Cal, you're late for the phone conference," Mary Archer called from the patio. "The board is waiting."

Still unsure what company he worked for other than the museum, Londyn wished his mother wouldn't interrupt. It was curious that she ran a business and roped him into it as well. He didn't seem to enjoy whenever she beckoned. He didn't look like the businessman type either. There was more to him than that. Plus she knew his passion was the museum, so the constant butting in from Mrs. Archer had her curiosity piqued.

Callum cursed under his breath. "I'm sorry, girls, but I need to go back to work. I'll see you later, all right?"

Bailey and Bethany grumbled and begged him to stay. Taking her cue, Londyn got to her feet and suggested, "Why don't we have a forest adventure and look for wild flowers?" She grabbed Bailey's hand. "We'll pick as many as we can hold, then put them in a vase for Gloria."

Both seemed appeased by this new alternative and led her toward the surrounding forest.

Before they disappeared into the tree line, Londyn looked over her shoulder and saw Callum give her a quick nod. It wasn't much, but it was a start.

CHAPTER FOUR

Tossing Sherlock the last bite of blueberry biscuit, Callum strode out of the office and down the hall. Darkness crowded the house, but plenty of lights were on as he walked through. *Good Lord, are all these necessary?* He didn't bother to shut them off, though. Bailey wasn't a fan of being in the dark, so she probably flipped them all on as she moved through the house.

The scent of fresh bread caught his nose and his stomach grumbled. He'd missed dinner. Again. It was mostly a mistake—he'd been so enthralled with the dig update from his archaeologist pal that he'd completely ignored the call for the evening meal.

He turned toward the kitchen and scrounged up a quick sandwich before moving toward the bedrooms, stopping short when the sound of show tunes caught his ear.

What the devil?

Switching directions, he came to his daughters' nursery and stood outside the door. The sight that met his eyes was mesmerizing.

Londyn stood on top of the couch, a straw hat in one hand and a baton in the other. Familiar music from *The Music Man* blared behind her as she recreated the famous "Ya Got Trouble" bit. His girls sat entranced by her silly dance moves and animated facial expressions. Clearly she was made for the performing arts if this sliver was any indicator.

He completely forgot the sandwich in his hand when Londyn went full-on Harold Hill and even tried to replicate the male voice, both singing and speaking. Bethany jumped up and started to sing along where the townspeople joined in. It didn't sound as good as Londyn, but it was cute to see her try. Meanwhile, Bailey patted on an empty plastic bucket, her tempo surprisingly on beat.

By the time Londyn and the girls finished, food was the absolute last thing on Callum's mind. All of them were sweaty and rolling in laughter. It looked too good to spoil, so he opted against saying good night to the girls right then.

"Okay, hop in bed," Londyn instructed, turning off the music.

"But there are more fun songs to sing," Bailey complained, though she walked toward the pink covered bed.

"Yes there are, but we can save them for another day." Londyn straightened the couch. "Plus, you just saw the movie tonight. Believe me, the Broadway version is so much better."

"Can we go?" Bethany asked through a yawn.

Londyn shrugged. "I don't see why not. I'll check the showtimes at the theaters around here and see if they have it anywhere, all right?"

Bethany and Bailey wrapped her in a giant hug and were instantly caught in her arms when she returned it. Callum's heart thudded at the scene. It was too beautiful to look away. He wasn't one to dance around, but if it meant his girls adored him….

He shook the thought far away. They loved him. He was their father. He didn't need to prove anything to them.

Londyn and the girls disappeared to the bathroom, and he stepped away from the door. Their giggles and operatic voices made him smirk. Before Londyn, they were goofy girls, but since the gorgeous nanny arrived, he'd never seen them happier.

Munching the rest of his sandwich as he headed down the hallway, Callum did his best to push aside the parts of Londyn's personality that irked him. *She's too energetic and spur-of-the-moment.* He frowned. It was a horrid reason to not like someone. He barely knew the woman, so judging her was premature. *Although, she is a bit immature.*

Recalling her sharp tongue and easy banter, he raked

his hands through his hair. Not many women could keep up with his dry brashness. That development was dangerous. If Londyn kept pushing back at him, he'd be forced to spend more time with her. Already the thought scared him. His physical attraction for her was swiftly merging with personal feelings.

It's time for another trip, he decided, reaching his bedroom. Although the museum wasn't expecting him, he was more than ready to put space between himself and the nanny. If he stayed at home, he was liable to narrow the space instead.

*****

"Don't fill it all the way to the top. We need to leave room to tie them." Londyn reminded.

Bailey carefully cupped the balloon as it filled with water from the faucet in the kitchen. "Like this?" She held up a red one, her brows knit together.

Londyn took the offering. "Perfection." The little girl beamed at her approval. "Get started on the next one while I put this one in the bucket. It's nearly full, so not many more."

The four-year-old nodded enthusiastically, then dug out a blue latex balloon and climbed the step stool.

Londyn grinned and plopped the tied water balloon in the rubber tote she'd found in one of the spare closets. Between the three of them, they were almost ready to head outside and play. She glanced to the window overlooking the backyard. Nothing but blue skies met her.

"Londyn, I found the slingshots," Bethany yelled, running down the hall. She slid on the floor in her purple socks when she reached the kitchen tile.

"Great. Those will be fun for our pending water war." She wiggled her eyebrows. "Think we can rope Theodore or Alfred to join us?"

Bethany giggled. "Maybe Theodore. He's young like my daddy."

Just as Londyn started to ask Callum's age, Bailey raced over to her with another balloon in need of tying. "Help, this one's leaking."

Laughing, Londyn eyed the pink balloon that had indeed sprung a ghastly leak. "I don't think this one will work." She patted the side of the plastic tote. "But we have plenty in here. Who's ready to fight?"

Both youngsters shrieked with glee and ran through the house, laughing and talking until they reached the back door. Londyn followed at a slightly slower pace thanks to the full basket.

As she neared the sliding glass door to the patio, she noticed Callum's office door ajar. Peeking her nose in, she offered, "We're going to have a water balloon fight in the backyard, and I'm seeking recruits for my team."

Callum's eyes lifted from the computer and a smirk played across his features. He looked business casual with a long-sleeved button-up blue shirt rolled to his elbows, though his thin blue and gray tie looked much too professional for a home office.

"Is that so?" His gaze lingered over her outfit. In retrospect, her camouflage bikini was probably overkill when she added thick black smudges on her cheeks and a ponytail braid. The girls wore similar football marks, but their swimming suits were much cuter.

"Yeah. Want to join? It's me against the girls so far." She rested the full basket against the doorframe. Water balloons were heavier than she remembered.

He splayed his hands to the files on either side of his laptop. "Sadly, I can't be of any help. I'm behind on these acquisitions, and I need to make a few international phone calls while they're awake or I'll lose my window."

"Ah, sounds like…." She stuck out her tongue. "Crap. Yep, sounds like crap. Come play in the sun."

He waved in dismissal. "Not today, Londyn. Perhaps tomorrow."

She pouted, but he'd already returned his attention to his work. During her short stay, Londyn had realized one thing: he was a workaholic. She never understood the call, but then again, she bounced from job to job. Finding a workplace she absolutely loved hadn't happened yet.

This one is a good contender, though.

Shrugging, she left him to it and stepped into the warm weather. Fifteen days into the job and she doubted she'd ever tire of seeing the views. The secluded woods—Black Forest, as she learned from

Bethany—was home to many types of wildlife and offered the ideal getaway and hiding place. She now understood why the Archer family built a home in the area—it was glorious and had plenty of privacy, something she gleaned was important to the United Kingdom-born crew.

"Are you ready?" she asked after dishing out the swollen balloons.

"Ready!" the girls yelled in unison. They looked adorable with their red hair in matching buns. She made sure to lather them up with sunscreen each time they ventured outside. She was still adjusting to it since she tended to tan more than burn, while the Archer girls were anything but tan.

"Fire at will!" she called.

Balloons of every color flew in the air. Bethany used her slingshot with the smaller of the bombs, while Bailey's left-handed throws went every direction. While some hit their mark—Londyn—others bounced and broke on the perfectly manicured lawn. Laughter and screams echoed around the backyard. Londyn tossed two balloons at once, catching both Bethany's and Bailey's legs.

"Is everything okay?" a man's voice asked, halting the shrieks for the time being. Theodore came into view, his normal suit discarded for khaki shorts and a T-shirt with a football team logo on the front.

"Yes, sorry. We're having a water fight." She held

up a balloon. "Want to be on the winning side?" She winked at the girls. "It's adults versus kids. So far, I'm winning."

"No you're not," Bethany called.

"Yeah, we're so beating you," Bailey added, squishing one of the balloons. Her cocky attitude ended up popping the yellow latex and splashing water all down her leg. Her face went from surprised to amused within seconds of the mistake.

Theodore pushed up his sunglasses and approached her, his dazzling blue eyes putting the sky to shame. *Holy hell, they're gorgeous.* She almost forgot he had eyes under those damn aviators he always wore. His equally jovial smile made her knees weak.

Maybe I chose the wrong guy for a fling. Because damn.

"Is there a prize for the winner?" he asked, picking up two water balloons.

"Londyn is buying Chinese!" Bailey called with a wide grin. "And I love Chinese."

Bethany rolled her eyes. "And we get to pick the movie we watch while we eat dinner on the couch." Her blue eyes beamed mischief. "I've never eaten on the couch before. Daddy says we'll get it messy."

Theodore smiled over at Bethany, then at Londyn. "How can I say no to that? Game on."

More balloons pelted from both sides at his words. Londyn hadn't had this much fun in years. It felt great to be a kid again and not worry about deadlines or bills.

Theodore crossed enemy lines, grabbed Bailey, and then swung her around on his shoulders. Bethany attacked him with a slew of balloons, and the gentle giant went down in a blaze of British glory when one of the watery bombs hit his groin.

"Avenge me," he yelled, falling dramatically to the green grass. Bailey and Bethany wasted no time dousing him in water and jumping on his conquered body.

Giggling, Londyn grabbed an armful of water missiles and ran toward the two redheads. She threw one that hit Bailey's back, and Theodore used the advantage to tickle her until she begged him to cease. It was down to Bethany and Londyn now.

"This is it, folks. England versus the United States," Theodore said in a funny commenter voice. "Two women, four balloons. Who will walk away victorious?"

Londyn grinned when she saw Bethany's serious war face. Glancing to the downed parties, she couldn't help but wonder about the story behind Theodore. He was young enough to be Callum's brother and handsome enough to make any sane woman drool. She'd shelve the thoughts for later.

"You're going down, Bethy," she heckled.

Bethany threw a balloon and it struck Londyn's chest. "It's Bethany," she corrected with a sassy grin. The four-foot cutie barreled toward Londyn, threw her last balloon, and then bolted toward the patio when she missed.

Not giving up, Londyn sprinted after her and let a blue balloon fly. She noticed too late that Callum was on the phone outside in the shadows, her aim way off. When the water balloon splattered against his chest, silence muted their war, and she skidded to a halt, inches from the concrete slab.

"Oh my damn," she mumbled, taking in the water stain on his shirt as it trickled to his pants. "I'm so sorry. I didn't see you there."

Callum held out his phone from his ear and lifted his chin. The normal fawn-colored eyes turned to a dark caramel. He said a few words in French, then hung up.

"We'll discuss this later, Miss Bellerose." He wiped a hand down his shirt. "After dinner, come to my study." He met her gaze, then slipped through the sliding glass door.

Londyn sighed. She wasn't making the best impression on her new boss. In fact, if she judged off the last few days alone, she'd imagine a teenager was the nanny and not a twenty-eight-year-old adult.

Pasting on a smile, she spun around. Bailey and Bethany wore shocked expressions, and Theodore was holding back a chuckle.

"Guess you guys won," she said with a shrug. "I wonder what movie you'll choose." She stuck out her bottom lip. "And I had my heart set on a Disney princess."

"Yes!" one girl cried while the other screamed,

"No!"

"Go whittle down the options, and I'll break the tie," she suggested.

They didn't need any more incentive, bounding toward the house. She laughed when they squeezed through the door side by side. They truly were the best kids she'd ever met. Proper, plenty of manners, and enough sass to make a mother proud.

"I better clean up the yard." She stooped and gathered shards of colored latex.

"I'll help you out before I return to washing the cars," Theodore offered with a smile. "After all, we're both the losers."

"I won't turn down the help." She returned the smile and glanced at his left hand. No ring or tan line presented itself.

He walked ahead of her and she caught herself staring at his built body. She'd never guess him to be a chauffeur if she met him on the street. His body screamed 'I live in the gym,' and his eyes hinted at something even more illicit.

"So, Theodore, have you been a private driver for long?" Londyn asked.

Theodore stuffed trash in his pockets. "I suppose so. It's a family job. My father drove the late Mr. Archer, and so on back four generations."

Londyn grabbed a stray piece of yellow balloon. "Very cool."

"It's not on the *Forbes* list of top jobs, but the

Archers treat me well. They're practically family." He took the smashed balloons from her hands. "Callum and I grew up together."

That piqued her interest. Her employer was anything but open, and she had to glean information when she could. "Then you're around the same age?"

"Actually, yes. While both Callum and I attended Oxford, I was more interested in partying than my studies. Not him, though. He was focused on his history and archaeology from day one."

"Hmm, that's admirable."

Theodore nodded. "Yeah, I guess so. I probably should've taken a page from his book when it came to school. He's the one with two degrees."

"What did you study?" Londyn asked, more interested in him by the second.

"Business." He rolled his eyes. "Boring, I know."

She grabbed the tote. "Not at all."

"I like to go with the flow and only barely convinced him to hang out with my friends and me from time to time." His eyes took on a faraway glaze. "If I could go back and force him to have more fun, I would. He's much too involved in his job nowadays. It's sad, really. We used to have such a good time together."

"Maybe he'll turn around one of these days," she hoped.

Theodore chuckled and shook his head. "I'd like to think so, but I doubt it." Grabbing the tote from her, he jutted his chin toward the house. "You go ahead.

I'll get the last of the carnage."

Londyn patted his arm—a very strong arm at that—and grinned. "You're a lifesaver. Come by later. I'll make sure they don't eat all the egg rolls."

"Perfect." He waved, then returned to the mundane task.

Jogging to the mansion, Londyn entered quietly. Callum's voice rumbled from his office, a slight Italian tint to his accent. She looked through a crack in the door and saw he'd shed his wet shirt and wore nothing underneath. He faced the window, and she instantly wondered if he'd seen her exchange with Theodore, but then the view muddled her thoughts. His back was better than she recalled from their swimming run-in: broad, muscular, and sporting a few freckles that begged for attention. When he turned slightly, her fingers itched to explore him. Her head tilted to the left at the deep V formation caused by his abs that deliciously snuck beneath his slacks. Callum shirtless was something she would beg to see on a regular basis.

The Italian words flowing from his lips sounded exotic and way too sexy paired with his shirtless torso.

I could stand here all day.

As if sensing her presence, Callum's gaze whipped to the door, brown eyes alert and searching. Afraid to get caught, she backed up and bolted to the other end of the house. Chinese and chick flicks awaited her. Thinking about the chat she'd have later with Callum, she figured she'd better check on her chocolate stash before dinner as well. Something about the man made her wish she had more than three Cs to get her through the day.

***

Pulse racing, Londyn cracked open the door to Callum's study. He sat in a high-backed leather chair, phone to his left ear. Waving her in, he continued his conversation about what sounded like a marketing debacle for the end-of-summer gala.

Londyn opted out of sitting across from him and awaited her turn for attention. It was the only constant she gleaned about him thus far.

A painted portrait of a man resembling Callum made her do a double take. She stared at the professional piece of art. No doubt about it, that was his father. She glanced to her boss, then back at the painting.

He's going to age well.

Walking along the bookshelves built into the walls, she read the titles. Most were history textbooks, scientific journals, and travel books, though the linguistic books gave her pause. There were at least ten different languages side by side. *I wonder if he knows all of these.* She recalled the Italian and French conversations she'd overheard. *Probably. It'd make sense with all the traveling he does.*

Running her fingers along the spines, Londyn grinned when she saw two lower shelves filled with children's mystery books. She glanced to Callum and saw him flip through a folder. No way they were his, but the weathered covers stood out. *Although....*

She stooped down and pulled one out. On the first page was Callum's name scrawled in juvenile handwriting. She tried to imagine a younger version of the man now speaking French in a frustrated tone. The quick switch between languages made her look up. It was rather attractive to see his lips move in a way she couldn't understand. His hand shot through his dark blond hair, ruffling it as he stood and paced.

I should've paid more attention in French class.

Sliding the novel back in its spot, she moved down the line. Some of the titles were foreign, while the modern art guide piqued her interest. His book collection appeared to be a decent combination of everything a museum curator would be expected to know. From anthropology to modern art, she could learn it all and still not come close to his intellect equal.

Londyn coughed when Callum switched to English long enough to say, "Bloody bureaucrats," before he tossed the phone to his desktop. He raised his eyes and the anger waned from his face. "Sorry, I forgot you were there."

She smiled at the paperbacks. "It's okay. I'm keeping busy with your library. It's fantastic."

Callum crossed the room and stood behind her. "If you're impressed with this, you should see my collection in England."

"It's more than this?" She eyed the three out of four walls covered in shelves, each one crammed with books.

He chuckled. "Goodness, yes. There's an entire library room. Perhaps someday you'll see it." He nodded to the chairs, and she slowly took a seat. Instead of taking his usual spot, he sat in the chair next to her.

"Is this the part where you tell me I'm great, but we should go our separate ways?" she asked at the solemn expression on his face.

"What? Of course not." He leaned up and laced his hands together. "Wait, has that chat happened before? Is it common for you to get fired after barely a month?"

"Er, no," she fibbed. She couldn't very well tell her current employer that she'd lost a few jobs because of her lack of dedication to the work, having been caught writing in the break room on more than one occasion.

"Right." Callum squinted at her, then spoke. "Well the girls adore you. I couldn't dismiss you without a very long and bloody uprising." He smiled. "I asked you to come by so we could go over summer goals."

"Oh, so it's not about me throwing a water balloon at you?" She held her breath for his answer.

"No." She relaxed until he added, "But I wasn't too fond of that."

"Okay, so goals, huh?" The idea of a structured summer break sounded as enjoyable as an enema. The warm months were meant to be lived on the fly, not forced by some doctor. Pun intended.

"Yes, goals," he repeated.

Londyn picked at her thumb cuticle, one of her habits when she was anxious. "Mmhmm, and what goals, pray tell, do you have?"

Snatching a notepad from the desk, he read aloud. "French lessons after breakfast, art class on Wednesday, swimming lessons in the afternoons, calisthenics after lunch, charity time at the animal shelter each Saturday, piano lessons on Tuesdays—"

"My, sounds busy." She peered at the list. He wasn't even halfway through. "Any time in there to squeeze in a little fun? You know, mountain climbing, riding bikes, etcetera?"

His brows rose. "All of this is fun, Miss Bellerose."

"I beg to differ, Dr. Archer."

His frown deepened. "Why do you do that?"

"What?"

He let out a huff, the sound sexier than he probably intended. "Switch between Dr. and Mr. Archer when we're talking."

Londyn crossed her left leg over her right knee. She needed to stop thinking of Callum. Especially how perfect his lips would feel on hers. "Probably for the same reason you switch between Londyn and Miss Bellerose."

"Etiquette?"

She snorted out a laugh. "Good Lord, no. I like to see your reaction. Pretty sure that's why you do it too. 'Miss Bellerose' is so uptight. Makes me feel like an old maid or something."

Callum's face dimmed. "I see. Well, I suppose I can stop calling you—"

"No," she interrupted, but wasn't sure why. On some level, she liked the way Callum called her by her proper name.

"All right, then." He flipped to the next page, then looked up. "Our last nanny kept the girls on a very strict schedule for their summer abroad."

"But I'm not your last nanny," she pointed out. If he learned anything from this chat, it'd better be that she was her own person. He'd better accept it too, since she wasn't about to give up her personality for a guy, even as hot as he was.

"No, not even close." His eyes widened as he caught his mistake and her mouth dropped open at the dry remark. "What I meant was, you're younger and have a career of sorts to get back to." He crossed his ankles. "Not that I consider flippant dreams a career, but I'm sure it works for you."

Londyn's entire body clenched at the way he tossed aside her playwriting. It was more of the same when people asked her about her life goals. They expected her to say, "Get married, have kids, and get a real job." No one ever saw the theater as sustainable or attainable for a livelihood.

She smeared on her best indifferent expression. "While you may have given up on your dreams, Dr. Archer, I have not and will not. Especially because some old curator 'bah humbugs' at me."

"Old? I beg your pardon." He flung the notebook to the oak desk. "Clearly you've no idea what you're talking about."

She came to her feet, not wanting to listen to another word he had to say despite enjoying his accent. "I'll make it to Broadway, just you wait and see."

He also stood and nodded mockingly. "Yes, yes, and I'll buy out the entire theater when that happens too," he said sarcastically. "I won't hold my breath, nor should you."

Her hands flew in the air at that last bit. "Seriously? What do you have against me trying to achieve my dreams?"

Callum let out a frustrated breath. When he met her gaze, she swore she forgot how to breathe. There was something painful in the brown depths that made her instantly regret raising her voice at him.

"Nothing. I have nothing against you, Londyn. I'm sorry." He clenched the back of the chair. "You remind me of someone who gave up everyone she supposedly loved to pursue her dreams."

Agony flooded through her at the soft tone of his voice. "Their mother?" she guessed. No one spoke of the girls' mom, so she assumed the woman had died. This turn of events made her stomach sour.

"Yes." He slumped in the seat and stared out the window into the darkness.

"I'm sorry." Caught between wanting to ask him

more and leaving it alone, Londyn stayed quiet. His personal heartaches were none of her business, nanny or not. Though his words did help her understand him a bit better.

"You can go. We're done." He waved her off, the act aggravating her more with each use.

"But what about the summer—"

His eyes meeting hers silenced the rest of her inquiry. Letting out a huff followed by a smirk, he said, "I'm willing to lessen my list of activities and try it your way for a trial period."

That caught her off guard. "Wait, really?"

Callum grabbed a crystal decanter and poured a brown liquid into a matching tumbler. "Yes, really. I shouldn't discourage Bailey's and Bethany's imaginations and dreams for what I think they should do with their time. Your free spirit may encourage them to look beyond our family business for their futures."

"Wow, all right. Thanks." She spun on her toes. "I'll still fit in some of your requirements when we have time."

He took a sip—bourbon, if her nose was right— then nodded. "Compromising already, are you? We may have a future yet, Miss Bellerose."

Londyn left him to mull over the woman who consumed his thoughts. She was assuming there, but she prided herself on knowing how to read a room, and the uptight curator was surely deep in thought over the ex she now wanted to hear more about.

Taking her time, she returned to her room. Bailey's stuffed purple giraffe sat on her pillow when she opened the door. *Such a sweetie to share her toys.* After watching *Mulan* and slurping egg drop soup with the two girls, Londyn didn't expect a positive outcome to her chat with Callum. Now as she sprawled out on the posh bed, she hoped there'd be more positivity when it came to the bookish English man on the other side of the house.

Her heart reached for him at the mention of his ex. She knew pain, and he was reeling in it. Clearly the woman hurt him badly if they didn't even speak her name. *I'll need to tread lightly on that subject,* she decided, crawling under the covers.

It bothered her how he likened the girls' mom to her because they both pursued their dreams. In her opinion, it was far from fair. His story of how his ex left them high and dry worried her. She was nothing like that, but how was he to know? She was determined to change his mind about 'free spirits' as he called them.

There's a difference between chasing your dream and losing yourself to a dream. He'll soon come to realize which path I'm destined for.

Londyn turned out the light beside the bed and hugged the purple stuffed animal in her arms. It wasn't a warm body, but it'd do until one became available. She was quite enraptured with Callum's, but the stuffed giraffe would have to do for the time being.

She grinned and closed her eyes. If anyone could

unravel the mummified heart of the museum curator, she was up for the challenge.

***

The familiar countryside of England rolled by the car window. Rain sloshed beneath the wheels, but Callum didn't mind. Rain was his favorite form of precipitation, though mostly because his homeland had plenty of it.

Scrolling through the emails on his phone, his eye twitched. The museum director was ruthless when it came to acquiring artwork, and Callum was his go-to person for the job. The piece in Paris the old man wanted didn't come easy for Callum. After a short banter with the owner of the sculpture and promising to return it within the year, Callum left triumphant. He preferred his trips to end that way. Thankful the recent trip to Paris went accordingly, Callum kept going down the list of unread messages.

A pang of worry clawed his stomach when he noticed an email from Jessica. The nerve of the woman to keep trying was beyond him. She was relentless when she wasn't bingeing somewhere.

Opening the message, Callum sucked in a breath. It was short, sweet, and full of shit, in his opinion. He deleted it upon reading, then stuffed his phone into his breast pocket. He couldn't help when his mind circled around thoughts of his ex. Jessica had been it. Well, he'd thought so, at least. She was outgoing, spunky, yet spoiled beyond belief. Having come from a poor family, the allure of a rich Brit seemed to be her main goal for her time in England years ago.

Doubtful she's changed much.

The driver pulled down the long drive to the Archer country house. Immaculate shrubbery lined the path, with tall trees on the left while the right opened up to a spacious clearing.

He never mentioned Jessica to Bailey or Bethany. They didn't remember the woman, and the thought of explaining why their mother wasn't around tore at his soul. He couldn't let them down like that. Not when his girls deserved someone better.

His conversation with Londyn the other day came to mind. She'd been dead set on doing things her way for the summer. At first, he wasn't keen on a carefree vacation, yet whenever he watched Londyn with Bailey and Bethany, his mind shifted little by little. The tall brunette didn't back down under his scrutiny and didn't try to weasel around to get her way.

The complete opposite of Jessica.

He shook his head, the thought of comparing them incredulous.

Still, watching a low-burning fire spark in Londyn's eyes at their argument made him smile days later. He was used to getting his way. It was why the museum sent him to retrieve artwork. It was also why he didn't give up on Jessica when she didn't want to marry him. He'd thought maybe, just maybe, he could change her mind about settling down. He was wrong on all accounts, and his heart bore the scars to prove it.

A phone call echoed from his pocket. *Londyn,* he noted when he saw the caller ID. *Lovely.* He cleared his throat. "Hello?"

"Callum, hey," she greeted. "So the girls were wondering when you'd be back."

He wished she didn't sound so friendly over the phone or in person. It made his usually stiff responses impossible. "Another day, I expect. Why?"

The driver came around and opened his door, giving her the chance to reply. "Well, they want to take a daytrip with you. Maybe a daddy and daughter camping trip or something."

Grabbing the umbrella from the driver, Callum hustled to the front door. "I don't know if I'll have time. Why don't you take them? They'll have more fun with you anyhow."

Londyn sighed. "Okay." It sounded like she was going to accept the rejection, but she surprised him. "You do remember what it was like to be little, don't you?"

Callum handed off the umbrella and smirked. He made his way toward the den, his favorite room in the entire mansion. "Yes, Londyn, I do."

She lowered her voice. "Then you understand how crucial it is to spend time with your daughters."

Her stubborn tone steered him directly to the bottle of bourbon. Pouring two fingers, he loosened his tie and slumped into an overstuffed chair by the large window overlooking the backyard. "I don't know what you want me to say, Miss Bellerose. My childhood was filled with tutors, boarding school, and rare visits from my parents." He paused. "Separately, never together."

"Oh, Callum."

The hushed reply sent a jolt through his body and settled in his groin. He could only imagine the same words being said in a sensual situation. The notion instantly made him hard. He coughed, hoping to disrupt further exploration. It didn't work.

"I'm sorry to hear that," she continued. "But maybe you can learn from your parents' mistakes and not make the same ones with Bailey and Bethany."

Sipping the bourbon, he closed his eyes. "Easier said than done." Girly voices shouted from the other end of the phone. "Sounds like you're being called away. We'll speak later."

Londyn's muted laugh wasn't lost on him. "Okay, enjoy your time away. And please think about what I said."

Callum disconnected before she could add more. Of course he'd think about it. He thought about every damn word she said. It was wrong, but his attraction to Londyn only mounted by the day.

He finished off the bourbon and grabbed the decanter for a refill.

"Cal, so good to see you at home."

His mother's voice caused the gulp of liquor to catch

in his throat. "Mother," he greeted after swallowing.

"This rain is quite dreadful. I wish it'd stop so I could enjoy the garden." She walked over to the window and looked out to the sizeable flower garden.

Sinking back into the leather chair, Callum stayed quiet. His mother would keep the conversation afloat, as she always did.

"The board missed you at the meeting today." Mary's eyes darted to him. "You'll take over the business, you know. You may as well get friendly with the members."

He threw back the remaining bourbon, the burn almost as bad as the one his mother dished out. "I'd rather not."

"Come, Callum. Your father would've wanted it." She returned her gaze to the rainy greenery.

He gripped the glass tighter. "No, he would've wanted me to be happy. Running two chocolate factories would *not* make me happy."

Mary stepped toward him and pursed her lips. "Happiness is a phantom, my son. Business, though, that is the way to happiness."

Officially done with the conversation, Callum stood and placed his glass on the side table. "Perhaps for you, Mother, but I prefer to find another route."

"You don't mean with love, do you?" She scoffed.

He stopped in the doorway and spun on his toes. It was no secret that his parents were never in love. Loved each other, sure, but mindlessly infatuated?

No. Their relationship was why he was adamant about finding a love that would never leave. Unfortunately for him, it hadn't happened that way. Even the possibility of loving again made his head spin. He craved the connection he'd seen in movies, but actually finding it? It seemed beyond reach.

"Yes, with love. I may be a father who travels often, but I want my children to see me happily in love. It wasn't something I saw from my parents."

Mary's brows rose. "Cal—"

"I believe I'll retire now, Mother. I'm off early tomorrow. I'll see you later." He didn't bother kissing her cheek as he'd done since childhood.

He'd meant what he said. How he'd achieve it was the conundrum.

***

"Come on, let's take a drive. I'm feeling Manitou Springs today." She laced her fingers with Bailey's, and Bethany quickly caught up with them.

"We've never been there," Bethany said. "What's there to do?"

"Oh, a ton." Londyn's eyes widened the instant they walked into the airport-like garage. It was deep enough to hold a private jet or two, but instead, twenty cars sat scattered throughout the building. "Whoa. What is all this?"

"These are Mr. Archer's hobby," Theodore explained,

appearing from the office on the right side of the structure. He smiled at the girls, then her. "Are you heading somewhere? Do you need me to drive?"

"Yes, but no. I'll drive. I kind of miss it," she said with a shy smile. "I don't get to drive much in New York since my car is in Iowa." She walked over to the cherry red 1957 Rolls-Royce Silver Cloud. "Holy crap, this car is amazing."

Theodore leaned against the side. "Yeah, she's one of Callum's favorites." His blue eyes scanned her in question. "You know about cars?"

"Oh, not a lot. My dad was obsessed with collectors when I was younger." She ran her finger along the Rolls-Royce. "We used to go to car auctions together. It was fun."

"That's great. Do you still do it when you're home?" he asked.

"No." She swallowed. "He's dead."

His smile drooped. "Shit, I'm sorry."

"It's fine." She waved his worry off. "It was a long time ago."

Surveying the rest of the building, Londyn spotted several other collector cars plus more modern ones. Infinity, Cadillac, Dodge, and Land Rover were among the newer models. A navy 1972 Chevrolet Nova 427 Yenko made her whistle low. "Damn, he sure likes his cars."

Laughing, Theodore nodded to the 1955 Mercedes-Benz 300SL Gullwing. "He does. He's a huge history buff, so there's that. He and his dad used to tinker on the cars now and then." He nodded to the older vehicles. "Some of these he inherited when his father passed, and the others I may have helped him with."

"It all makes sense. You find the collector cars and use his money to buy them," she teased.

"Guilty." He went to the box of key rings and plucked one off. "But he enjoys them too, so it's a win-win."

"I suppose so." She noticed the girls were waiting next to a late 90s Land Rover Defender. "Is that my car for the day?"

"No, that's Callum's car. Yours is the Infinity SUV." His brows furrowed, but then he shrugged. "But since he's in for the day, why not? I'll use the Cadillac SUV if he needs to go somewhere."

Londyn snatched the keys from his hand. "Perfect. We're off."

He grinned, then asked, "Where to?"

"Manitou Springs."

"I've heard it's a sight. Have fun," he called as they piled into the car.

She waved fast, then started the engine. If she wasn't already addicted to this lifestyle, the car alone would get her there. It was a soon-to-be classic. "I could get used to this."

Six hours later, they rolled back down the long driveway. Theodore smiled at their approach and guided them into the garage.

"Okay, girls, go wash up. You two got so dirty at the cliff dwellings."

Bailey and Bethany hopped out of the car and ran toward the house before she could say another word. After grabbing her purse and cleaning the back seat of their drive-thru dinner wrappers, Londyn closed the door. Callum's stern face met her once it was shut.

"Holy shit, you scared me!" She placed a hand over her chest.

"Why'd you take my car?" he asked, not bothering to greet her.

Londyn slung the strap on her shoulder. "Because it was there, and the girls wanted to."

"And you do everything the girls want?"

Londyn scrunched up her face. He was awfully invested in a car's well-being. Maybe she shouldn't have taken it. "No. It's a car. Theodore said you wouldn't be going anywhere, so I didn't see the problem."

"The problem is that I did need my car this afternoon. And when I came to get it, I found out you took it."

Rolling her eyes, she moved toward the house. After an afternoon of wrangling the girls, she didn't want to deal with him.

"We aren't done, Miss Bellerose." The authoritative tone in his voice made her stomach churn. She wasn't huge on confrontation when she was on the other end.

She whirled on her toes and glowered. "I am."

He caught up with her without any hassle. *Damn long legs of his.*

"You're to use your car from now on," Callum stated with finality.

Swinging her purse to the other shoulder, she shrugged. "You have nineteen other cars you can use, Dr. Archer. You can survive if I ever take your car again."

His brows rose so high she was afraid they'd merge with his hairline. "God, you're infuriating. Can you be controlled at all?"

"Nope." She placed a hand on her hip. "Not when you're being ridiculous. It's a car, Callum."

"It's *my* car, Londyn." He took a step closer, the fury still prevalent in his brown eyes.

Still not sure why it was a big deal, she moved toward the house. "So?"

"It was the last gift my father gave to me," he said quietly. "I don't want it harmed."

Understanding flooded her, but not forgiveness. "Oh wow. I'm sorry. I didn't know. I should've taken the other car."

Silence simmered between them. The desire to scurry into the house and away from him nearly overwhelmed her. As much as she liked being near him, she didn't trust herself not to act instead of think.

"You know, it's fine." He let out a breath, eyes fixed on the setting sun. "I just realized what I was fighting about, and it's stupid. Sometimes I pick fights for no reason. I'm sorry. I don't know why I overreacted."

"Hey, it's one of your favorites." She offered him

a small smile. "I get cranky when Abi steals my collector's edition of *Pride and Prejudice*, so I get it." She eyed the car. "Sort of."

He chuckled. The change in him calmed her down as well. She understood the attachment to everyday items, even if hers was a television series and his was a collector car.

"Did you have a good time in Manitou?" he asked, falling in step with her.

She rather liked being in someone's shadow for once. It made her feel safer somehow. "We did. Our first stop was the Cliff Dwellings."

Callum placed a hand on her arm. "You took them to a historical place?"

"Of course. Why wouldn't I?" Londyn fought the urge to kiss his shocked face. No doubt he'd never expected her to like the same things.

Huh, I guess we have more in common than I thought. First the cars, now history. She'd judged him too quickly. It wasn't her finest habit, but it happened more than she liked to admit.

He looked lost for words. "I, uh, wasn't aware you liked history."

"It made humans who we are, so yeah, I like to dig into history whenever possible." She held up a hand. "But don't get me wrong, I have no idea what I'm talking about half the time."

He chuckled and scratched his nose. "That's all right. We usually make things up." He lowered his voice and winked. "Nobody knows but us."

Londyn smiled over to him. She liked this kidding side of Callum. It was even more attractive than his brooding side.

Of course, the brooding is still hot. How could it not be? He is British, after all.

"Bailey and Bethany loved seeing the structures, I think. They each got an arrowhead necklace from the gift shop, and then we checked out the mineral springs. After that, we went to Cave of the Winds." She shivered. "It was a little spooky there, so we had to stop by a restaurant and get some ice cream. We ended the day shopping, then grabbed dinner on the way back."

He held open the door to the house for her. "Sounds like you had a good time."

Pausing over the threshold, she gazed up at him. "It would've been better if you were there."

Closing the small distance between her and the door, Callum's body grazed hers as they stood neither inside nor out. His eyes dipped to her lips and then back up to her eyes. The act made Londyn's breath catch. Anytime she was around him, she wanted this to happen, to be touching him.

Then a buzzing sound broke into their locked gazes.

"That'll be the museum," he said, clearing his throat.

"You mustn't keep them waiting." She stepped backward. "You might actually have a life if you didn't answer."

Callum sighed at her snide remark and tugged her

back to him. Surprised at the act, she didn't have a chance to object. "I have a job, Londyn. One I must maintain or someone else will steal it out from under me."

"It's a job, Callum." She pressed her lips together. "Just like it was a car." Patting his chest, she gulped at the hard plane. "Those things can be replaced. Your family cannot."

He scanned her eyes, his face hard. "You're right, but a nanny can be."

Appalled he'd even suggest it, she shoved at him. The act backfired when she tripped over her feet and nearly face-planted on the marble entry. Callum's steady arms caught her and hauled her upright.

"Really, Miss Bellerose, you need to learn how to take a joke." His brown eyes lit up with mirth, and he pulled her close until her chest was pressed to his. "I can't replace you either."

"You can't?" she asked, surprised at both his teasing and the statement.

He offered a lopsided grin. "Well, I could try, but I think my children would disown me." She gave him an annoyed glance, so he added, "Plus I'm rather fond of you. Free spirit and all."

"Oh." It was all she could muster. Between being enclosed in his arms and never wanting to leave them, Londyn wasn't sure what to say next. It was a rarity in her line of work, and one she didn't like one bit. She was always prepared to offer quick wit or a sassy retort, but Callum turned her brain to mush.

And I like it.

His eyes darted between her lips and her eyes. She rubbed her lips together instinctively and a pained expression covered his face. "You really need to stop doing that, Miss Bellerose. I'm liable to kiss you one of these times."

Londyn's mouth dropped open. He wasn't joking that time. He was serious, and it only made breathing that much harder.

"I'd best find out what they wanted," he said, breaking free from their tangled arms when his phone rang again.

"Yeah, sure." She turned away and took a deep breath. "I better check on the girls. They're probably filling the tub with way too many bubbles." She set her feet into motion and didn't look back until she was safely in her own bedroom.

"What is going on with me?" She tossed her purse to the dresser and stared into the mirror. Her cheeks were flushed, eyes dilated.

Callum. He'd done that to her.

The longer she looked at her reflection, the more she liked the residual effects of the museum curator.

CHAPTER FIVE

Rolling out of bed, Callum winced at the pain in his lower back, and frowned at the top-of-the-line mattress. It was new and not his type of comfortable. Naturally, his meddling mother had ordered it while he took a quick trip to Germany. When he came home yesterday, he'd been too tired to give a shit.

He tugged his robe and slippers in place, then yawned at the time on the clock. It was half past two in the afternoon. He'd slept much longer than usual, but traveling had taken its toll on his body. It was the same whenever he went abroad. A little part of him wished his job didn't include constant red-eyes and late-night flights.

Not bothering to check his phone, he headed downstairs after brushing his teeth. Following the sounds of laughter and girlish voices, Callum paused in the shadow outside the kitchen door. The serene scene he came across was one he could easily get used to seeing. Bailey's fingers were covered with dough, while Bethany rolled the sticky concoction into globs, then placed them on baking sheets. Londyn was somehow covered in what looked like flour as she offered tips and kind advice to the chefs-in-training.

Watching for a minute, he gathered more information about her personality. She was always nearby to lend a hand, but didn't micromanage their baking creativity.

He leaned an arm on the doorframe, a smile swiftly spreading over his face. It was mesmerizing. He'd always wished to see his children and their mother doing precisely this. He swallowed a lump in his throat at the thought. Bailey and Bethany would never have such an opportunity. Their mum preferred modeling, rock bands, and recreational drugs over her flesh and blood. The memory brought up the bitter past, but he pushed it down. Dealing with Jessica wasn't something he'd ever have to do again.

For now, he was content with Londyn. She was the closest thing they'd have to a surrogate mother. Her demeanor was caring, yet she could give the best 'mum' stare he'd ever seen when they crossed a line. Without question, she was the best nanny to grace the Archer family. *Plus she looks stunning in black athletic shorts and a yellow racerback tank top.* He swore that was all the woman wore, but he didn't mind in the least.

As he admired the long legs of his nanny, a burning

scent reached his nose. *Surely she knows how to bake.* When the fire alarm shrieked at the opening of the oven, Callum found the answer to his own question.

Bailey and Bethany placed grimy hands over their ears as Londyn frantically raced around the kitchen in search of oven mitts. She found them just in time, on top of the island buried beneath cooling racks.

"Crapolony," she mumbled, pulling the baking sheet from the smoky haze. The once-edible treats were toast—well, burnt toast.

Deciding it was as good a time as any, he walked into the kitchen and made a beeline for the alarm system. Quickly punching in the code, the high-pitched scream shut off within seconds. The last thing he needed was the fire department showing up. One of the hunky fireman would undoubtedly sweep Londyn right off her feet.

He shoved the thought aside. *Why do I care who she dates?*

"There. I'm glad I got up when I did," he said, pushing open the window above the sink before moving to the others and doing the same. Glancing at Londyn, he noticed her face was forlorn as she examined the biscuits.

"Thanks," she said, then huffed in defeat.

Bailey rushed to his side, and Bethany licked her fingers clean. He didn't even want to address the sanitary conundrums he was witnessing right then.

"Go wash up, girls," he said.

They scampered off to the bathroom down the hall, leaving him with a disappointed nanny.

Peering over her shoulder, he held in a chuckle. The black blobs couldn't look worse. "So, uh, I'm curious. What kind of biscuits were they supposed to be?"

Londyn scraped one off the sheet and smelled it. Her nose scrunched up in the most adorable way at the foulness. "Chocolate chip." She dropped the biscuit in the sink. "I'm not usually the one in the kitchen. My roommate does most of the baking, and we order in a lot." Her shoulders sagged, and the French braid slipped to her back. "I'm such a failure. No wonder I'm single. What man would want a woman who can't bake?"

Leaning closer, the mixture of chocolate and cinnamon assaulted him. It couldn't have been the biscuits. He inhaled quietly. No, it was Londyn herself. Somehow she bottled the essence and combined it with a poignant cinnamon stick.

His pulse raced as new memories flooded his mind at the sugary fragrance. Until her, he hated anything having to do with chocolate. Now, as he gently turned her around, he'd sell his soul to have her chocolatey scent consume him at all times.

"You may not be able to bake, but you did something better." His fingers itched to move from her shoulders and explore more of her. She smelled too damn good to pass up. Instead, Callum continued. "You made my girls smile and taught them something new."

"I guess," she mumbled, her gaze on her toes.

Lifting her chin with his index finger, Callum's words caught in his throat. Small tears lined her stormy blue eyes when they met his. "Ah, Londyn. None of those. They're only biscuits." He moved as close as possible. He didn't want any space between them, but he held back from completely demolishing the line of employer and employee. It was a constant battle he struggled with every time they interacted. "Don't be discouraged. The single memory Bailey and Bethany will have is what fun they had today." He smirked. "And how you aren't to be left unattended in a kitchen."

That earned a reaction from her. Gray-blue eyes flashed, but she merely shook her head and laughed. "You're right. It's not a big deal. I just wanted it to be special like when I was little. Some of the best times with my mom were in the kitchen." She bit her bottom lip. "I know I'm not their mom, but I hope they're getting a sample of what a real mom does with her kids."

If he didn't already have flickers of feelings for her, Callum would've burst into a full-fledged bonfire at her soft words. "You really are something, Londyn Bellerose." His thumb drifted over her lip, and he reveled at how soft it was. He shouldn't be anywhere near her lips, but the desire to kiss her overwhelmed him.

"Is it something good?" she asked, her gaze dropping to his mouth.

So she's thinking it too. Good.

He swallowed a smile. The thought that she wanted him a fraction of how much he wanted her encouraged his tentative mind. "Oh yes, very good." Her racing pulse carried across her face to his finger. "And Londyn?"

"Yes?"

He grazed her ear with his lips. "I don't give a toss that you're horrid in the kitchen." Meeting her eyes, he added, "In fact, I rather like it."

The gorgeous depths to her blue eyes glazed over with a gray hue. God, he could stare at her forever and never tire of it.

"Daddy, tell Bailey I made the best biscuits." Bethany's voice hastily broke them apart.

Bugger. He continued to curse silently as Londyn skittered to the disastrous biscuits.

Hunkering down to his daughter's height, he wiped a smudge of chocolate from her cheek. "My darling, your biscuits look divine. Do I get to try one when they're baked?"

Shaking her head, the oldest of his children bounced to the sheet of raw dough. "Once they're done, I'll bring you a whole plate full of them. With milk too."

Callum kissed the top of her head. "I can't think of a better snack." He tickled Bailey's side when she pouted. "And I'll want to try one of yours as well."

The redhead in pigtails jumped up and down and clapped her hands. "Yes! Then you'll see why my biscuit is deliciouser."

Even sparring, his girls were the light of his life.

While the two argued about their cooking skills, he grabbed a mug and poured tea into it. *Thank goodness Gloria keeps the pot on all day.* After a drop of honey, he stirred the hot liquid with a tiny spoon.

"Now there's one thing you both must assure me," he began with a serious tone.

"What, Daddy?" Bailey asked, eyes huge with wonder.

He looked to Londyn, who hadn't stopped scraping the tray with a spatula. A tuft of her brown hair came loose from the braid and settled at her jaw. "Make certain Gloria is back in here before Londyn tries to bake anything else, all right?"

"Hey!" Londyn retorted, eyes locked on him.

Callum shrugged and took a sip. It hit the spot, just like the fiery expression on Londyn's face. "Maybe steer clear of the laundry room too. I'd hate to wade in suds."

Bethany and Bailey giggled in agreement, then added their own cute jabs. Londyn took it like a champ, her hands on her hips and a secretive smile on her lips.

This is how life is supposed to be. Easy, fun, inspiring. How did I not know this until now?

***

"Whoa, are these all comics?" Bailey asked, scanning

the hole-in-the-wall shop.

"Yes, ma'am." Londyn steered them toward the female superhero section. "And each of you get to choose two comic books to take home. If you like them, we can come back for more."

With glee-filled faces, they scattered in the direction of the tables bursting with comic books. Londyn fingered through the latest *Wonder Woman* graphic novels, noting which ones she had and those she didn't. It wasn't a pastime many women had, but she and her dad were superhero junkies since she was a kid. That love tumbled over to comics, movies, and television shows. Reading side by side with him led her to write comics of her own, though she couldn't draw a lick. With his encouragement, she penned her first play at nine years old. It was a disaster, but he raved about it to all his friends.

Thumbing through an older edition, a sad smile crossed her face. Missing her parents came in waves, and being in the one spot where her father would've stayed until close brought a fresh one to bay. In retrospect, her dad's love of comics—including an entire room dedicated to them—led her to read every novel he kept behind glass. She kept them all after his death. They were one of her prized possessions, even if most of them were in a storage locker. Some of the comics were worth thousands of dollars, but she couldn't ever part with them. They were as much a part of her as Callum and his cars.

Pausing on that thought, Londyn felt a tiny bit bad for getting upset with him the other day. She'd do the same if she caught him going through her dad's comics. *No, I'd be worse.*

"Londyn, I found a girl who can fly!" Bailey yelled from the other side of the shop.

Eyeing the *Supergirl* comic, she grinned. It was one of her favorites too. "That's awesome! Did you find anything, Bethany?"

The other girl held up a comic Londyn wasn't familiar with. "It's called *Gotham Academy*." Bethany's eyes skimmed the thin book. "It looks pretty cool."

"What'd you find?" Bailey asked, now at Londyn's side.

She pulled out a *Batgirl* comic and handed it to her. "I was thinking about getting this one and maybe a *Wonder Woman* comic. What do you think?"

Bailey's brows knit together and she quickly flipped through the pages. "I guess it's okay. I like mine better."

Laughing, Londyn tugged on the girl's ponytail. "Yeah, yours is pretty cool."

"Have you read a lot of these?" Bethany asked, joining their group.

"Actually I have. My dad and I used to read them together." Pushing a comic back in its place, Londyn watched the girls closely. "Do you and your dad do anything special together?"

"Sometimes he takes us to new art exhibits," Bailey replied with a sour face. "I don't particularly like it.

Art is boring. I want to play, but you have to be quiet at the gallery."

"Hmm, that is a problem." She turned to Bethany. "Do you like art?"

Bethany shrugged and opened her comic. "It's all right. Daddy likes when we go, so I try to be good. I'd rather go horseback riding, though."

Londyn looped her arms around the girls and led them toward the cashier, who wore a bright pink Wonder Woman shirt. "You know, we haven't seen your horses at home in a couple days. Why don't we do that when we get back?"

The agreement was unanimous, and after purchasing their comics, the three returned to Archer House. She was driving her SUV after the last run-in with Callum. Really, she didn't mind arguing with him. It was rather cute the way his face reddened and the vein on his forehead stuck out. She smirked and shook the thoughts aside.

After spending an hour in the horse barn, Londyn was relieved to have air conditioning again. The ninety-degree weather crept up on her, and even though the girls didn't complain, the stuffy barn coupled with warm horse bodies made it more like a sauna with hair. A sticky combination all around.

"Yes, AC," she sighed, flopping onto the couch. Closing her eyes, Londyn wondered if all summers were like this for the Archers. She could get used to it, heat wave or not.

Bailey rustled through the bag from the comic book store. "I'm going to read," she announced. The soft thud that followed told Londyn she was on the miniature rocking chair. It was the girl's favorite spot aside from her nanny's lap for nightly movies.

"Me too," her sister added from the love seat.

Opening her eyes, Londyn smiled at the scene. Both girls had their noses stuck in comic books and appeared to be enjoying themselves. After hearing they'd never read one before, she had to rectify the mistake immediately. Now, hours later, Londyn was proud of herself for introducing the imagery of graphic novels. The world needed more girls who read and enjoyed all things superhero- and comic-based.

Digging out her books, she pried open the first one and started reading. The fan overhead oscillated speedily, slightly rustling the pages. Propping a pillow under her head and crossing one leg over the other, she snuggled into the comfortable couch.

"Wonder Woman, huh? I would've guessed Batgirl."

Slowly lowering the book, Londyn spotted Callum at the end of the couch with an amused smirk on his handsome face. His light blue polo was untucked and accentuated his wide chest. If she peered hard enough, she could make out the muscles of his pecs. The light tan slacks didn't hurt matters either, but it was his eyes that did her in—full of mischief and a hint of longing. Staring into those until her own eyes dried promptly rose to the top of her to-do list.

"Damn, you're beautiful." She slapped the comic against her lips when his brows rose. Instantly, she realized her thought was said aloud. The heat creeping on her skin made the sauna from the horse barn insignificant. If she looked in a mirror, she was positive she'd be as red as a tomato. "Crap, uh, yeah, Wonder Woman is one of my favorites."

Callum snatched the novel and flipped through it. "We're just going to ignore what you said, then?"

"Yeah, that'd be great." She grabbed the comic back and changed the subject. "The girls and I went to the local comic book store in Colorado Springs." Pointing to the duo engrossed in their stories, she grinned and met his gaze. "I think they like them."

"I'd say you're right." He walked over and studied each of the comic covers before returning to her side. "I never thought they would."

"Girls can like comics too," she reminded him. "There's a whole slew of them just for the female gender, in my opinion. With all the superheroes, an everyday person can be one. I think that's why I like them so much. The opportunity to be a completely different person with one wardrobe change. It's a lot like the theater, now that I think about it."

"I never thought of it like that." He picked up one of the comic books from the couch. "Do you relate to any of the superheroes? Or villains?"

Pressing her lips together, she thought it over. There were plenty she could say, but she went with her childhood favorite. "I'd have to say Supergirl. She's honest, a defender of the innocent, and the whole flying bit and super speed would be amazing."

"You know, it does sound like you." He chuckled. "I'm impressed you like comics. Not many women do. It's different."

She gave him a pointed look. "Bad different?"

"No, not in the least." His eyes met hers, and she wished the air conditioning would be turned lower. "I like finding out these surprising things about you, Miss Bellerose. They're charming."

"Who would you be, Daddy?" Bailey asked, suddenly involved in the conversation. Londyn was grateful for the interruption. Having his sole attention was nerve-racking. Somehow, he managed to make butterflies swirl in her stomach by simply talking to her. She was growing fond of it more and more. And the fact that he wasn't repulsed by her love of comics, well, that was icing on the top.

Callum crouched in front of his daughter. "Who do you think?"

"Hmm." The four-year-old tapped her chin. "Superman!"

"No way. Definitely Aquaman, because he likes to swim," Bethany argued, holding up a photo of the comic she referenced.

Looking over to Londyn, he asked, "What about you? Who do you think I'd be?"

Londyn swallowed the boulder in her throat. While

he would make a fabulous Superman or Aquaman, her mind was made up when she first arrived. "Definitely Batman."

He stood and grinned at his daughters. "Oh?"

"Yeah, because you have a butler named Alfred."

"Any other reason?" he asked, somehow right next to her.

The light tanginess from his cologne met her nose, and she tried not to close her eyes at the intoxicating smell. "Plus you like to dress sharply, have all sorts of fun cars, and I'm pretty sure you have a hidden office behind all those books," she teased.

"Hush now, or you'll give away my secret," he whispered, tickling Bethany under the chin. "If the children find out, I'll never hear the end of it."

Catching on to his play, Londyn put a finger over her lips. "Don't worry, I won't give you away."

"I will!" Bailey shouted, throwing down her comic and running toward her father. She rammed his leg, which resulted in him playfully toppling over. Bethany joined in, messing up his hair until it stuck up in every direction possible.

Hopping out of the way of the impromptu wrestling match, Londyn sighed at the family in front of her. Little by little, she learned new tidbits about Callum. Her initial perceptions of him were skewed, though not entirely off base. He still needed to loosen up, but watching him tickle his girls like a monster shifted a piece of her heart toward him.

If she kept it up, there wouldn't be anything left.

***

Typing a response to an email, Callum heard his office door open. The rush of hot air when Sherlock panted on his leg made him glance down. The old basset hound was always around, a fact he loved yet sometimes detested when slobber was involved.

Reaching down, he scratched Sherlock's floppy ears. "I haven't seen you for hours. Where've you been hiding?"

"With Londyn and the girls," Theodore stated, entering the room.

"Was he now?" Callum's fingers paused, causing Sherlock to grunt softly at the interruption. He met Theodore's gaze. It'd been some time since his old friend visited him. Mostly because of Theodore's boyfriend. The two were adorable yet made him envious of their connection.

"Yep, she's got a real way with animals and children." Theodore sat in the chair across from him. "And with you."

Callum frowned. "I don't know what you're talking about."

"Mmhmm, sure you don't. I see the way you look at her." His friend wiggled his eyebrows.

"Like an employee, yes."

Theodore snorted and crossed his arms. "More like

an employee you wouldn't mind shagging."

Returning to the laptop, he hit the button to send his email. "That would be inappropriate, Teddy."

"Yes it would." Theodore grinned. "Which is why you should do it."

Callum rolled his eyes. "You can't be serious."

"But I am."

"She doesn't like me in that way."

It was Theodore's turn to roll his eyes. "Oh, bollocks. She looks at you like you're God's greatest gift."

"Well, I am." He couldn't help but say it. At university, that was always Theodore's line.

"Yeah, yeah, but seriously, Callum. At the very least, she thinks you're attractive."

Standing, he retrieved two glasses and a bottle of bourbon. After pouring one for each of them, he said, "It doesn't matter. We're professionals, and it's safer to stay that way."

Theodore sipped his drink. "Perhaps, but what if Londyn is the woman you're meant to be with?"

"A struggling playwright from Iowa?" he scoffed. "I doubt it."

Shaking his head, Theodore chuckled. "The fact that you're fighting this affirms my thoughts." Before Callum could interrupt, he continued. "She asks about you, you know? Plus, I doubt her tiny bikinis when you're around are by accident."

"What about the girls?" he asked, wary of putting his thoughts into action. Of course he wanted to kiss Londyn. His dreams at night only reiterated the craving. But he couldn't.

"They love her. Plus, it's not like you'll do anything when they're around. I know you too well," Theodore said with a tilt of his cup.

It wasn't far from the truth. Callum's parents had raised him with the upmost respect for women, which included no public displays of affection. In retrospect, he wished he'd rebelled a bit. It could've been why he wasn't successful with Jessica.

He shook his head. *No, she had her own problems. I wasn't one of them.*

"What're you going to do, old friend?" Theodore asked.

Callum patted Sherlock's head. It was a good question. He'd been struggling with the temptation ever since Londyn set foot in his house. It wasn't just her looks—not that those didn't hurt at all—that drew him to her. There was something about Londyn that made his heart beat as though it was the first time. Which was ridiculous, since he barely knew her, yet somewhere in his mind, Callum couldn't let the chance go.

"I'll see if she has similar feelings."

Theodore's head bobbed. "And then?"

"Then I'll woo her."

"Pardon?"

Seeing the odd expression on Theodore's face, Callum smirked. "You know, pursue her without being a jackass." He sipped the bourbon. "I'd prefer to keep Londyn interested in me. The best way I know how is to be a complete gentleman."

Theodore blew a raspberry. "Sounds horrid. Just grab her shoulders and kiss her. You'll get your answer faster."

"I'm not a caveman, Teddy." He chuckled when his friend gave him a pointed look. "All right, I can be, but I don't want to rush this."

"She's only here for the summer, Callum," Theodore reminded him.

The thought had crossed his mind more than once. Still, Callum couldn't shake the idea that if he and Londyn had a connection, it wouldn't be destroyed by a timeframe. "Yes, well I suppose I'd better hurry and be my best dashing self."

Coughing on his bourbon, Theodore wiped his mouth, then stood. "Don't wait too long. A lady like Londyn doesn't come along too often."

"Duly noted." Nodding in agreement, he watched his friend disappear through the doorway. Sherlock nudged his hand, so Callum scratched the dog under his chin.

He'd take Theodore's advice, even if it scared him. Moving on was overdue. Whether or not Londyn was the woman for him, he'd have to find out sooner rather than later. If he waited too long, she'd be gone in more ways than one.

***

A dance party. It was how Bailey wished to spend Saturday night. It didn't take any convincing of her sister either—they were both thrilled to host in their nursery. And not just any regular dance party. A karaoke and costume dance party.

Chucking a sparkly pink pillow onto the rearranged furniture, Londyn surveyed the room that served as both a bedroom and playroom for the Archer girls. Of course, it was bigger than her apartment in Queens and held two canopy-style beds side by side on one-half of the room. A set of stairs led to a play area loft above making it ideal for two girls becoming more independent by the day.

"You guys ready yet?" she called. The play area had been cleaned until it shone, and the couch now faced the window. A karaoke machine sat ready for use, and the girls had even created a makeshift stage for the activity. She grinned as she plugged in the twinkle lights. It took thirty minutes, but they shaped a square on the carpeted floor in front of the bay window until it resembled a stage.

"Coming down," Bethany yelled.

"But don't look yet," Bailey added.

"Yeah, close your eyes." Bethany called.

"All right, all right. They're closed tight." She squeezed her eyelids shut and heard the gentle swish of skirts and rustle of taffeta.

"Open," they said as one.

The sight she was met with made her mouth drop open in amazement. They weren't wearing cheap dress-up clothes like she did growing up. They wore authentic gowns made specifically for their little bodies, and no cost was spared in the details.

"Oh my goodness, girls. You look stunning." She twirled her finger and they both spun around to show off their outfits. "Wow. I'm officially jealous." She patted Bailey's dress. "It looks so real. Are you sure you didn't steal this from Cinderella's castle?"

Bailey's blue eyes squinted as she smiled. The color of the dress perfectly matched the azure hue. "No, silly. Daddy had it made."

"He did well." She switched her attention to Bethany. "You are the epitome of a Victorian mademoiselle in that lavender gown." She fluffed the skirts. "How can you even walk in this thing?"

Bethany spun around, dress swelling in a large poof as if to prove she could do anything. "Easy. Now go change," she commanded, taking charge.

"Oh, I think this is good enough." Londyn pointed to the strapless purple sundress Abi had made.

"No way." Bailey shook her head and yanked on Londyn's hand. "There are big girl dresses in the closet." The little girl pushed her nanny closer to the walk-in. "Don't come out until you're beautifuller," she said before closing the door.

Not sure what she'd find, but given no other choice,

Londyn emerged five minutes later wearing the single item that fit her tall frame, a flowy blue and white kimono. Judging by the texture of the dress, it was straight from Japan. The long sleeves hit at her elbow, and the skirt part of the silky fabric touched above her knees. Obviously it wasn't made for a woman almost six feet in height.

"Ready or not," she called, opening the door. To her delight, Theodore had joined the judge's panel on the couch.

Bailey rushed over and slid her petite hands up and down the soft dress. "You look very pretty," she said, looking up at Londyn.

The adoration in the little girl's eyes was too much for her to handle. Such a small act of dressing up meant the world to the four-year-old. "Shall I spin too?" She started her rotation and was glad she'd left her shorts on underneath. "What do you think, Bethany?"

The older girl scrutinized every inch, then nodded once. "It'll do."

Londyn laughed at the adultlike reaction. It sounded like a response Callum would offer.

Pushing her jumbled feelings for the good doctor away, she sat next to Theodore. "How did you luck out and not have to change too?"

Theodore pulled out a hat from behind him. "I brought my own props." He plopped the blue tweed cap over his brown hair and instantly looked as if he'd stepped out of an English moor.

Rolling her eyes, she was glad Bailey started the sing-off with a familiar yet agonizing rendition of "Let It Go." The child may be cute, but singing was not her forte. Both Londyn and Theodore clapped enthusiastically when the youngest Archer finished with a ballerina twirl.

Bethany followed with a moving song from *Pocahontas*, complete with dance moves thrown in here and there. The ballet lessons were really the best thing Callum could've done for the girls. Neither could sing a note, but she loved them even more because of it. They weren't afraid to mess up or be embarrassed; they were simply happy being themselves.

More applause followed a dramatic bow and plié from Bethany. Bailey ran onstage to join in on the fame. Theodore may have gone a bit overboard with the whistling. Glancing at him, Londyn was glad he was genuinely involved with the girls. They adored him, and for obvious reasons.

"Your turn," Bethany stated, holding out the microphone.

Palms instantly sweaty, Londyn looked at the pleading faces in front of her. Bailey was much too good at the puppy dog expression. "How can I say no?"

"You can't," Theodore said with a wink.

Standing, she blushed when he let out a few whistles and catcalls as she made her way to the square of lights and flipped through the book of songs. Their karaoke machine was much nicer than the ones she'd used at the bars back home.

There's no way I'm singing a Disney song. She moved the pages until she found the adult section. When her gaze caught some early 2000s bands, she looked to Theodore. "Hey, do you want to sing with me?"

"Well—" The girls grabbed his arms and hauled him off the couch. "I guess I do," he laughed, stepping over the lights. "What did you have in mind?"

She eyed his in-shape body. "How's your dancing?"

Worry lined his brow. "Uh, dancing? I've been working on it, but I must warn you I'm not the best at some styles." He looked over her shoulder at her choice. "You can't be serious." She wiggled her eyebrows. "No, can't do it."

"Aw, come on," she begged, tugging on his hand. It was soft, definitely not what she expected from the burly man. "I know every move to the song. Well, at least I used to. You can play puppeteer if you aren't comfortable."

A mischievous glint flashed in his blue eyes. "Oh, no. This genre of music is right up my alley. I'll dance circles around you, girl," he heckled, stretching his muscles and hopping up and down like a fighter. "I'll hit the lights so there's more ambience. This is going to be epic."

Once the lights were down and only the string of white holiday lights lit up the room, Londyn cranked up the boy band melody. Bailey and Bethany bounced on the couch as *NSYNC 's "Bye, Bye, Bye" blared.

In unison, Londyn and Theodore started the easy introduction hops. She laughed when her feet crossed and she nearly fell. They let the boys take each chorus while they kicked, arms mimicking the group's movements, and twirled around during the routine. They weren't in sync the whole time, but with practice, they would've been incredible. No longer was she worried about the kimono getting in her way or the possibility of falling on her ass. She was dancing, singing, and having more fun than should be legal.

Both she and Theodore took turns belting out the easy lyrics in the tiny microphone. Getting close enough to harmonize, Londyn couldn't help but wonder how his voice was so angelic and his moves so professional.

Thankfully, the karaoke version of the song was shorter, but by the time they sang the last note, perspiration dripped down her back and her hair was officially a mess. She had to approve of the flowy kimono, though, as it gave her plenty of wiggle room for the dancing.

Glancing to Theodore, she saw he was equally worn out from the pop song. "Well, what'd you think?" she asked, catching her breath. "I'm a little rusty, but the singing was solid, right?"

"I think if nannying and writing don't pan out, you have a great future in music videos," a new voice said.

Londyn froze. A bead of sweat slid off her forehead, and she let it fall to the floor. Peering into the dark audience, her eyes adjusted enough to see Callum sitting on the couch with Bailey and Bethany on his lap. An amused smile played across his handsome face.

"I… uh… I didn't realize you were there," she stammered.

Callum moved Bethany's hair out of his face. "I snuck in midway through your puppeteer bit." He smirked at Theodore. "I see your dance lessons are paying off."

Theodore's face flushed and he toyed with his cap. "I'd like to disagree, but I was bloody amazing."

Londyn stepped off the stage and ran her hands over the front of her dress. Her sweaty palms slid right off the silk. "Not the best material for dancing."

As the girls chased Theodore, who snagged Bailey's fairy wand, Callum stood and lowered his voice. "Maybe not, but you looked good moving in it."

Warmer now than during her ancient dance moves, Londyn fanned her face with the large sleeves. The look in Callum's eyes told her much more than how well she mimicked a pop song. The temptation in those light brown eyes made her throat dry. It was the same every time. Callum didn't speak in many words, but why would he when his eyes did more than enough communicating?

"So, are you going to give it a go? Maybe a nice Frank Sinatra song?" she asked as Theodore wrestled both girls to the ground and tickled them. He was such a natural.

She peered at the man beside her, watching with a polite smile. *Why isn't he joining in?* She'd seen him do so just the other day. *Maybe it's because Theodore's here.*

"You and Theodore looked quite compatible up there," he said with a grin.

Startled at the subject change, she shrugged. "He's an impressive dancer. I can't figure out how, though. Most guys are horrible. Then again, his lessons probably help."

Callum's hand caught one of the kimono's long sleeves. "He's always been better at certain things, such as dancing." He met her gaze. "He and his boyfriend are incredible together. I swear they're even better dancers than professionals."

The instant the words were aired, it all made sense. The majority of her best friends in life were gay—a fact she should've picked up on earlier. "No wonder he knew how to match makeup for the girls better than me."

"Theodore's been like a brother to me over the years. He was always great with the girls, and they see him as an uncle figure," he filled in the lingering questions she'd left unasked. "Being childlike is easy for him. I don't share the same quality." He turned his head toward her. "Which is why I won't be singing Sinatra or any other great crooner. I'm not the outgoing, 'leave it all out there' type of person."

"I gathered as much," she mumbled, then bit her lip.

Dammit, Londyn.

He chuckled, making him appear younger. "Yes, I'm sure you have." He looked straight ahead. "I don't do something unless I know I can succeed. I've always been like that. The few times I didn't think it through ended poorly."

His ex. No doubt it was the decision he referred to. His wariness pained her. Love wasn't supposed to be gut-wrenching, but as easy as breathing instead.

Londyn shifted her gaze back to his profile. He truly was the epitome of how she imagined an England native. With his straight nose, curved lips, and hard jawline, he was beautiful in a way only a man could be. "Then how do you know you're pushing to better yourself if you don't try?"

Scratching his wrist, he bobbed his head in agreement. "Good question, Miss Bellerose. I don't have the answer." His eyes met hers. "But I'd like to find it."

The clock struck ten at night, breaking their concentration on each other. "I'll put the girls to bed tonight, if you don't mind?" he asked, moving toward the two who were now fighting over a doll.

"Sure, no problem. I have some laundry I need to catch up on." His eyebrows shot up in alarm, so she amended, "And by that, I mean taking it to the laundry room for Gloria to handle."

"You had me worried for a moment." A relieved grin met his lips before he hustled to break up the hair pulling his daughters were caught up in.

Londyn slipped out of the nursery and waved to Theodore before she closed the double doors. It made her feel much better to understand Callum and Theodore a bit more after the night. And all thanks to a dance party.

She grabbed her phone the moment her bedroom door shut. Dialing Abi, she paced when her best friend didn't answer. When her aunt didn't answer either, she huffed. "What the hell? They can't have lives without me," she moped. Neither one surprised her, though. Abi was notorious for missing calls, and Glenda was probably off in la-la land with Stew.

Still, she needed to talk to someone about the mounting attraction she felt for Callum. It shouldn't be possible. He was mostly a grump, but he also showed a side that possessed a heart of gold. She let out a sigh. Being in numerous situations where she could've leaned in and kissed him only made her frustration worse. He didn't try to kiss her even though he wanted to. Hell fucking yeah, he wanted to kiss her. She'd recognized the lustful tint to his eyes that extended to the rest of his body.

Tearing out of the kimono, she slid on her swimming suit and grabbed a long T-shirt. A few laps around the pool were in order after the sweaty evening. *Too bad the sweat wasn't caused by another activity*, she thought with a smile. *I know just the guy.* And he was far from making the first move. A fact she both appreciated and found aggravating. She loved that he was a gentleman, but her body craved a little rough and rowdy attention too.

***

The next week, Callum added a dab of milk to his tea, then headed back to his office. It'd been a long workweek thus far. Unexpectedly, the museum sent him to Copenhagen to retrieve a sculpture on loan. Any other time, he wouldn't have minded, but lately he was drawn to being home instead of abroad.

Shaking his head, he cursed under his breath. *It's because of Londyn.* He liked being around her more than should be proper for an employer and employee. There was something sprightly about her that lulled the workhorse in him. Instead of taking a trip to Rome, he'd delegated it to the assistant curator. *I still can't believe I did that.*

He padded down the hall and recalled why he was missing a stamp in his passport—because she asked. The girls had a horseback riding competition, and somehow Londyn convinced him he needed to attend as well. Looking back, he was glad for her persistence. Bailey won first place in the barrel race, and Bethany snagged second in jumping. Needless to say, he was the proudest parent in the audience. In England, they competed regularly, but he never had the time—or made it—to go to any of the events.

Damn woman is going to kill my career, he fumed, though a smile split his face. He took a sip of tea as he rounded the last corner to his study. To his surprise, Londyn was inside when he arrived.

"What can I do for you this evening, Miss Bellerose?" he asked, eager to speak with her. Ever since seeing her dance, he couldn't get her out of his mind.

As she turned, Callum's throat dried. The lighting in the room bounced off her auburn highlights amid brunette strands. She offered him a shy smile, and he nearly dropped the china cup.

"I wanted to take you up on your offer to teach me about art." She splayed her hands to the portraits. "Other than that being a painting, I know very little."

Setting down his tea, Callum slipped off his tie and tossed it to the desk. It felt like it was strangling him. *Or it could be the tiny blue shorts she's wearing.*

"Of course." He nodded to the door. "There's not much in my study, I'm afraid, since books line the walls, but we have plenty around the house."

Londyn fell in step beside him. Her hair swayed gently around her shoulders, capturing his attention so he nearly bumped his head on the wall lantern his mother insisted on keeping. *One of these days, I'm taking it down.*

He pointed down the hall. "Did the girls give you any trouble tonight?"

She laughed. "Oh no, they never do. They're angels."

"For you, perhaps." He snorted and held out an arm to the formal sitting room. "Since the girls are a bit rambunctious, we keep the expensive art in places they don't frequent. In here, you'll find an original Peter Max. My mother picked out some of the paintings, so if you don't like them—" He paused and winked. "—don't tell her."

Tilting her head, Londyn reviewed the rainforest-inspired canvas. He didn't mind that one, but it wasn't his favorite.

"What drew you to art? And history, for that matter?" she asked.

He pointed out the Wai Ming oil painting before he replied. "Like you, I admire creating worlds from nothing. You can do it with writing, whereas I like to see how the imagination manifests on a canvas and with ordinary objects."

They paused as she delicately studied a Marko Humphrey-Lahti sculpture. His mother would scream bloody murder for being so close to the art, but he didn't utter a word. It was beautiful merely watching her eyes scan the smooth marble.

Finally she met his gaze and nodded. "I like that. And history?"

Callum led them to the formal dining room where a large foliage landscape of their home in England hung on the wall. "My father used to read these dusty books to me about civilizations lost to us. Naturally, I imagined myself digging up the remains of cities and bones and becoming world famous." He chuckled. "Then I realized archaeologists don't exactly roll in the money, so I steered more toward the artistry side of history. There's plenty of lost artwork there too."

"Interesting." She tucked her hair behind her ear. "I guess science doesn't pay."

He shook his head sadly. "Not unless you discover gold, I'm afraid."

They moved back toward his study. In honesty, they really didn't have many famous pieces at their summerhouse for safety's sake, so their tour was shorter than he'd hoped. He managed to give tidbits about different styles of art and the way they shifted over the years. As much as he wanted to spew facts all night, she deserved more than an information download. Londyn was someone who learned over time—at least, that's what he'd gathered from knowing her thus far—and she was a polite and intent student despite listening to him drone on. Spending time with Londyn was natural, and he craved it more as each day passed.

"If you could have any painting or piece of famous artwork in your house, which would you choose?" she asked when they reached the door of his study.

Callum thought it over quickly. He could've said any, but the one he coveted was extremely out of his reach. "*Wanderer above the Sea of Fog,* by Caspar David Freidrich."

She lifted her brows as if asking him to explain.

"He was a romanticism artist in 1818." He stared out

the window as if seeing the landscape in front of him. "It shows you the infinite potential and possibilities of man and the mystery of nature. I've seen it a number of times in Germany, and I stop by the museum whenever I have time. I've been kicked out a time or two for staying too late." He scratched his forearm when he noticed she was staring at him. "Sorry, I'm rambling."

"Don't be. I enjoy listening and learning about you." Her eyes darted to Sherlock when he stood and yawned. "You're a very interesting person, Callum. It's fun to find out more about you."

Before he could ask exactly why he was interesting, she bent down and patted the basset hound's ear. The dog turned his head into her hand until his back leg started thumping in delight.

Traitor, he thought when Sherlock glanced at him with a satisfied face.

"So, Bethany told me you have a new exhibit in London. Tell me about it," she urged.

Callum opted for the seat beside her instead of at his desk. It felt more informal that way. And with the way his mind was spinning at her in that lace-trimmed tank, informal was the only direction he could go. "Our archaeologists found a promising dig site for Nefertiti, one of the early Egyptian queens."

Londyn tucked her legs under her and leaned forward. "Really? That sounds intriguing."

"It is." He crossed his right leg over his left. "And they found her about six months ago." He grinned. "It was the biggest find for our museum in some time, so naturally we had to celebrate it."

Her eyes lit up excitedly. "So, they found the queen and the pharaoh too?"

"Sadly, no. Just Nefertiti herself. Akhenaten has yet to be found." He met her eyes and found them enthralled. It was easy to catch since her entire face lit up when she was excited. "Many legends swirl around the two of them."

"Why?"

"It's said that Nefertiti and Akhenaten had a love that was deep and inseparable. Back then, their marriage was one of duty, so any type of affection was surprising."

Londyn propped her chin up with her fists as she listened. It was captivating, the way she homed in on his tale. "Sure."

He leaned forward and continued. "While Nefertiti was said to be a goddess of fertility, she couldn't produce a male heir. It's believed that insurgents tried to have her killed because of her abnormality to only give female heirs. One day she disappeared, never to be found again."

"No!" Her brows shot up and the cutest frown covered her lips. A life in theater made sense with her unique facial expressions.

He nodded. "Some believe Akhenaten had her murdered or banished her."

Londyn tapped her chin. "But you don't, do you?"

Callum sat back and shook his head. "No. I wrote my thesis on Akhenaten. Every ancient scroll and sliver of data I found showed how much he loved her. Back then they didn't write it so plainly, but he wished her a long life along with their six daughters. A man on the verge of murdering his wife wouldn't say such things. Nefertiti was a fearless warrior both in court and outside. She radicalized religious changes and was his steadfast supporter. Akhenaten wouldn't allow her banishment or murder."

Londyn's eyes were as wide as saucers. "What do you think happened?"

"I believe Akhenaten loved her so dearly that he sent her away. Had she stayed, their love story would've ended abruptly, as well as his reign." He watched her process that possibility, then added, "It's said that Akhenaten would visit a burial ground each year on the anniversary of her disappearance. Many historians believe they would meet there and share one night together until the next year."

A sigh escaped her lips, the sound much too dangerous for the love story he was spouting. "That's so romantic. What ever happened to Akhenaten?"

"He died not long after." Callum patted Sherlock's head when the dog wobbled over to him. "It's said he died of a broken heart, but it's all legend. No way of proving it."

"I'll take a legend any day of the week if it tugs at your heart and makes you imagine," she replied with a grin. "That's the kind of stuff I need for my plays." She pressed her lips together. "In fact, it may make a good script."

"If you say so. I'm not fond of the theater, to be honest." He held up his hands when her face turned ashen. "But the last time I went, I was a youngster. Perhaps it's gotten better."

"Oh my God. We have to take the girls to a show." She stood and started pacing. "I promised them I would, so you may as well join us. I was initially thinking *The Music Man*, but seeing how you're iffy, we better go to one you may enjoy."

"If you're in attendance, I have no doubt I will." The quiet words settled around the room. He didn't regret saying them. They were true. *Talk about scary.* He stood and opened the back door for Sherlock. "Set it up and let me know when."

"Oh yeah, sure." She moved to the exit, then paused. "Thanks for tonight, Callum. I really had a good time learning about art, history, and you."

The bourbon on his desk tempted him, but he met her gaze instead. He didn't need booze when her blue-gray eyes muddled his mind. "As did I. Sleep well, Londyn."

A red tint crept to her cheeks and she nodded.

"Oh, and Londyn, I'm catching a flight first thing in the morning." He couldn't let her leave without at least trying to put himself out there, even if he failed. He'd promised himself and Theodore that he'd try. "I'll call you tomorrow evening, if that's all right?"

A shy smile crossed her cheeks. "Sure. Safe travels."

Without another word, Londyn skated from his study and left him all alone once more. The tasks on his desk were long forgotten; with his emotions spinning on thoughts of the pretty American within his grasp, he couldn't focus on a damn paper clip, much less work.

It amazed him how easy she was to get along with. Sure, she was a spitfire and sassy to a fault, but she was incredibly smart as well. The select few women he dated couldn't—or wouldn't, he wasn't sure—comprehend all that his job entailed and his passion for history and art. They were more interested in the checkbook attached to his family name.

Sitting at his desk, Callum realized Londyn wasn't interested in the monetary value of his inheritance. She wanted to frolic with the girls and enjoy summer. *It doesn't sound like a bad idea either.*

He sat back and watched the clock strike a new hour. Londyn wasn't like the other women he'd dated. *Hell, she isn't even like Jessica.* His thought crippled his stereotype of dreamers. Surely he wasn't right. If Londyn was indeed a new breed of dreamer, he was in for one hell of a ride, because each moment he was around her, Callum wanted nothing more than to kiss those pink lips of hers.

CHAPTER SIX

Callum's quick trip turned into a weeklong venture. One of the museum's largest benefactors was wavering on the next donation, so his job shifted to arse-kissing.

Packing the last smidge of biscuit into his mouth, he let out a relieved breath as the plane neared the airport. As much as he loved talking art until the sun rose and then set, he desperately missed being home. Well, as close to home as his mother's house could be. It wasn't home, per se, but it was where his girls were currently. It was enough for now. Plus, a certain nanny made returning to Colorado even more enticing.

He fired up his cell phone when the plane came to a stop. Judging from the excess of photos Londyn sent his way, Bethany and Bailey were having a grand time without him. This nanny was by far the best they'd had. Still, he needed to do more as a father.

He gripped the back of the seat in front of him and let a blue-haired woman cut in line to the exit.

Each night he could, he Skyped with the girls. They gushed about racing go-carts, shopping at the mall, giving each other pedicures, swim competitions, and of course, cooking a new spaghetti recipe. Evidently Londyn wasn't the best cook either. Or so Bailey let on when he'd called the day before. He smirked, picturing the tall woman floundering in the chef kitchen. It was a sight the first time, but no doubt she perfected the definition of lost.

Callum walked down the carpeted plank and into the bustling airport. He waved at a fellow frequent flyer but didn't stop to chat. Not once did Londyn stick her pretty oval face in front of the camera, but he did catch her in the background a time or two. She'd looked gorgeous each time, though the last, she'd sported marinara in her hair. How she accomplished that he'd never know.

Making his way toward the exit, he waved to Alfred as he approached. The butler was more of an uncle figure than an employee, and he never missed one arrival or departure. "Good to see you."

Alfred bobbed his head. "And you, sir."

Callum swung his carry-on bag to the other shoulder. "Cut the shit, Alfred. No one's around."

The other man eyed him. "Yes, of course." They moved in the direction of the luggage carousel. "Have a nice trip?"

"Schmoozing benefactors mostly, so tiring. I swear this isn't what I thought the job would be." They stopped and watched the silver conveyer belt lurch to life. "How're the girls?"

"Oh, just fine." The longtime friend cleared his throat. "Having fun with Miss Bellerose."

Callum laced his hands together. "No doubt."

Other than the surrounding people waiting for their baggage, the arrival port was quiet. Static rasped over the airport speakers and a dog barked from the check-in desk.

At last, Callum had to ask, "And Londyn? How is she?"

Alfred spotted the bag and pointed it out. "I dare say you should ask her yourself."

Callum grinned and snatched his suitcase. "Very well, I will."

Once they cleared the airport, he took a deep breath. The scent of rain lingered in the air, while mountains capped in snow stood in the distance. Reaching the car, he eyed the looming clouds. "Is it supposed to rain?"

Climbing in the driver seat, the butler gave him a sarcastic glance. "Do I look like a meteorologist?"

Callum closed the door. "Quite right. I think it'd be a good day to visit the factory with the girls." Rain spat on the windshield. "Think Londyn would fancy tagging along?"

The driver looked at him through the rearview mirror. "I can assure you, anything to do with chocolate and Miss Bellerose will leap at the chance to attend."

Curious as to how Alfred came to such a conclusion, Callum took out his phone and scrolled through the contacts. He was interested in understanding more about their nanny, even if his brain warned the opposite. Ever since meeting her, he couldn't keep from thinking about her. Their run-in at the pool that first day was one of his favorite memories, though. How the pink-striped swimming suit hugged each of her gangly curves, how the shade of her skin matched that of a light caramel treat, and how much it hurt to not kiss every inch of her.

He needed to stop before he embarrassed himself. The time away hadn't helped. *Hell, it made it worse.* In London, he'd gone to a pub, had a pint, but didn't want to take one of the bar babes back to his hotel. He only wanted Londyn and her smart mouth.

He cleared his throat and adjusted his pants. Merely thinking about Londyn had an immediate reaction. He'd surely die if she felt an iota of that same desire toward him.

Focusing on the task at hand, he dialed and didn't have to wait long for an answer. "Hello, Mother. We're planning to stop by later this afternoon. Can you see to it that we're given one of your fancy tours? I have a hunch we'll need plenty of chocolate samples too."

***

"A chocolate factory? Your family owns a chocolate factory?" Londyn's eyes widened until she had to blink from the dryness. She glanced around the ginormous building, landing on Callum's smiling face last.

He stood near the front desk and straightened a plaque. "I thought for certain you'd have known that coming into the job." He pointed to the name of the company above his head. "It is called Archer Chocolatery, after all. We have locations in England and the United States. Didn't you Google the family you were nannying for before agreeing to the job?"

Londyn wanted to squeal like a child, but instead she grasped his hand and squeezed. "No. I had no idea. I'm not so great with technology. This is so cool. Is there a chocolate river like in *Willy Wonka*?"

Callum chuckled and shook his head. "Um, no. That's a movie, and it would be incredibly difficult to maintain for a number of reasons. Not to mention the health codes." His face took on a horrified expression at the mere thought.

"Oh, have a little fun." She nudged him with her hip. The act seemed to catch him off guard and he tripped over the tiled floor.

Catching himself on the railing, he pointed to the hall. "We have a tour awaiting us." He glanced around the lobby. "And from the looks of it, the girls are already there."

She followed him quickly, totally fine with her viewpoint. The dark jeans and orange polo appeared more natural on him. When she'd first seen him return from the airport, the urge to spar with him tempted her. He'd all but abandoned them for a week. Sure, the girls had fun and acted fine, but she wasn't. She should've been, of course, but she'd missed running into him and hearing his dry humor break the ice.

How is that even possible?

"Come now, Londyn," he teased over his shoulder. "I know your long legs can keep up with me."

Taking the bait, she quickened her pace until they were side by side and finally caught up to the tour. Bailey and Bethany were up front, helping the guide along the path. Callum's hand rested on the small of her back as he directed her to a better spot to see.

"Rose is the best," he advised in a whisper. "She's been with the company for almost thirty years. She's one of the few employees my mother actually likes."

Londyn couldn't focus on the sixty-year-old tour guide if she tried. Having Callum's body against her back, his cologne tormenting her senses, made it impossible.

His grand surprise of taking her and the girls to a chocolate factory thrilled her more than the children. Now she knew why—they'd been there more than once. If she guessed right, the Archer girls would inherit part of the massive factory too, both that one and in London.

An hour later, Londyn's arms were full of goodies while she and Callum sat on the bench outside and watched the girls play on the monkey bars. Since the chocolatery had a daycare for their employees, it was second nature to have play equipment nearby, and it allowed the adults a hint of privacy.

Unwrapping a caramel covered in dark chocolate, she moaned when it hit her taste buds. "This is so good."

"My, aren't you a regular chocoholic," Callum laughed, looking over at her.

Londyn chewed, then nodded. "As it turns out, yes, I am." She held up the bag stuffed with concoctions from the factory sample area. She couldn't resist filling the tote. "And I'm loading up for a rainy day." A drop of rain landed on her nose and she grinned. "Like today."

The mist didn't seem to bother Bethany and Bailey as they hopped toward the swing set.

Callum moved closer and peeked inside the bag. "I think you grabbed every sample they offered." She nodded enthusiastically. "So, is chocolate your only vice, or are there more I should know about?"

She liked this side of him. He wasn't uptight or worried about appearances. His slight teasing and gentlemanly manners throughout the tour baffled her. *I mean, what man holds my hand to make sure I get down the steps without tripping?*

"Mostly chocolate." She held out a piece of nougat, but he declined. "I live by the three Cs."

Callum's light eyebrows furrowed. "And they are?"

She held up three fingers and ticked them off as she spoke. "Chocolate, Chinese food, and chick flicks."

"Ah yes, the trifecta," he teased.

"I'm serious." She crumpled a wrapper and playfully tossed it at him. "If I ever come across a problem, I use the three Cs."

Laughing outright, Callum stole the tote and clucked his tongue at the numerous empty candies. "And what happens if they don't do the trick?"

"Hmm, well I don't know. It's never happened before." She scratched her head. The mere thought disturbed her. Everything could be solved with either chocolate, Chinese, or chick flicks. She just knew it.

He stood and offered his hand. "Perhaps you need to find a few more Cs, Miss Bellerose, for surely such a time will come."

Taking his hand, she stood to her full height, only a few inches shorter than him. She rather liked looking up to a guy for a change. When he didn't immediately drop her hand, her heartbeat quickened. "Perhaps you're right, Mr. Archer."

Callum pushed back a lock of hair that had fallen across her eyes. She held her breath, willing him to kiss her. It drove her insane, but she wasn't just going to press her lips to his. She was outgoing, but not when it came to making the first move.

All at once, his touch vanished when he waved for the girls to return. She held in a disappointed sigh. She shouldn't want him, but she did anyway. The flirty way they interchanged their formal names and their first names only made it worse for her.

"Oh, Miss Londyn, you forgot your purse," a friendly voice called over the rumble of thunder.

Turning her neck toward the approaching man, she recognized him as one of the employees who'd crammed chocolate in her hands.

Smiling, she walked toward him. "Thanks"—she glanced at his nametag—"Mark." She retrieved her oversized satchel from the man with blue eyes and couldn't help but notice his shy smile.

"You bet. See you around?" the man asked.

"Probably, if you keep giving me chocolate," she said, holding up a candy, and they both laughed. He disappeared as quickly as he appeared, and when she moved the other direction, she ran straight into Callum. "Oof."

"He's a bit young for you, Londyn," Callum noted, bracing her shoulders to keep her from toppling over.

Looking up, Londyn met his cognac-brown eyes. There was a hint of jealousy in those captivating depths. It was an emotion that never used to be attractive in a man, but on Callum, it was mesmerizing. "He's, uh, not my type anyway," she said in a voice barely above a whisper. Evidently that was what happened when she was nose-to-nose with a man—she lost her tongue and brain all at once.

Not any man, though. Just this man.

"Pray tell, what is your type?" His eyes dropped to

her lips, and she instinctively rubbed them together. Bad move, since it made him lean in closer until his minty breath collided with hers.

British. Say British, her mind screamed, but she couldn't utter anything except "Um, tall and nice eyes." She wanted to smack her forehead. *Seriously, Londyn, that's all you could come up with? God, I'm an idiot.*

Callum's lips curved in a smile. Leaning to her ear, he said, "Then I see you have lofty requirements." His thumb swiped across her top lip. "You've a bit of chocolate there." He licked his finger, eyes never once leaving hers.

Immediately, she wanted to smear more chocolate on her lips just to see how he'd wipe her clean. With his tongue, she hoped.

His hands disappeared again, though not where she'd prefer them. "Better be careful. I'm suddenly quite fond of chocolate, and this flavor in particular is growing on me."

Londyn stood mute, unable to fabricate a comeback quick enough to his sultry words. Then he winked at her, the act only furthering her dumb nature.

Watching Callum retreat toward his daughters, she finally shook herself free from his spell. He liked her. Right? Normal men didn't go around licking fingers and making slight comments with sexual intones without liking her, did they?

She watched him chase Bailey and Bethany, smiles on all their faces. In reality, he was an excellent father.

He simply had a few stumbling blocks when it came to his priorities.

Rain spat down on her, and she raced toward the SUV. Looking over her shoulder, she spotted Callum scoop both girls in his arms like footballs and run toward the sleek Cadillac. All three were drenched and laughing, the grins fully worth the plastered clothes.

Buckling up, Londyn felt her heart shift toward Callum. There was more about him she needed to grasp, but he was a genuine gentleman who loved his daughters.

I just need to figure out what's holding him back.

She found the towels she'd thrown in the back in case of a rainstorm and tossed them to the girls as they clambered inside. Their dad was soaked to the bone, but his eyes shone with mirth.

In one day, she'd gone from cursing Callum and his endless trips to nearly begging him to kiss her. She needed to get her act together and fast, or she'd have no control left.

***

Londyn turned the knob on the stereo and Disney tunes filled the living room as she took a quick look around the space. After shoving the couches, tables, and random memorabilia to the walls, the hardwood floors were the perfect spot for dancing.

"You know, we could've used the patio out back.

It's big enough for dancing," Bethany pointed out.

Londyn shrugged and tied her hair back. "I know, but it's more fun when you can slip and slide. My parents and I used to do it all the time. Nothing better than skating on wood floors."

"I slid down the bannister once," Bailey added, tugging on her shirt.

Londyn eyed the stairwell. "That sounds fun. Should we do that next?"

"No!" both girls shouted.

"Grandmother was so cross," Bethany informed her.

"Yeah, plus Daddy was out of town and we got in big trouble when he came home," Bailey included.

"Fine, fine. We won't." Londyn chuckled. "Today."

Bethany rolled her eyes, then moved to the center of the makeshift dance floor. "You know we have a ballroom at home in England."

"I didn't, but it sounds great." Londyn stared at her feet. "I'm not the best dancer, to be honest."

Bailey laced her fingers into Londyn's. "We can teach you. It's easy. You just follow the beat."

Londyn let the girl lead her, but it was no use. Dancing and being tall didn't get along in her experience. The few times she tried to be graceful, she swore a drunk flamingo would've looked better.

"Sorry, girls," she apologized after half an hour of attempts. "I'm a little clumsy."

Bethany and Bailey linked arms, then began to waltz

to the popular *Beauty and the Beast* song. "Watch us and you'll pick it up."

Unsure of where they found their faith, Londyn stood off to the side and followed the girls with her eyes. They were enchanting even in pajamas.

"Ballroom dancing. Now this is more my style. Why didn't I get an invitation?" Callum asked from behind her.

Turning, she offered him a shrug. "Sorry. They said they wanted to show me how to dance. It didn't go so well." Eyeing his athletic getup, she wondered if he was pre- or post-workout.

Offering his hand, Callum said, "Well, perhaps it was because your dancing partner was half your size. Let me try."

"Okay, but I apologize in advance for stepping on your feet." Tentatively, she accepted his hand. *Preworkout,* she noted when he twirled her and then pulled her to his body. A hint of bourbon clung to his breath amid the normal cologne scent.

"Visualize a box and stay relaxed, for goodness' sake. I won't bite you," he teased at her stiff arms. "Step back with your right foot, bending your right leg slightly as you step so you land on your toes."

She tried the first step and actually completed it.

"Good. Now keep your body straight and then slide your left foot so your feet are parallel." He carefully moved her.

"Like that?" she asked, afraid to mess up. It'd be

just her luck to stomp on his feet or trip them both.

"Perfect. Next, slide your right foot next to your left. Bend your knee slightly so you're on your toes again. Finally, slide your left foot parallel to your right so they barely touch." He smiled down at her. "And there you have it."

Londyn concentrated on her feet, the steps much easier than she expected. Soon Callum walked them faster. She fumbled over her large toes more than one time, but it got easier the more they practiced. "Hey, this is kind of fun."

"It is."

Once she was sure she could handle it, Callum slowly moved them around the room. The swell of the music perfectly matched Londyn's excitement the longer they circled the makeshift dance floor.

"Stop looking at your feet. You're doing brilliantly, and I'd much rather see your face than the top of your head," he chided with a hint of humor in his voice.

Looking up, she beamed. Never did she imagine she could dance the waltz. It was in nearly every play and musical, but always seemed out of reach no matter how many times she attempted.

Meeting his light brown eyes, she sighed in contentment. *I didn't have the right partner,* she decided as the song hit the crescendo. Without a doubt, Bailey had hit Repeat, because there was no way in hell the song was that long.

"You're not half bad," he complimented.

She rubbed her lips together, suddenly in need of more lip balm. "Thanks. I have a pretty good teacher."

His hand tightened on her hips as their eye contact never wavered despite the clapping from Bailey and Bethany. On the last turn, Callum twirled her out and then back to him. Her hands hit his chest and she slowly lifted her chin. His lips hovered inches from her own, and his eyes spoke of the delightful things they could do alongside the rhythm of music.

"You have beautiful eyes," he murmured.

Heat flooded to her face, and the temptation to reach over and taste him overwhelmed her. "You have nice everything," she replied, then shut her eyes at how sultry it probably sounded to him.

Damn, Londyn, pull yourself together.

"You're too kind, Miss Bellerose," he said on a chuckle. The humor in his voice made her eyelids flick open. She could've stayed there all day simply staring into his eyes, which held a hint of desire.

"Londyn, your phone's ringing," Bethany called, shattering their connection.

"I should, uh, see who it is," she said, moving out of his embrace and instantly shivering. She hadn't expected his loss to be so great that she felt cold.

Londyn eyed the caller ID and walked to the door. "It's my aunt. I'll be back." She nodded to the girls. "Why don't you show your dad how you can slip and slide along the floors?"

Bailey didn't waste time before doing exactly as

suggested. Her sister soon joined her, and both begged their father to do so as well. Stopping at the door, Londyn looked over her shoulder and caught Callum's gaze. A half grin covered his face while his eyes watched her every movement.

Damn. I should've learned dancing a long time ago if this is what it does to guys.

She waved, then escaped to the outside world. At least there it made sense. Unlike her increasing attraction to the British man mere feet away.

***

Three days later, Callum closed his study door and made his way to the kitchen. It was one of his favorite spots in the entire house, mostly because Gloria consistently had freshly baked goodies. They were for the girls, but she'd been with the Archer family long enough to make extras for him.

"There you are. I thought the smell of scones may tempt you out of that lair of yours," Gloria said with a wink.

"What can I say? You make the best." Snatching one of the lemon scones, he took a bite of the flaky crust. "Delicious as usual."

Gloria went back to her baking and asked, "How is the nanny coming along? She's quite terrifying in the kitchen, but the little misses seem to like her."

Swallowing his bite, Callum took a seat on a

barstool. "Yes, Bethany and Bailey adore her. I think she's one of the best they've had."

"And what about you?" Gloria paused her busy hands. "Do you fancy the American beauty?"

Callum met the twinkling eyes of the woman he saw more as an aunt. She'd taught him to bake as a child, though it didn't go well, and endlessly offered advice whether he wanted it or not. "Londyn is lovely."

The chef snorted and placed the unbaked treats on the cooking sheets. "That isn't what I asked, Callum."

"She reminds me of Jessica," he admitted, finishing the scone. "And it terrifies me, because there are enough differences between them to make me like her."

"Ah." Gloria stopped her task and wiped her floury hands. Coming over to him, she placed a hand on his shoulder. "Londyn isn't Jessica. Goodness, that redhead wouldn't have touched a kitchen with a ten-foot pole, whereas Londyn is atrocious here but tries anyhow."

"Yes, but—"

"I've watched her these last weeks with the girls. She acts more like their mother than their own flesh and blood." The older woman moved away and shoved the scones into the oven, then pointed at him. "And I've seen you too. Don't think I haven't. And you aren't obsessed with work—well, not as much, I should say. It's nice to have you around more. I think your daughters enjoy it too."

"It's slow this time of year," he interjected. It wasn't

anywhere near the truth, but he had to say something to defend himself.

Gloria perched both hands on her wide hips. "Don't lie to yourself, Callum. Londyn is good for all of you. It's a pity she's only around for the summer. She'd be a good addition to the house."

Standing, he leaned over and kissed Gloria's cheek. "I'll keep it under advisement. Now if you'll excuse me, I'm off to catch up on some reading."

He grabbed two more scones, then left before any argument could leave the woman's mouth.

Just as he reached the hallway, two voices met his attention from the music room. Curious, he stopped outside the room and saw Londyn and his mother inside. *Oh dear. It seems she's back from London already.* For the majority of the time, his mother was occupied with the business and stayed out of his hair, which he preferred.

"Miss Bellerose, you really must do something about Bailey's piano lessons," his mother complained. "She hasn't been practicing. I heard her the other day and nearly died of a heart attack at the sound."

Londyn picked up the discarded piano books from the floor. Clearly his children weren't good at cleaning up after themselves either. "I gave them a break this week. They had a lot going on."

Mary narrowed her eyes. "Decisions as to their schedule aren't up to you. Cal should've made it clear—"

"He did. We agreed to ease off on the mandatory lessons and the like for the summer."

"I don't believe it," his mother huffed.

She shrugged and folded a blanket on the blue chaise. Callum didn't even want to know what happened in the room that looked like a hurricane had hit. "Ask him yourself." She moved the settee over a smidge. "Plus, you're not their parent, so it shouldn't matter."

"I'm their grandmother and I pay for their education." Mary's brows furrowed, and she looked down her nose at Londyn. "Unlike their father, I provide them with an upbringing that will lead to successful careers. Cal wasted his training on art and history, but I won't let his children follow his mistakes."

"Callum provides for them." Londyn crossed her arms over her chest. "And I think he does an excellent job too. If he thinks Bethany and Bailey need more time to be wild and free, then I agree with him. I don't put too much stock in pushing kids throughout their childhood. They'll just end up unhappy as adults."

A slow smile crossed his face. Londyn didn't back down from his mother. It was admirable even if it was stupid. Mary Archer was a viper. He should know.

"You're simply saying that because you're 'wild and free,' as you put it."

"Don't forget outspoken," Londyn added, returning her attention to the toys scattered across the floor.

"I should've never hired you," Mary said venomously. "You're nothing like what I imagined."

Londyn stood to her full height, a good three inches taller than his mother in her heels. "I'd hope not, because if I were a stuffy nanny, the girls wouldn't enjoy their time with me."

"Well I never," the matriarch scoffed.

"Oh, and about Callum's career." Londyn paused as if searching for the right words. "He loves what he does at the museum. So what if you don't understand art or history? He loves it, and you should too as his mother. Perhaps if you did, your relationship with him would be better. Supporting your child should always be your first priority."

Mary's lips parted in surprise and her eyes flashed rage. Still, the woman didn't utter a single word. In a huff, she turned on her heels and strutted out the door.

Callum stepped into the shadows just in time to miss his mother's hasty retreat. Thankful she didn't look his way, he waited until the coast was clear to resume his spying. The way Londyn defended him and his career choice sent a tremor through his heart. He wasn't thinking about the uneaten scone in his left hand anymore, too busy watching Londyn finish her tidying.

After a moment, he entered the room. "You didn't have to do that, you know."

Londyn gasped at his soft words and whirled around. "Callum, you scared me." Her hand fluttered over her chest. "How long have you been there?"

Callum set the scone on the coffee table and walked

closer to her. "Long enough to hear you put my mother in her place."

Terror spread over her face but was quickly replaced with anxiousness. "Oh shit. I probably should apologize, right? It wasn't proper of me. I mean, you guys are very British, and I stepped over a ton of lines, and I—"

"Londyn, you talk too much," he said, taking her hand in his.

Her gaze dipped to the floor. "Yeah, I've been told."

"I wanted to thank you." That brought her blue-gray eyes up in a hurry. He smiled at the curiosity he found in them.

"For what? I didn't do anything." She wrung her hands together.

He rubbed her hand. "But you did. I need to stand up to my mother more. She's a bit overbearing at times, and I let her get away with it because she's my mother. Nevertheless, you defended me and my profession. It doesn't happen much."

Londyn's cheeks flushed red. "I guess I'm so used to doing it for my job that it comes naturally."

Callum squeezed her hand, then walked back to the door. "It's a commendable trait, Miss Bellerose. Don't you dare lose it."

He nodded once another flash of red crept up her long neck. She was gorgeous all the time, but seeing her blush was hurriedly becoming one of his favorite looks on his nanny.

****

"Londyn, it's so good to see you!" Abi squealed on the other end of the Skype call. "It's been forever."

Rolling onto her stomach, Londyn grinned cheekily. Dramatics were too common with the roommates. "It's not like we don't talk every day, Abs."

"Yeah, but this is different. I get to see your face." Abi squinted. "And a very tan face, I might add."

Londyn's free hand flew to her face. "Yeah, we're outside a lot. It's great."

Abi walked through their apartment, then stooped and picked up Oreo. The cat batted at his owner's arm until she sat on the couch. "So, tell me what's new. Has the sexy professor given you a tongue-lashing yet?"

"He's a museum curator, not a professor," she corrected.

"Okay, fine. Has he dusted away the cobwebs in your lady bits yet, then?"

Giggling, Londyn shook her head. "God, I miss you. And no, we haven't done anything."

"Boo. Why not?"

"Because it's not that simple. He's my boss—"

"Which makes it hotter."

"Yes, but also why I need to be careful."

Abi pouted. "You're a grown-ass woman. Make the first move. It's not like you need the job." She cleared her throat, looking away. "Unlike some of us."

While it was true that Londyn really didn't have to

work for the summer, her friend did. They were out of college and no closer to successful careers. Londyn had her aunt to fall back on if times got tough, but Abi had no one. "What would you do if you were in my shoes?"

Oreo hopped into the frame, nuzzling the iPad. Both women laughed at his pink nose as it filled the screen before Abi snuggled the cat in her arms. "I'd go for it."

"But—"

Abi held up her hand. "I know you're scared after what happened with Blake, but you can't let it control the rest of your life. You deserve a good guy, one who will do whatever it takes to make you smile. If you think, even for a minute, that Callum could be that guy, act on your feelings." She bumped noses with Oreo, then grinned. "Your heart's abroad this summer, Londyn. Enjoy the ride."

Soaking in the serious wisdom from her best friend, Londyn slowly nodded. "You're right. I won't close off the chance." She blushed. "Plus, I think he's great."

"There's my girl." Abi clicked on the television. "Are you any closer to figuring out if you're staying in New York or heading back to Iowa?"

Londyn let out a noisy breath. It wasn't a subject she'd broached but once since being in Colorado. Broadway wasn't knocking down her door in Queens, and her aunt suggested she return to Iowa to take over the real estate business. She wasn't keen on that, but she was nearly thirty years old. Life was quickly passing her by, and she had nothing of note to show for it. She'd hoped her time away would help her figure out what she wanted to do after the summer ended, but she rarely thought about anything other than the Archer family.

Standing, she walked over to the window and pulled back the shade. Bethany and Bailey were riding bikes in the driveway, seemingly having a good time. It hurt to think about leaving them now or ever. Though they weren't hers, Londyn felt a kinship with the beautiful redheads.

"You still there, Londyn?" Abi asked, breaking into her thoughts.

"Yeah, sorry." She focused on the screen. "I haven't given it much thought since the last time we talked about it. Going back to Iowa is always an option. I just don't know if I want to give up my dream for stability."

"Hmm, too bad you can't be a nanny forever."

Shaking her head, Londyn knew she couldn't do that. She wanted a family of her own. "Nah, they'll get sick of me eventually."

Abi snorted. "Doubt it."

Changing gears, Londyn asked, "Any special guys I should know about?"

"Nope." Abi stuck out her tongue. "But even if I was shaking the bed with somebody, I wouldn't have to tell you until you came back to New York."

"Oh, so there is somebody." Londyn bounced her brows up and down.

Her roommate shook her curls. "Uh, no. Wishful thinking." The doorbell rang from the other end of the call. "Hang on, I need to get dinner." Abi set the iPad down and Londyn heard her run to the door. A moment later, two bags of Chinese food came into view. "Tada!"

The sight made Londyn's mouth water. "Oh, God, I miss Chinese dates with you." Her stomach rumbled. "And eating chocolate while we watch chick flicks."

Abi unpacked the white cartons and broke apart her chopsticks. "Then come home." She pinched the chopsticks toward her in jest. "Or I'll get you."

Londyn laughed at Abi's antics. "All right, well on that note, I'll let you eat your food in peace." She checked the clock on the wall. "Plus it's almost time for dinner, and Gloria makes an amazing roast."

"Spoiled rotten. You won't want to come back to lukewarm Chinese now," Abi pouted, slurping a noodle.

"Oh please. I can't leave you alone too much longer. You're liable to adopt another cat or two," Londyn said when Abi offered a piece of chicken to Oreo.

Abi shrugged. "You're just jealous."

"True." She blew Abi a kiss. "Talk to you later. Stay out of trouble."

"Do my best." Abi puckered her lips at her. "Don't forget to show your hunky boss how you feel."

Signing off, Londyn instantly missed her best friend. This was the longest they'd been apart, and even though they were adults, Abi was her rock.

Whatever happened in the coming months, Londyn was confident she'd always have at least one person to go home to.

Shaking her head once, she tossed her phone on the bed and went over the plans for the next day. *Maybe Callum wants to join us since he's in town.* She grinned like a fool. She'd noticed he didn't jet off as much anymore. While she wanted to think his feelings for her had something to do with it, she couldn't be sure.

I'll just have to find out myself.

CHAPTER SEVEN

Callum pushed aside the portfolio of artwork recently sent from the museum. Several new artists were vying to have a spot in the end-of-summer gallery, and he was tasked to pick one. Usually the decision was simple, but the competition was stiff this year, as the focus was historical cities in honor of the Egyptian excavation.

He held up one sketch and studied the bold brush marks with red and gold over the city of Barcelona. It wasn't bad, but not up to par with previous pieces. He scratched the artist's name from his list and shoved the sketch into a folder labeled 'rejected.' Upper management in the museum expected perfection, and his reputation was on the line. Everyone who was anyone in the museum and art business knew of Callum Archer and his eye for a fine piece of art; should he fail, his position at the museum may waver.

Sherlock yawned loudly from his basket. Callum glanced over and watched the old hound flip to his back and stretch his stubby legs. Once upon a time, the dog was a great hunting companion, but nowadays, lounging and slobbering kisses were all he was good for. Callum didn't mind in the least, since he wasn't fond of hunting anyway. He much preferred to be inside by the fire with a new book.

"Hey, Professor, what're you up to?" Londyn asked from the doorway.

"Going through submissions for the gala." He dropped the file in his hand and looked up. "What are you doing?"

"Do you want to come with us to Garden of the Gods? I'm taking Bailey and Bethany horseback riding. I went years ago, and it was splendiferous."

She said the last bit with a faux accent. He more than approved of how she always acted like herself around him. It was refreshing. "It seems our way of speaking is rubbing off on you."

She shrugged. "What can I say? I'm impressionable."

He looked at the pile of art, then to the woman dressed in jeans, a pink tank top, cowboy boots, and a pair of braids tucked beneath a light brown Stetson. The view was much better than studying modern art, in his biased opinion. Then he scolded himself for even thinking such a disgrace since art was his life.

Slowly, he stood. "I have a deadline."

Londyn's hands rested on her hips. They weren't

itty-bitty, but held the right amount of width with just enough flesh to make them ideal for gripping. "Oh, fudge the deadline and come with us. The girls would be ecstatic." She snorted. "You in a cowboy getup would be hilarious."

The notion of her imagining him in chaps made Callum change his mind in a hurry. "Well, when you put it that way, I suppose a break is in order." Already, he heard the screams of delight from the two miscreants who made his world go round.

One hour later, they reached the Garden of the Gods outside Colorado Springs. Bethany and Bailey ran toward the stables, wide smiles on their faces. He watched Londyn help the girls on their horses. They didn't need it, but they didn't reject her aid either.

Resting his arms on the fence, Callum couldn't help but stare at the way Londyn mounted the black mare. She told him she'd done it before, and he could tell. Her movements were fluid and mesmerizing, even for a man who'd been around horses most of his life. He realized too late that he wasn't paying any attention to the guide, who was yelling at him to get a horse.

"You ride the girl, not stare at her," the male guide teased with a knowing smile. Snickers and more innuendos drifted around the group at the joke.

Callum cleared his throat and kept his gaze down until he was fully astride the chestnut mare and in line with the group of riders. To his relief, Londyn didn't search him out. *Perhaps she didn't hear.* He wasn't normally dumbfounded, but it happened nearly every time he looked at the gorgeous woman.

The guide offered tidbits of information while Callum snuck up behind Bailey's painted horse. Each of the girls had on a hard helmet, but they didn't appear to mind when the horses climbed the first row of steep hills. The views couldn't have been better for him. Sure, he'd ridden with the girls on their property and in England, but he'd never given Colorado Springs a try. Pike's Peak stood in the not-so-far distance, and a cool breeze drifted between the rock formations. Dust kicked up from the hooves in front of him, creating a swirling of red and brown.

"Having trouble keeping up, Professor?" Londyn called over her shoulder. Her gray eyes were hidden by sunglasses, but Callum knew what he'd see in them: merriment and teasing amid blue flecks.

"I'm not Indiana Jones, Miss Bellerose," he replied with a crooked grin.

Londyn chuckled and flicked her braids over her shoulder. "Of course not." She lifted her shades. "Mr. Jones wouldn't have been caught ogling."

Guess she heard after all. Callum's smile deepened. God, her eyes were magic in an otherwise boring world. "I wasn't ogling." He pointed toward the nature around them. "I was merely appreciating my surroundings."

He almost missed her subtle roll of the eyes when the tortoiseshell frames fell back in place.

The remainder of the ride was uneventful as the

group of tourists meandered through the lush greenery offset by the rich red columns. At one point, they even took a break to pose for photos. It quickly became obvious that this wasn't Londyn's first attempt at riding. Watching her became one of the highlights of his day. It warmed his insides to see his girls so comfortable with the tall screenwriter. She was a natural.

When he saw her dismount, he noted her talents weren't solely with children and theater, but also trickled to horses. She stroked the mare's neck as her lips moved in hushed words. Such an act shouldn't have been beautiful, but it was to Callum.

"You've been around horses before, then?" he asked, wiping his hands on the back of his jeans. He nodded to the stable hand and patted his horse before moving closer to Londyn. Bailey and Bethany played on the small rock wall at the entrance along with five other children.

Londyn glanced over and smiled. "Yes, but not as much as the girls. Just a few trail rides on vacation, to be honest. I would've loved to have one as a child."

"You and every other child." Callum rubbed her horse's nose. "You're a natural, you know?"

She grinned at the stable hand who retrieved the reins from her and led the mare away. "Thanks."

He opened his mouth to suggest they hit up a popular ice cream shop, but his phone rang and cut off his thought. Seeing the museum's number on the screen, he held up a finger. "I'm sorry. I need to take this. It's work."

"Sure, sure." She moved to the rock wall while he headed away from the loud crowd and screaming children.

"Yes?" he answered.

"Cal, did you get my email?" the assistant curator, Maddy Jones, said with a strained voice.

"Uh, no. I've been otherwise disposed." He ran a hand through his hair and kicked at a chunk of dirt in front of him. "What did it say?"

Maddy grunted. "Mr. Nathaniel wants you back here tomorrow. Apparently he needs your expertise with the upcoming gala again."

"What? Why?" He wiped a bead of sweat off his brow. "I've already sent my proposal for the event."

"It wasn't enough."

Bailey called to him from the top of the tower, but he waved her off without looking. "You can't be serious. It's my finest idea yet." He gritted his teeth. "He approved it last month."

Keyboard typing came from Maddy's side in London. "I'm just telling you what I was told. They want something big. Flashy even. We're unveiling the latest finds from the Egyptian dig, so a normal soiree won't do. Not since we need new donors to fund the rest of the expedition."

Callum clenched his jaw. He'd worked for two months to perfect his designs and it wasn't good enough all of a sudden.

Story of my life.

Bethany's voice drifted to him, and he glanced over and saw her wave. He haphazardly returned the act, too distraught over the newfound failure.

"Fine. Back to the drawing board. Tell Nathaniel I'll be there tomorrow night to go over the new expectations," he mumbled, hanging up. The day went from amazing to awful in record time.

He scrolled through his emails in search of the one Maddy spoke of. Sure enough, the board director wasn't fond of his pitch anymore. *Bloody bastard.*

"Callum?"

Whipping his head up from the screen, he met Londyn's perturbed face. "Yes?"

"Didn't you hear Bethany and Bailey?" she asked, her body language full of attitude.

He hit Reply to the email and started typing with his thumbs. "Um, yes." He looked up and noticed her lips pulled into a flat line. "Er, no."

Huffing, Londyn stomped to his location beneath a tree. With one swift swipe, she grabbed his phone.

"Hey—"

"Oh, no you don't." She stuffed the phone in her back pocket when he moved to grab it, then pointed to the rock wall. "The girls were trying to get your attention, Callum. They wanted to show you their success at scaling the wall." She tipped her hat back. "But you're too wrapped up with your damn phone to give them any of your time."

Her gumption didn't surprise him, but he noticed her action and volume had drawn onlookers. Causing a scene wasn't something he preferred at any time, but especially with his nanny.

Reaching around, he snagged the phone, the temptation to linger on the swell of her jeans nearly overtaking him. "Isn't that what you're here for? To pay attention to their trivial achievements? Let me know when they've discovered a lost colony." He didn't mean for the words to come out sarcastic, but they did anyway.

Londyn's face turned such a deep shade of red that he was afraid she'd go completely purple and her head would pop clean off. She inhaled slowly, then crossed her arms over her chest. "You're an ass, and you've no clue what you're missing out on with those adorable girls. One of these days, you'll wake up not knowing who they are or why they hate you." Her words were daggers to his already slivered pride. Jamming his phone in his pocket, he lowered his voice. "Perhaps you should get back to work, Miss Bellerose." He took a step closer, his temper near boiling. "I can handle my children."

Raising one eyebrow, she snorted. "Yes, I can see that." She tugged the Stetson low over her eyes, obscuring his vision into their stormy depths. Turning around, she strutted toward Bailey and Bethany, never once giving him another glance.

Callum let out a long, steady breath as he watched her hasty retreat. He'd screwed up, sure, but he hadn't expected a scolding from anyone. He did the best he could with his time.

Though, after watching Londyn usher the girls to the car and drive off without him, he decided maybe he needed to step up on his definition of 'best,' since clearly his nanny wasn't cutting him any slack. A fact he'd somehow grown accustomed to in her short time at Archer House.

***

Chocolate ice cream. It was the one and only solution she could come to since Chinese was out of the question at that time of night, and she doubted a chick flick would do the trick.

Opening the freezer door, Londyn scanned the contents. After moving bags of frozen vegetables and something resembling a fruitcake, she found it—her favorite type of ice cream, and in a perfect pint-sized portion.

"Thank God," she mumbled, breaking the seal on the brownie batter concoction. She'd asked Alfred's wife, Gloria, to pick up a few snacks for her at the store. The lady clearly came through, since she found six more pints in the back of the freezer.

Pulling out a tall bar stool, she slouched with her elbows on the kitchen island, spoon in hand. One bite in and she sighed in delight. "The only two men I'll ever need," she reminded herself around a hunk of brownie. Her spoon skimmed the chocolatey goodness and the time flashed above the door that led to the pantry.

Five hours ago, she'd abandoned Callum at the Garden of the Gods riding stable. Crossing her legs, she frowned. *I so shouldn't have done that.* She licked her finger at the trickle of melted chocolate. *I need to find him and apologize.* The look on his handsome face when they drove off haunted her even then, a combination of hurt, enraged, and amused. He didn't track her down even after Theodore went and retrieved him.

Instead of facing him head on, Londyn had ignored his presence completely. She and the girls swam, then ate pizza by the pool when they returned home. After tucking the girls in bed, she called Abi—who didn't answer—then meandered the halls until she ended up in the kitchen.

Now, hours later, her stomach churned at the repercussions of her act. It would make sense if Callum fired her. She'd called him out. Loudly. And in front of a ton of people. She cringed at the memory.

But then, shaking her head, she vowed she wouldn't take all the blame.

She stabbed the ice cream with the spoon. "Well, if he wasn't a cocky ass—"

"Please do finish that sentence, Miss Bellerose. I'm curious as to whom this cocky arse is."

At the sound of the deep British voice, the brownie in her mouth went down the wrong tube and she sputtered for a breath.

Callum slapped her back gently. "Are you going to survive, or shall I call for someone who knows CPR? I do not, I'm afraid."

Clearing her throat, she nodded and wiped her mouth. She must've been quite the sight: hair in a messy bun atop her head, shorts, and a cutoff T-shirt, all while chocolate stuck to her face.

Real attractive, Londyn.

"I'm fine," she lied, standing and shoving the chair backward.

Callum's hand slowly dropped from her shoulder. He took the seat next to hers and chuckled. "Ice cream? I didn't think Gloria bought this stuff."

Londyn grabbed the pint protectively. "A girl needs her chocolate."

He eyed her warily. "Not very healthy, is it? I usually ask her to get frozen yogurt for the girls."

"Not everything has to be healthy, you know."

"Can't disagree with you there." He moved to the freezer and waved a juice popsicle at her. "Though these are much better for you."

She snorted. "That's boring."

"Then I suppose I'm a bit boring at times." He put away the popsicle and returned to the island counter.

Scooping a brownie bite into her mouth, she shrugged. "Don't you ever just have fun, Callum? You know, wear sweats, throw popcorn at corny movies, and let your hair down type of fun."

He pointed to his head. "My hair's a smidge short for such nonsense."

"Smartass." Sitting down again, she dug out a large spoonful of ice cream and shoved it toward his mouth. "Now, eat this and prove to me that you're not always a fuddy-duddy."

He took a long look at the chocolate. "Uh, no. I'm good. Thank you."

"Eat it." She pushed it closer.

"No."

"Come on, eat a little," she pleaded.

Callum's face scrunched in exasperation. "Londyn…."

She positioned her body in front of his chair to avoid his escape. "You know you want it, Callum."

She flew the spoon in like an airplane, and when he opened his mouth to object, she snuck in the brownie ice cream. Chocolate smeared all over his lips at her hurried act and she froze, not sure what his reaction would be.

When he licked his lips and laughed, she grinned. "Well?"

"It's actually not bad," he said after swallowing.

"Psh, not bad? This stuff is amazing. Got me through many rough nights." She took a bite for emphasis. "A girl can't go wrong with Ben or Jerry."

Callum's smile slipped when his brown eyes dipped

to her lips. Impulsively, she licked them. No doubt there were remnants of dessert there.

"You're an enigma, Miss Bellerose," he confessed softly, leaning on the edge of his seat.

"Yeah? Why's that?"

He reached over and stole the spoon from her. After he took another bite, he pointed the utensil at her. "My plan was to scour the house for you once the girls were asleep and scold the living hell out of you for leaving me high and dry this afternoon."

She gulped, now worried for her job. "And now?"

Callum used the spoon to gently trace her lips, the cold steel touching but only briefly. It was hypnotic and spread chills over her body as his eyes clashed with hers. "Now all I want to do is find out if you taste like the chocolate you so adore."

Londyn's heartbeat pulsed in her ears. She'd known him barely two months and had thought of nothing else but kissing him. To see if he was still polite and snarky with his tongue tangling with hers.

"What about you, Londyn?" He set the spoon aside. "What do you want?"

She dropped his gaze and gripped the pint. Melted ice cream spilled over the carton, but she couldn't focus on the mess. *Surely I'm dreaming. This is all a symptom of too much sun and not enough hydration.*

Her eyes searched his out.

Right?

"I, uh, um…." She couldn't put together a sentence

no matter how hard she tried. *How am I supposed to react to that?*

"All right, I—"

"I shouldn't have left you there," she blurted.

He chuckled. "No, but I did deserve a little punishment for having my priorities flipped."

"Okay." It was a step in the right direction, at least. She couldn't fault him for that.

"It's late. I'll let you get some rest," Callum said, standing. "I'm off to London tomorrow, and judging from my boss's email, I may be there a week or two."

She nodded, then stopped when he locked her in the chair, hands on either side of the counter behind her. Brandy-hued eyes pinned her to silence.

"When I return, I'd like to hear your answer, Miss Bellerose." He stared at her lips. "Because I have a feeling it's the same thing I want." His nose grazed hers briefly before he softly pressed his lips against hers. His tongue traced the seam of her lips, and she moaned in frustration when he didn't invade her mouth.

Callum pulled back and smirked. "Oh, and I do believe I just took chocolate off your list of quick fixes." He stood to his full height. "Because I doubt you can ever eat chocolate again without thinking of me," he added before slipping from the room.

Only when his footsteps became faint did Londyn let out her breath, her hands shaking as she clenched the ice cream. After his short kiss, her cutoff top was suddenly flaming on her skin. She loved it when he touched her, but a tiny part wondered why. He acted aloof and curt when others were around, but when it was just the two of them… damn. He set her on fire, and she wanted to rip his clothes off until all he wore was that tie of his.

Fanning herself, Londyn opened the freezer door again and stood there as the cool breeze swept over her. She put the pint of brownie batter back in its safe hiding place. Apparently not even Ben and Jerry could solve her current predicament. An unusual feat for any man.

One C down.

He was right. Chocolate and Callum would be synonymous with one another from that moment on.

As to which tasted better on her lips? She wanted to know now more than ever.

CHAPTER EIGHT

Staring at the screen in front of him, Callum studied the new layout for the gala. The archeological finds in Egypt would be the centerpieces, but around them would be the evolution of cities stemmed from the Egyptian inspiration. He'd tweaked his initial idea, and the museum's board director loved it. Giving up on his dream for the event wasn't in the cards for him, so he pushed through until he got his yes.

The digital clock on the computer struck midnight. The museum itself was closed, but the private offices were lit up here and there with late-night workers; it was common among the employees, and Callum was glad he wasn't the only workaholic. A group of paleontologists down the hall was celebrating a new find along the Siberian territory, but he didn't feel like joining in on the festivities.

Drumming his fingers over the wireless keyboard, he saw a new email pop up in the lower right corner of the computer. The last week and a half had been nothing but work. From morning until the late hours of the evening, he was at the museum or asleep, and it wore on him more as each day passed. It certainly wasn't what he'd had in mind when he imagined a future in the museum.

Cracking his neck, Callum picked up his phone and noticed a missed call from the girls. Doing quick calculations, he shook his head. They'd be nigh on dinner, so he opted against returning the call. Swiping through the pictures Londyn sent, he smiled at the collage of activities they'd ventured upon during his absence. The white-water rafting shocked him, but the rock climbing, hiking Pike's Peak, and new archery course in their backyard made sense. His girls were made for the outdoors. They played among the woodland creatures back home in England too, but Colorado was especially fun for the duo.

His finger stopped at the selfie of the three of them, snapped during a spa day at home. Each had on a green facial mask, a stigma he'd never understand. Bailey's hair was in Princess Leia buns, Bethany's red locks curled in ringlets.

And then there was Londyn.

He let out a sigh at the sight. Her chestnut-brown hair resembled Pippi Longstocking's, perfection amid chaos. His heart panged. How was it possible that he felt something for a woman he barely knew? *Hell, we've hardly even seen each other.* It was the physical attraction, he was positive. She was gorgeous and oh so wrong for him. But still, Callum knew it went beyond the surface. At least, he wanted it to.

He sank back into his seat and ran a hand over his face. It was in desperate need of a good shave, his routine having been tampered with since his departure. *I wonder if Londyn would like my bristles.* Rubbing the sides of his chin, he closed his eyes.

"You're being ridiculous, Archer. This is ridiculous," he chided.

"What is?" a woman's voice asked.

Startled, he tipped over the bottle of water on his desk, the contents spilling on his lap. "Lovely."

"Oops, sorry, Cal." Maddy came into his office and leaned against the doorframe.

"It's fine." Wiping off the water, he decided it was time to call it a night after seeing what she needed. The younger woman was always pestering him for one thing or another, and that night was no different. "What're you doing here? This is the latest I've seen you at the museum."

Maddy closed the door and perched on the edge of his desk. "I had a report to finish. Plus I saw you working, so I thought I'd stick around." She batted her big brown eyes at him and twirled a strand of hair between her fingers.

Her proximity disturbed him, so he rolled his chair

backward. When she skootched closer, he regretted his movement. The familiar scent of scotch lingered in the air. *She's been drinking. Great.*

He reached for his phone, but she pushed his hand away. "Um, Maddy, what're you doing?"

"Making my move," she slurred. The moment the words left her mouth, she hopped off the desk and onto his lap. Her lips collided with his before he could react.

Damn liquid courage.

He didn't kiss her back. Years before, he'd thought about pursuing something with the thirty-year-old, then came to his senses. *Work and love don't mix.* That thought brought him to a screeching halt. *Or can they?* He desperately needed to know the answer. Not for the woman currently licking him, of course, but for another.

He abruptly pulled away from Maddy and met her eyes. She was beautiful in the science girl type of way, but she didn't fit him.

And Londyn does?

He wiped off his mouth. *Oh sod it.* He'd only kissed the tall brunette back in Colorado once, but he knew she'd fit him in every possible way.

"I can't, Maddy. I'm sorry."

The geologist by degree gasped. "Oh, right. Sorry. That wasn't very professional of me. I've had a drink of two." She stood and tucked her hair behind her ears. "Is there someone else?"

Getting to his feet, Callum powered down his

computer and grabbed his phone. "Not yet, but I hope so." He smiled and opened an app for last-minute flights. "Will you make sure the catering is all set for the gala? I'll be back in a few weeks to go over the final details."

"Um, sure." Maddy cringed. "Cal?"

He paused. "Yeah?"

"Can we pretend my epic failure didn't just happen? I've had the biggest crush on you and couldn't control myself."

Callum loosened his tie. "Yeah, Maddy. We're good. Don't worry about it." Opening the door, he paused. "I have a plane to catch. See you in a few weeks."

Racing down the hall, he heard her call after him but didn't stop to listen. He may have known virtually nothing about Londyn Bellerose, but he wanted to learn more. *She may be the biggest mistake of my life.* He grinned and prayed he was wrong. *Or the best thing to ever happen to me.* Either way, a month of bliss was better than loneliness.

Callum quickly sent a text message to Londyn. He needed to hear her decision when he got home. He'd done nothing but fret over it during the plane ride over the pond. Surely he hadn't read her body language incorrectly. She'd leaned in every time their bodies were close and had enjoyed his kiss, that much he was positive about.

Making a mental note to pick up at least one of the items on Londyn's ridiculous list of Cs, he raced down the polished stairs and into the balmy weather outside. For the first time in four years, he felt light and hopeful for a future. Whether it was long or short, a future with Londyn was well worth the trouble.

***

Turning on her phone, Londyn yawned as messages popped up and chimed. During one of their adventures the day before, her phone had plopped into a bucket of water. Needless to say, the blow-dryer method was one of many she tried to revive the aged technology. Eventually she gave up and left the device in a bowl of rice for the night. From the sounds of it, the rice suggestion from Theodore worked like a charm.

She dragged her slipper-clad feet to the bathroom, eyes still adjusting to the light. Two messages from her aunt Glenda. She checked those and rolled her eyes at the photos of Glenda and Stew at the Grand Canyon. *Apparently she didn't need me this summer after all.*

The three messages from Abi did little to excite her. She wanted to know if the sexy professor had made a move yet. *Technically, no.* She'd circle back to that particular subject with her best friend later. It was too complicated to explain over text anyhow. The next text gave her a recap of her ex's failure on the community stage, which put a little more pep in her step. The third one was a photo of Oreo—who looked like he'd gained a few pounds—and a letter of consideration from the

Broadway executives. Londyn didn't put too much faith in the piece of paper, though; they sent those out to anyone who submitted a play.

Finally she scrolled down to the last message. It was from Callum. As she read it, the toothpaste dripped off her toothbrush and into the sink.

Callum: Taking a red-eye. Be there in time for tea and biscuits.

Londyn checked the time of the text. It was well over fifteen hours ago. *The one day I drop my phone in water.* She went to type a reply, then bit her lip. *He's already home.*

Glancing in the mirror, she scrunched her nose. Her hair was in pigtails courtesy of Bailey, and the pieces not tied down were sticking up every which way. "Well, I look delightful."

After sliding in her contacts, she took a speedy shower, then pulled on a dark blue shirt and khaki shorts. A fast dab of eye makeup and she headed to the kitchen.

Reaching the haven of comfort food, Londyn smiled at Gloria. The woman cocked her head to the right when Londyn grabbed a teacup.

"Is this a new fashion trend?" she asked, pointing to the younger woman's head.

Londyn remembered then that her hair was still wrapped in a towel. Hands flying to her head, she groaned at the mass. "Of all days," she muttered, grabbing the kettle and pouring tea into her cup. She'd never really liked the British staple until she tried Gloria's brew. The breakfast blend was exactly what she needed that morning too.

"I'll be back in a few minutes to start breakfast." Gloria chuckled, then hustled from the room, a second pot of tea on a tray along with scrambled eggs, a slice of ham, and a piece of toast made from homemade bread. From the limited time she'd been there, Londyn had learned the cook liked to take breakfast to her husband in bed now and then. It was sweet, really, how the two of them were very much in love despite all their years together.

I wonder if I'll ever be like that with someone.

Londyn glanced around the kitchen with a small eat-in table. No one was up and around yet, reminding her to wake the girls soon. She missed their rambunctious antics and addictive accents; they were too cute on children. She sipped the sweet liquid and shook her head. *Of course Callum isn't down here waiting for me. He'll be sleeping after such a long flight.* Still, Londyn's face fell at getting herself flustered for absolutely nothing.

"Guess I should do something with my hair." She unraveled the towel, the wet hair slapping her face.

"Or you could leave it." Callum's voice rippled through the empty room and surrounded her like a warm blanket.

Turning to face him, Londyn's breath caught in her chest. He looked incredibly sexy with ruffled hair, at least a day's growth on his jaw, and still in his nightclothes. Well, if pajamas were silk pants, no shirt, and a robe with his initials embroidered on the lapel.

"You're back." The words felt as breathy as they sounded to her ears.

He crossed his arms over his chest, the gray robe coming open at the top. A generous tuft of curls caught her eye. On him, it looked distinguished and not at all cheesy. "Last I checked." He pointed to her mass of hair. "Is this what your morning hair always looks like?"

"Definitely not." She scrunched it with her hands. "It's usually much messier."

He leaned the small of his back to the counter. "Hmm, well I'm interested in seeing that fine specimen."

For a moment, they stood there simply staring at the other. She twiddled her thumbs, unsure what to do next. She knew what she wanted to do. Ripping off his robe and kissing him sounded ideal, yet she was wary of making the opening move. He was her employer, after all.

Taking a step toward her, Callum tugged at a strand of hair. "If it's anything like this, I won't complain."

Londyn's face heated the closer he got. It was like being intoxicated, but her mind was working on every cylinder.

"What, now you're speechless?" He smirked and reached for the kettle. Pouring a cup, he grazed her body with his.

"We weren't expecting you until next week." She grabbed a blueberry bagel and stuck it in the toaster.

"Well, I can leave and then come back if you'd prefer," he suggested, taking a sip of tea.

She whirled around, eyes wide. "No! That's not what I meant."

"Need time to hide your boy toy before I got back, then?" he ribbed.

Londyn's brows rose when his face darkened slightly. She couldn't help but tease him back. "And what if I did have a guy hiding in my closet? What would you do about it?"

Setting down his mug, Callum sauntered over to where she stood. "Do you?" His brown eyes locked with hers, his nose close enough to kiss.

Londyn's hand trembled at the huskiness in his voice and the jealousy filling his gaze. She set her tea on the counter lest it shatter on the floor. "No," she whispered.

"Good." He cradled her face and stared into her eyes. "Because if you did, I'd be forced to unleash my extensive rugby experience on the twat."

Londyn doubled over in laughter at the serious yet hollow threat. "Rugby? You played rugby?"

He chuckled, the sound delicious to her ears. "Don't believe me?"

His hands settled on her hips, the sensation shooting excitement through her body.

"I never thought of you as a jock, that's all."

Callum feigned a knife to the heart. "Ah, Miss Bellerose, you pain me. I have plenty of surprising secrets, should you choose to want to know me better."

Toying with the loop on his belted robe, she grinned. "I like surprises."

"Good to know." He laced his hands with hers. They were rough and completely dwarfed hers. "I'm not a huge fan myself."

"Oh, then I really should sneak the guy out of my window, shouldn't I?" She stepped toward the door, but his arms snaked around her waist and dragged her back to him.

Giggling, Londyn pretended to struggle, but it was no use. He was much stronger than he looked. Clearly his workout regimen did wonders beneath his tweed.

"Maybe I should start sleeping outside your room to ward off the other men," he suggested.

The mere idea of having him close at night made her shiver in anticipation. "Now why would you do that?"

Callum tipped her chin up and traced her bottom lip with his thumb. "Because I like you, Londyn. And quite honestly, I want to spend more time with you. Alone. I can't do that with a harem of guys around you, now can I?"

She playfully swatted at his chest. It was more solid than she anticipated. "Be serious, Cal."

"Good God, don't call me that, please." His face wrinkled in disgust.

"But why not? I've heard—"

"Yes, my mother likes to use my father's nickname for me. She knows I hate it too." He shook his head as if to ward off those thoughts. "Callum would be great."

"All right, Callum." She fingered his lapel. "What's your goal here? I'm only in Colorado for another month."

"I'm aware, but there's something about you that makes me forget deadlines and work. I enjoy your companionship and adore how you feel in my arms. I want to see if it goes anywhere." He pressed a kiss to her cheek and retrieved his tea. "However long—if you're in agreement—will be enough for me." He took a drink. "What do you think?"

Abi's words floated across her mind. He wasn't looking for anything serious. She needed to be clear she couldn't fall for him. Her life was in New York, not Colorado. "The summer works for me." She smirked, then teased, "If I end up liking you."

Callum grinned and raised his cup. "Now that we've cleared the air, I'm going back to bed. Jet lag is a bitch."

He headed to the doorway and then paused, looking back at her. Shaking his head once, he set the cup on the counter and crossed the room. With one smooth move, he pulled her into his embrace and overwhelmed her lips with his own. Londyn gasped at the unexpected act but didn't argue with the way his lips moved over hers. He let go much too soon for her liking.

"Right, I think that will hold me over for a few hours." He tucked her hair behind her ear and smiled. Londyn swore her heart would burst. "And give me something to dream about." Nodding once, he retrieved his tea. "Oh, and tell the girls we're taking them away to the mountains for the weekend. They'll love it."

Her eyes widened, and she couldn't help the grin on her face. "Sounds like an adventure to me. We'll get packing."

Callum snapped his fingers. "And Londyn?"

She turned toward him. "Yes?"

"I'll do bed checks at eleven each night from here on," he joked with a wink, then disappeared down the hall.

Londyn didn't bother to stifle her giggle. The beginning of whatever this was felt like a monsoon of emotions. *Oh my God, wait until Abi hears.* Her best friend would be ecstatic. She'd probably even overnight her enough condoms for a frat house.

The summer was looking up, and she still had a little over a month to go.

CHAPTER NINE

The sleek black Infinity SUV eased into the last parking spot outside Woodland Lodge in Aspen, Colorado. The exterior resembled a modern log cabin, complete with carved wood totem poles and authentic rocking chairs on the wraparound porch. The two-story A-frame looked torn straight out of a woodsy fairy tale.

How do people even leave after being here? she wondered, unbuckling her seat belt.

The majority of the ride from Colorado Springs was uneventful until Bailey swiped the DVD her sister wanted to watch. *The joys of sisterhood.* Surprisingly, Callum handled the disaster calmly and diplomatically from the driver seat. It still amazed her hours later. No wonder he was so good at his job. Dealing with children was probably much like dealing with aristocrats and artists. If the accent didn't calm you down, his rational conversation would do the trick.

As the Archers clambered out of the vehicle, she took her time to take in every glorious part of their lodging for the next few days. "This place is stunning," she cooed, closing the passenger door.

"We stay here every time we come to Aspen," Bethany said, grabbing her favorite stuffed animal—a Siamese cat with blue eyes and chocolate points on the face, feet, and tail. It was almost too pretty to sleep with, but the oldest Archer child didn't have any trouble toting the giant cat around no matter where they went.

"I better stick with you, then, or I might get lost." She followed Callum to the back hatch and grabbed the straps to her duffel. "How often do you visit?"

Bailey answered as Callum dished out the remaining luggage. "Usually every summer. We didn't come two years ago because I was sick."

"I see." She grinned at Bailey. "So there's stuff to do around here even when it isn't snowing? I thought this place was mainly popular during the winter months."

They entered the outdoors-themed lobby, which was tasteful yet showed it was one of the higher-class lodges. The bellhop and gold keycards also tipped the scales to that conclusion. Elegant moose and bear carvings were etched in wood behind a glass panel along one wall. A giant fireplace sat in the middle of the room, dividing the large expanse, while the other wall boasted a long aquarium complete with fish native of Colorado. Everywhere she looked, leather couches and comfortable-looking chairs sat ready for use. Judging from the parking lot, there was no vacancy either. Clearly Aspen was busy year-round.

"Oh yes, Aspen has it all." Callum stepped up to the desk while she and the girls watched the large fish swim along the length of the freshwater tank.

"What should we do first?" she asked when he came back. They followed the bellhop to the elevator and waited for it to return to the first level.

"Swimming," Bailey suggested.

"No way, let's go hiking," her sister argued.

"Okay, okay." Londyn held up her hands to stop a full-fledged brawl. From her time with the girls, she knew they were edgy because of all the time spent together in the car and lack of food. *Easily remedied.*

"How about we let your dad choose how we kick off our weekend?" She looked to Callum for his response.

The elevator arrived and they crammed inside. "Hmm, that's a hard one. So many choices." He tapped his chin with his index finger. "I do fancy a stroll in the local shops." Bailey bunched up her nose, but the devious gleam in his eyes continued despite her reaction. "Or there's the art gallery. I heard they have new exhibits." Bethany crossed her arms over her mermaid T-shirt with a huff.

The elevator stopped on their floor and Callum waved off the bellhop. Once they were clear of eavesdropping ears, he stooped down to the girls' level and whispered, "But first, let's show Londyn how the two of you ice-skate. Will that work for you?"

Bailey wrapped her arms around his neck and squeezed. Hard, if the choking from him was any indicator. "You're the best daddy in the whole world."

Londyn gripped the duffel bag tighter. The scene in front of her was too sweet, something she'd never forget. He was a good dad, she was 100 percent sure of it. Her hasty judgments before were precisely that— hasty. But the only way to truly know Callum was to get to know him without two nosy girls around all the time.

"Yes, well I do my best." He kissed his daughter's cheek, then pointed up ahead. "You girls and I will share a room, and Londyn has the one opposite us."

"Aww, why can't we sleep with Londyn?" Bethany asked, reaching the neighboring rooms.

Callum handed the other key to Londyn, then opened their door. "Because I have the double beds and she doesn't." He gave Bailey a pointed look. "Some people don't enjoy being kicked in their sleep either." He chuckled when his daughter offered him a sassy sashay into the room, Bethany following closely. "Plus she deserves some time to herself," he added when his children started chattering about snacks from the minibar.

Londyn swiped her key. "Maybe not all to myself." She opened the door and slowly walked in backward, her eyes glued to Callum's. "Even nannies get lonely."

His smile broadened, and he leaned against the doorframe. "Is that an invitation, Miss Bellerose?"

"I do believe it was, Mr. Archer." She let the door close, his soft chuckle making her press her lips together tight. They had chemistry, that much was clear. Now Londyn wanted to see how they'd react together. Preferably in an explosion she anticipated more than fireworks on the Fourth of July.

Surveying the room, she felt a little more at home. The warm cream color of the wall enhanced the nature scene painted in the large panel above the bed. The deer drinking from a calm river with mountains in the background made her believe it was based on the nearby woods. She investigated the rest of the room, finding a full bathroom with proper toiletries that made her grin. Though the large tub made her think twice about ice-skating. A nice, long soak in bubbles would do her body a world of good. All in all, she was impressed with the woodsy room; it held the right amount of class to not be seen as manly.

From the confines of her purse, Abi's ringtone rang out, capturing her attention. Digging through the tote, Londyn answered before it went to voice mail. "Finally," she greeted sarcastically.

"Don't 'finally' me," Abi laughed. "How's it going? I feel like I haven't talked to you in forever."

Londyn tossed her bag onto the bed. "It has been a while. What're you up to?"

"It's laundry day, so blah."

"Aren't you glad I'm not there to screw up the machine?" she joked.

"Um, yes. You and technology are not chummy." The sounds of detergent being shaken over clothes and the water knob cranked filled the air. "How's nannying today?"

"Well, we're in Aspen, so it's more of a mini vacation. Who am I kidding? This job is a vacation most of the time." She unpacked her sweatshirt and pants. No doubt shorts and a tank wouldn't work with ice-skating.

"Whoa, really? Just you and the girls?"

"No, Callum's here too." She tossed the bag to the floor. "It was his idea."

Abi let out an inaudible girl shriek. "Have you guys… done anything?"

The insinuation made Londyn's cheeks burn. "Just kiss, which was freaking amazing, by the way. I'm pretty sure something will happen while we're up here too." She changed into the jeans and buttoned them. "At least I hope so. This blatant yet somehow sly flirting is killing me. I don't get it. Maybe it's the Englishman in him. He's so thoughtful and doesn't rush anything. I guess he likes to take his time. It's frustrating, but I like it. Is that weird?"

"Damn, girl, he's straight-up wooing you," Abi pointed out. "As in old-timey, sweep-you-off-your feet wooing."

Londyn shook her head. "Please, I'm not a woo girl."

"You are now." She laughed, and the apartment door screeched open. Oreo meowed at her entrance, and Londyn suddenly missed the chubby kitty.

"Maybe. He seems kind of shy when it comes to this. He's hinted at being gun-shy, but I don't know why he would be." She glanced out the window. "He's gorgeous and funny. Not to mention richer than God."

Abi clucked her tongue. "You know what they say about the quiet ones?"

"No, what?"

"They're the ones you have to watch out for."

Londyn rubbed her eyes and pulled on a sweatshirt. "Oh, pishposh."

"I'm serious. I can see it now." Abi's voice lowered to a sultry tone. "He may act like a gentleman in public, but, girl, he'll go savage on you in the bedroom. Chain you up, whipped cream on your stomach, tease you until you scream. Rip those red panties off and kiss you until you're numb. And not only your lips. Everywhere." She chuckled. "Oops, I think I just turned myself on a little."

Londyn couldn't help but laugh at her friend's description. It sounded nothing like Callum. Although, the imagery made her bite her bottom lip and heat creep down her body. *Could he act like that?* She didn't know, but she sure as hell was interested in finding out. "All right, nympho, you're done. You seriously need to stop reading those erotica books."

"Why would I?" Abi sighed. "I don't have a sexy

British guy to keep me warm at night like you. Fictional men are all I need. Oh, and B.O.B."

Glancing around the room, Londyn tucked her hair behind her ears. "Lalala, I'm not hearing this."

"Whatever. I keep you up to date on all things sexy, and you love it."

Londyn grinned. Abi wasn't wrong, but telling her so would only encourage the antics. "Debatable."

"Either way, you better call me right after he claims you for England." The television flicked on in the background. "Because I have a feeling you'll be speaking with an accent after he does. It'll be *that* good."

"You're giving me way too high hopes, Abs. I'd be good with a month of decent sex with a hot guy. I don't need fireworks or romance. That'd just make it harder to leave in August."

"Hmm, yeah, you're right. Better keep it plain." She snickered, then made a sexy, guttural growling sound. "Plain in public and spicy in the bedroom."

A knock on the outside of her door pulled Londyn back to the present. "I've got to run. Wish me luck. I'm attempting ice-skating."

"Luck! Oh, and send me a picture of him sometime soon. I'm dying to see what he looks like," Abi begged.

Londyn hung up before her best friend could add more photo requests. When she pulled the door open, Callum's handsome face met her gaze. She could get used to seeing it on a daily basis.

"Ready?" he asked. "The girls are waiting downstairs."

"You bet." Her gaze skidded over him quickly. She couldn't help it, as his dark jeans and red wool sweater looked out of place amid the upper-eighties weather. Despite the faux pas, he was every woman's dream.

He held out his hand and she took it without recourse.

Every woman including me.

***

Aspen's solitary indoor ice-skating rink was exactly as he recalled. A decent crowd of people milled about the lobby while some ate pizza and chatted. The Zamboni finished the last pass as they laced their skates.

Bailey and Bethany shot across the ice the moment they were given the all clear, whereas Londyn stared at the rink as if it would swallow her whole.

"Have you ever skated before?" he asked, coming up behind her. The red scarf around her neck offset the pure white sweatshirt and made her lips that much more desirable.

"Yes, but the last time I did, I ended up smashing my face on the ice." Londyn winced. "I'm a tad clumsy at times, if you hadn't noticed."

"It caught my attention a time or two." Callum didn't have to rack his mind to know that. Whether it was the way she spoke her thoughts instead of thinking them or bumped into things, Londyn wasn't nearly as graceful as other women he knew. He smirked at the thought. It was why he liked her. Despite the bumps and bruises she always sported, she was genuine 100 percent of the time. That quality wasn't common in his opinion.

She frowned and touched her jaw. "Anyway, I wore braces back then." She scowled at the memory. "My mouth was all cut up and my lip split thanks to the mandatory field trip. So since then I've shied away from the sport."

"Well now." He straightened the scarf, inching closer to her. Somehow, the cinnamon perfume overwhelmed her usual cocoa-laced skin. He needed to figure out how she smelled that good all the time. It was ridiculously distracting to be around. "We can't have a repeat of that disaster. Come on, I'll show you how to glide like a pro."

Apprehension filled her pretty features, but she took his outstretched hand and followed him onto the slick ice. Her fingers curled around his forearms as he skated backward, leading her to the point of no return.

"Shouldn't we stay near the edge, so I can grip the side?" she suggested, panic in her voice.

Callum navigated them to the middle. "Do you trust me, Londyn?"

Her eyes lifted from her skates. "Yes."

Her confidence bolstered his pride. "Then you have nothing to worry about. I'll make sure you don't kersplat."

She tilted her head and scoffed. "Right, because you

can keep me upright."

"You don't think I can?"

Londyn scrunched her nose. "Nope."

He smirked, determined to right her misconception. With one quick tug, Londyn slid straight into his arms. Her legs wobbled worse than Bambi's as they intermingled between his. A puffy cloud from her mouth collided with his lips.

"I'm very sure I can keep you upright." He smiled down the few inches to her. It was liberating to have a woman close enough to kiss at any given moment. "And on your toes."

She shook her curls—God, she looked sexy in loose ringlets—and gasped when they moved forward. "I thought this was supposed to be fun. I'm terrified."

Pointing to Bethany doing a twirl, he agreed, "It is." Her eyes bugged when she looked over at his daughter. "Though I think they have a few years of lessons on you."

"You think?" Bailey skated around them backward, and Londyn clenched her teeth together. "Show-off," she muttered, setting her feet into motion.

After a few minutes, her posture straightened, and her grasp was no longer like a vise on his arms. Little by little, he released his hold until they skated side by side. Letting her take the lead, Callum skated alongside the determined playwright, his hand never far from hers. "All right, be careful on this turn. If you try too hard, you'll face-plant. And I'm quite fond of the way your face looks."

Londyn's arms flailed as she kept her balance on the slight turn. It would've been a success had Bethany not whizzed by her too close. The fall was hard, fast, and painful from his point of view.

"Bethany Marie." He glowered at his daughter when Londyn toppled to the floor. The six-year-old's face took on an anxious and sorrowful expression as her eyes turned down, but she didn't stop. In fact, she raced to the far end of the rink. "You'll pay for that later," he warned with a knowing look. He doubted his eldest heard him, but she would later.

Focusing on Londyn, he dropped to his knees to help her up. Her shoulders shook violently, immediately worrying him. If she'd hit her head and had a concussion, all bets were off. "Are you all right? Nothing's broken, is it?"

"Purple monkeys," she mumbled.

"Pardon?"

"The flying lions are so pretty."

Dear God, my child rattled her brains loose. He maneuvered closer despite the chilly ice. "Londyn, talk to me, love." He scooped her off the ice and studied her face intently as he cupped it gently. Humor filled her blue-gray eyes when she came into view. "You're joking?"

Londyn laughed and wiped the ice off her jeans. "Sorry, I couldn't resist." She doubled over, the hearty sound warming him despite her teasing. "You were so worried that you broke me."

He helped her to her feet. "It did cross my mind, yes."

"Don't worry, I'm hardy." She patted his chest. The chuckles tapered off when her hands lingered.

His heart pounded beneath her touch. It felt right, normal even, to have any part of her on him. He wanted to kiss her. *But here? Now? In front of all these people?* He couldn't muster up the courage. Not when there was a chance she'd reject him.

"I'm glad to hear it. Would you like to try again?" He nodded toward the girls. "I promise to stay as far away from my energetic children as possible."

Rubbing her hip, she winced. "Actually, I think I'll take a short break and get something to warm my hands. That ice is cold."

Callum pushed aside the disappointment circulating in his mind. Being near her made his heart light and worries dissipate. He led her to one of the exits and made sure she was safely off the ice before returning to the rink. Bethany and Bailey were racing along one side, a definite no-no if the faces on the other parents around the ice told him anything.

Setting a course to them, he hoped whatever injury his child caused wouldn't be permanent. He needed Londyn alive and well for more than his own selfish reasons. She was becoming someone he could rely on and trust, two qualities that weren't easy for him without due cause.

He checked over his shoulder and saw her settle at one of the benches with a hot beverage in hand. She looked cozy and safe. *And way too beautiful.* He'd scorn himself if he didn't at least attempt another stolen kiss. Hell, he'd like a whole lot more from the woman who fit in his arms better than a puzzle piece.

***

Londyn watched Callum skate toward Bailey and Bethany. After a quick chat—no doubt about safety—the trio started sliding across the ice as a team. It was beautiful, the way the two girls knew more moves than anyone out on the rink.

She sipped on the large hot cocoa from the sidelines, her posterior sure to have a bruise or two from her colossal fall. Blaming Bethany would've been pointless. It was an accident. She'd have done the same at her age.

Bailey showed off for Callum, who in turn clapped and offered quiet advice for her next trick. It flabbergasted Londyn how flawlessly the youngster spun and twirled without any fear. In a way, Londyn could relate to the blind trust in the frozen water; she'd all but skated on thin ice her entire time in New York, after all.

That notion made the paper cup filled with chocolatey goodness pause at her lips. *Is it really true?* She thought over her adult life—minus college, because come on, that wasn't real life—and couldn't deny it.

There was no stability in the theater. Writer or actor. It's what everyone told her, employer and friend alike. She didn't believe them; it was the bullheadedness to her personality. She just kept trying and working. *And for what?*

She took a sip and thought it over. In reality, she had nothing to show for her efforts. Sure, her continued work with the theater in Queens kept her in the performing arts business, but she had absolutely nothing. She worked a dead-end job, and that was exactly what she'd return to. *Maybe it's time I found something more secure.* That scared her more than moving to New York in the first place. In the fall, she'd be another year older with no clear future in store.

She licked her top lip free of whipped cream. *I guess there's always Aunt Glenda's offer.*

Bethany's laughter brought her head up. The girl in pink leggings picked up speed and did a perfect single Lutz. Shock and awe circulating through her mind, Londyn stood and then teetered when her legs recalled she still wore ice skates. Cheering loudly, she wobbled to the edge of the rink. "Holy cow, Bethany. I didn't know you could do that. You're amazing!"

Cheeks flushed, the girl stopped in front of her. She perched her hands on her hips, a proud smile on her face. "Thanks. That's the first time I haven't fallen."

"How long have you been skating? You look like a

mini Olympian."

"Dad signed me and Bailey up for lessons when we were little. We're on the ice every week back home." She pushed off the side with one last wave.

Home. The smile dropped from her face. They were going home in a few short weeks. It wasn't the same as her going home, as theirs was across an ocean.

Callum and Bailey skated backward in her peripheral vision. Somehow she already missed them, and they were only fifty feet from her.

Slowly she returned to her hot chocolate and stirred it. *Where is my home? New York? Iowa?* Her gaze caught Callum's and her heart fluttered when his smile reached his brown eyes. The more time she spent with the Archers, the less she knew where home truly was for her. It was all a jumble of feelings, and she didn't want to face any of them.

Abi's words from earlier tumbled around her head. She cared deeply for Bailey and Bethany. Their dad, though, he was a mystery. One thing was for certain, she'd know his intentions by the end of the trip. If he was simply stringing her along, she could accept it.

But what if he's not? What if he like *likes me?*

She shook her head and finished her drink.

No. This is a summer job, Londyn. Only for the summer.

Callum waved at her.

Even if that sucks.

CHAPTER TEN

"Snow!" Bailey said as she and Bethany rushed out of the car toward the dusting of white fluff.

"Slow down, it may be slippery," Callum warned, climbing out of the car. It'd be just his luck for them to break a bone while at twelve thousand feet. He glanced over toward where Londyn should've been, but she was among the children, frolicking in the snow.

"You'd think none of you had seen this white business before," he teased, nearing the end of the gravel on the turnabout for cars to stop to review the majesty of the mountains.

"Summer snow is special," Bethany said matter-of-factly.

"Yeah, we're so high up that it's like Christmas here."

He tromped through the soft ground to the piles of

deep snow. While the majority of Independence Pass was lush and green, large spots of snow remained on the mountains.

"Do you get much snow in Iowa, Londyn?" he asked. "I've never visited, but I heard you have lots of corn there."

Londyn stopped rolling snow into a giant ball and looked up at him in bewilderment. A small chuckle escaped her mouth. "It's Iowa, so yeah, we get snow. And we have corn. Lots and lots of corn." She pulled up her gloves. "But not as much snow in the middle of the state where I'm from. We get enough to make the bitter wind chill feel like home." Sniffling at the cold, she returned to her task of creating the bottom of a snowman. "What about England? I've never been, but I hear you get plenty."

"Actually, we don't get that much," Bailey stated.

Londyn put on a shocked face. "No, really? I don't believe it."

"It's true," Bethany said, working on the middle section of the snowman.

"And when it snows, it gets boring after a while," the youngest admitted, her ball of snow looking more oval than circular.

"Boring? That's no good." Londyn rolled her ball a couple of feet, then stopped and dug her gloves in the snow. "Don't you know all the fun things you can do with snow?"

Both girls shrugged. He caught wind of what

Londyn was doing when a small ball formed in her hands. He was looking forward to the next part more by the minute.

"Well, there are snow forts you can build. We used to make the best ones. Igloos, really. Of course, there's sledding, though you need a good hill for that." She glanced to him and winked. "Then, my favorite of all, snowball fights."

She let the first ball fly toward Bailey. It hit her in the leg and the screams of delight began. The girls ran and hid behind the large ball for the snowman while Callum ran over to where Londyn smashed snow together. She was rather quick too.

"Adults versus children, I take it?" He crouched and quickly created ammunition for the pending battle.

Londyn nodded, the fuzzy ball at the end of her winter hat bouncing. "Wouldn't have it any other way."

Before he could reply, snow flew at them from two directions. *All those tactical shows are paying off*, he thought when Bethany came in from the left and Bailey on the right. They were officially boxed in thanks to two girls under the age of seven.

Shrieking, Londyn jumped to her feet and started throwing the snowballs at Bethany. Callum took to the other enemy, Bailey, throwing loose snow when his supply ran out.

"I think we're losing momentum," he called when Bailey jumped on him and covered his head with snow.

"I think you're right." Londyn's loud giggle warmed

him despite the frigid temperatures. Glancing over, he saw she was in a similar predicament.

Pulling on the front of his youngest's coat, he whispered, "Let's switch sides, shall we, and join forces."

The blue-eyed beauty grinned and nodded once. Within moments, the tables turned, and they pommeled Bethany and Londyn with freshly packed snowballs.

Startled by their traitorous partners, the two exchanged a silent agreement, then ran toward Callum and Bailey, snowballs flying. The fight was fair until the snowballs ran out. After that, it was a shock that the girls didn't draw blood. Their fierce cries of war were nothing compared to how easily Londyn let them win.

Callum had never laughed so hard as when Bailey hopped on Bethany's back like a jockey. The act caused Bethany to fall, which resulted in snow being forced into her face by her loving sister. The older girl gave it right back to Bailey when she rolled over and let her sister eat a mouthful of snow.

Seeing the girls so happy at a spur-of-the-moment game made him act instead of think for a change. Snagging Londyn around the waist, he pulled her to him.

"What're y—"

His lips over her cold ones cut off the rest of her question. The snowballs in her gloves crumbled and dropped to their boots as she wrapped her arms around his neck to kiss him back. Good God, she tasted like he'd remembered—warm, passionate, and a hint of chocolate.

Deepening the embrace at her satisfied moan, Callum pressed her closer until almost every inch of her body was against his. He could stand there forever merely kissing her and feeling her come alive under his tutelage. From the way Londyn clung to his shoulders and tangled her tongue with his, Callum wasn't the only one feeling the magnetic tug between them.

A snowball to the side of his face halted any further act. *They're going to pay for that too.* He slowly eased his mouth from hers, though the soft groan of disappointment tempted him to go back for more. The giggles from Bethany and Bailey swayed him otherwise. Her eyelids were still closed, but when they opened and stormy gray eyes flicked to his face, Callum's entire body begged him to not do the proper thing for once and rebel instead.

"Whoa," she managed in a hoarse voice, fingers toying with the back of his wool cap.

"Is that a good 'whoa' or a bad one?" he asked, ignoring the pelting of snowballs. Evidently the children didn't approve of him monopolizing their nanny's attention.

Well, get used to it, girls. I'm going to be doing a lot more of it.

She licked her lips, the act pushing his self-control. Those were his lips to lick now, and he wanted to badly. His eyes dropped to her neck. *And not her lips alone.*

All of her.

"Oh, it's good." Red crept onto her cheeks, the hue almost matching her scarf. "Very, very, *very* good."

Callum's hands tightened around her hips. "Good. Maybe we can do more of it later, then."

She just blushed again, but she didn't have to say anything. He already knew the answer. It was crystal clear when she unabashedly returned the kiss.

She's an amazing kisser.

"Come on, let's go build the snowman we abandoned." He grabbed her hand and led her back to reality. He didn't know where the bloody hell the sudden urge to kiss her came from, but he guessed it was from the woman beside him. She brought out a side to him he'd thought lost after Jessica left. Now he was afraid he might smother the flicker before it became a flame.

Londyn quickly fell back into her nanny nature with the girls as if nothing had changed. Well, it had for him, at least. The whole damn mountain shifted under his feet when their lips met. She wasn't merely the caretaker to his children anymore. He couldn't just have one taste of her and be done.

"Callum, come join our selfie," Londyn called from the fully built snowman. He hadn't even noticed when they completed it. Vaguely, he recalled wrapping his scarf around the neck, but he'd lost all sense of time when Londyn smiled at him.

Walking to the open spot on the other side of the

snowman, Callum took in the view. Bailey and Bethany kneeled in front of their creation while he and Londyn crouched on either side, the snowman the only thing keeping them apart.

Giving her a sideways glance, he determined any photo with her in it was well worth the space on the walls and in his heart.

***

Londyn sank into the large leather couch across from the roaring fire the next evening. Yawning, she reviewed the day's events while Callum tucked the girls in bed. They'd hiked one of the trails outside Aspen most of the day. She'd scraped her legs pretty good on the overgrown weeds along the path, but the pain was well worth it when they crested the top and looked down on the bustling city stuck between the Rockies. They stopped in the picnic area for lunch, and after the girls chased birds and bunnies, she managed to snap a few photos of the group. Callum had to carry Bethany on his back on the return trip, which meant she'd been roped into giving Bailey a piggyback ride too.

Rolling her neck from side to side, she tucked her legs under her. After hitting up the local shops, they'd stopped at a park, ate ice cream, and then ordered pizza when they returned to the lodge. All in all, her time in Aspen was much better than she'd hoped.

And that kiss. Oy vey. She sighed in remembrance,

her lips still tingling. Nobody kissed like Callum. She hated to admit it, but Abi was right. He was prim and proper until his lips met hers. She shifted on the couch at the thought of where else his enthusiasm would transfer. Their first kisses were nothing compared to that one.

"From the sounds of their quiet snoring, I'd say they're fast asleep," Callum said, taking the open spot beside her. The lodge was scarce of people, and the couch was ideally tucked in the shadows as if anticipating lovers canoodling and affairs beginning on the property. With the stunning views at every window, it didn't seem an impossible idea.

"They had a big day." She watched him slowly relax as he stared into the flames. "I almost don't want to leave in the morning."

His hand sought out hers, and he laced them together tightly. "Neither do I, because once we leave, so do I."

"The museum?" Her heart sank when he nodded sadly. One of the positives about their trip was he didn't answer one call or even check his phone for emails. He was fully present in all aspects of their time together. She almost considered tossing the damn phone in the river, but ultimately decided against it.

"Unfortunately, yes." Leaning his head to the back cushion, he sighed. "The new exhibit and summer gala are quickly approaching." He swung his eyes to her, lids heavy. "Apparently they need the curator for such a job."

Tousling his sandy-colored hair with her free hand, Londyn took in his comfortable attire. He'd officially succumbed to sweat pants and a tee, both fitting him better than should have been legal. "They can't live without you. It's a good problem to have."

"I suppose." Sitting up, he kissed the back of her hand. "Now that it's just the two of us and nobody's vying for your attention, let's chat."

Sitting cross-legged facing him, she prepared herself for the worst. Surely he couldn't be as fabulous as he seemed. Everyone had flaws. She admired his slow nature, though. It wasn't what she was used to when it came to her dating life. Normally the guys were fast, easy, and sleazy, but Callum was different, and she couldn't get enough. "All right, go for it."

Callum eyed her alert position and replicated it on the couch. His long legs tucked beneath him looked completely out of place, but she had to commend his dedication. "So, I already know your age, but I haven't been graced with knowing your birthday."

"Starting easy. I like it." She tightened her ponytail and pulled out a stray twig. *Damn thing must've snuck in there midhike.* Laughing, she tossed it aside. "November 27th. I'm a Thanksgiving baby."

"Very nice. I know I'd be thankful for you every year," he said with a boyish grin.

"Yeah, yeah." She pushed at his arm. "When's your birthday?"

He took a breath. "As it turns out, it's December 24th."

Her mouth popped open and she howled with mirth. The sound echoed in the high ceiling and caused a passing woman to glare at her. "Christmas Eve, huh? You must have magical powers being born on such a day."

His smile deepened. "Well, I got you to kiss me, so yes, I'd like to think so."

She rolled her eyes. "We're both holiday kids." She nudged him with her elbow. "I knew I liked you for some reason. And you're what, thirty?"

Callum's deep chuckle rumbled past his straight teeth. "Close. I'm thirty-five."

"What? No freaking way." She lifted one eyebrow. "You don't look it at all." Her eyes traced him from head to toe. "Definitely not."

"Alas, I am, but I'll take the compliment. I try to stay in shape. My father failed to do so and died young. I don't want that for my girls or myself, which is why I strive to stay young." He shrugged and scratched his ear. "Well, physically that is. I'm afraid my psyche is more of an old man's."

"Nah, I don't think so. You're classic, not old," she encouraged.

"Thanks."

"You look like him, you know? The portrait in your office." She paused. "Your family ages gracefully."

"You're too kind." He moved closer to her on the couch. "But if you don't mind, I'd rather steer far away from any conversation about my mother if you were going there next. She's an entirely different dragon."

She chuckled, the same thought having come to mind. "Agreed."

"What about your family? You mentioned losing your parents." His face softened and the bristles from his day's growth shone in the firelight. It made him appear more human, rugged even. "If it's too difficult, don't feel obligated."

"No, it's fine." She waved off his concern. The story had been told many a time over the years. "They died in a car accident. Slick winter roads combined with a tree. I was ten when I found out they were gone. My aunt Glenda was all I had left, and she took me in." Smirking, she added, "She's a bit kooky, but I wouldn't have her any other way."

"I'm sorry to hear that. Having one parent ripped from you is tough, but two at once at such a young age is catastrophic." He comfortingly rubbed her forearm. "I think your situation is why you're so passionate about children and their parents. You lost yours, and so many people take them for granted."

Tears welled in her eyes. "Exactly." It scared her how intuitive he was compared to other men.

No, comparing Callum to anyone else is ludicrous. He's his own man. And a damn fine one at that.

They ceased talking when another couple walked by. Once clear, he asked, "I have to know because it's been killing me. Why are you so obsessed with chocolate? You even smell like it."

"It's always been my favorite for as long as I can remember." She shrugged. "A combination of sugary and bitter sometimes. Just like life."

"I like that. It fits." He leaned over and lightly kissed her lips, but didn't give her the opportunity to return it. "You taste like chocolate. It isn't fair. Are you made of the damn cocoa bean? Because if so, love, I'll demolish every semisweet morsel."

Chills scattered down her spine at the shameless glint in his eye combined with the pet name. She secretly adored when he used the phrase. There was something sexy and sweet about the common term of endearment when it came out of a Brit's kissable mouth.

"It must be my lotion. My aunt got me hooked on it. It's called 'hot chocolate delight' or something along those lines." She sniffed her arm, then held it up to his nose. "It's kind of worn off by the end of the day."

Callum smelled her offered arm, his fingers lightly tracing up and down the appendage. "And the cinnamon? Where does that come from? It's almost as strong as the chocolate."

"Honestly? A popular chain store in the mall," she laughed. "I've always loved the fragrance, and the body spray I use is like waking up to fresh cinnamon rolls."

His lips grazed her wrist. "Chocolate and cinnamon. You're trying to kill me with food, aren't you?"

"I'd never dream of it."

"I hope not." He followed her vein up her arm with

one finger. "Your last boyfriend, what happened?"

"Oh geez, how long do you have?" She forced a laugh, but quickly realized he was serious in his query. "He's an actor and screenwriter too. We met at the theater in Queens." She thought about Blake and shuddered. It wasn't a happy rabbit hole. "He was very full of himself and decided one day that I wasn't what he had in mind for a girlfriend."

"What do you mean?" he asked, tracing circles on her arm.

Wishing she had a shot of strong tequila, she hastily muscled through the next part. "Among other reasons, like I was a better writer than him, the one that killed me was that he said I was too tall. I mean, we were about the same height, but with any heel, I was taller." She chewed her bottom lip at the memory. "Oh, and then he went back to his ex-girlfriend, who was also an actor, so yeah."

"I beg your pardon?" He growled the words as if they disgusted him, each syllable worse than the next.

"Yeah, we were around the same height, and I guess he couldn't handle it." Her gaze dropped to her lap. "Some guys aren't okay with a girl over five-foot-seven."

"That's absolutely atrocious." He huffed in aggravation. "Should you ever see him again, pop him in the nose. He deserves no less from a gorgeous woman with a perfectly proportioned body." He eyed her legs. "Plus those legs of yours are simply mouthwatering.

He's a douche and not good for you at all."

"Thanks. I think so too." She rather liked this side of him. Somehow, even discussing her past made Callum more approachable.

He nodded as if to never speak on the subject again. She was more than all right with such a decision.

"Tell me about the girls' mom." The second the request left her mouth, she regretted it, his face clouding and his brows furrowing into a blond caterpillar. "I'm sorry. You don't have to. I just thought…." The sentence tapered off with her voice.

Instead of dropping her hand, he kissed it again. "It's fine. You should know about Jessica." He let out a slow breath. "I met her during her summer abroad in England. She was in university at the time and very much American. Before you ask, she's a taller version of the girls, though not by much."

Londyn's stomach pitched at the realization that his Jessica was short. They were always short.

His eyes took on a faraway gleam. "I fell hard, but she didn't want to marry me when she found out she was pregnant with Bethany. I held out hope that she'd change her mind when Bailey came along a couple years later, but she didn't."

Londyn nodded. It was hard to see him struggle through the past.

"Anyway, I woke up one night—Christmas Eve, to be exact—and she was gone. Poof. Adios. Not a trace of her remained, which is fine in retrospect. She left a note saying she needed to find herself and pursue her dreams in music and modeling, and she couldn't do that with a family dragging her down." His smile turned bitter. "I didn't find out until later what she meant was being a groupie to a rock band and doing drugs."

"Oh, Callum." Her heart ached for him already and he wasn't even done with his tale.

He held up his hand to finish. "It's how it was meant to be. Her parental rights to Bethany and Bailey were terminated the year after she left. Every now and then, she'll try to contact them through me, but I never reply. She doesn't deserve to know them. Not when I'm the parent who stayed." He patted her hands. "I wasn't enough for Jessica, and it's made me wary of pursuing anyone else. I'm worried the same thing will happen again and I'll be right back where I started. Alone with a shattered heart."

Words had never broken her heart before, but those fractured her.

Climbing over the couch, she cupped his strong jaw in her palms. His cognac-hued eyes were vulnerable and guarded at the same time. "Not every woman is Jessica. She sounds like a lost soul to me. You weren't meant for her in the long run, and it wasn't your fault or anything you did. She wasn't ready for someone like you." She rubbed her thumb over his pointed chin, the stubble a stark contrast to her soft skin. "I'm sorry she hurt you, Callum, and that she made your birthday suck. You deserve so much better." She leaned in. "And if you ask me, she wasn't good enough for you. I may be a smidgen biased, though."

Callum's slow smile warmed her more than the fireplace. "Thank you, Londyn. You truly do have a way with words. I see now why you haven't given up on your dream. I'd love to read one of your plays to get the full effect."

"Oh, I don't know. They're not that—"

"Shut those gorgeous lips and kiss me." He lowered his voice, eyes darting to her mouth. "Please."

Not needing any other incentive, she closed the minimal distance. The force behind his kiss left her just as breathless as the first time did. Sitting on his lap, she explored his mouth with her tongue, tracing his lips, tasting the hint of mint on his tongue; it all short-circuited her nerves. Callused fingers threaded through her hair, unraveling the ponytail until her brown locks flowed around their faces.

"You're breathtaking," he murmured, coming up for air.

Emotions fuzzy, she ran her hands over his head and wrapped her legs around his waist. "You're one to talk," she teased, gently massaging his scalp. "Your accent alone makes my entire body excited."

"Oh yeah?" Callum's eyes twinkled with mischief. "I don't hear that a lot."

"What? No way. It's a huge turn-on." She shrugged. "But maybe it's just me."

"Well, if you ever get sick of the British accent, I can switch to French." He kissed the tip of her nose. "Or Greek." His tongue darted out and traced her upper lip. "Or maybe Italian, if you're lucky." His teeth nipped her bottom lip, tugging on it slowly.

If Londyn thought other men had turned her on before, she was dead wrong. It was overwhelming, but she wanted more. She needed more.

"*Il tuo bel*," he whispered in her ear. The Italian words washed over her and sent a jolt straight to what lay beneath her lacy black underwear.

"I have no idea what you said, but I could get used to foreign words in my ear," she replied, kissing his neck.

Smiling lazily, Callum's voice turned raspy. "Then I'd better keep learning more languages."

Capturing his lips again, Londyn's mind blanked at how perfectly compatible they were. His touch, while passionate, was still stifled. He had more to give, but he held back. She felt it in his taut muscles and the healthy bulge now pressing against her ass. He was polite yet engaging, and it took every molecule of her will not to push him to his back and ravage him on the couch in front of everyone.

"Ahem." Someone cleared his throat behind them. Londyn shot off Callum faster than a bolt of lightning.

Callum took his time, a particularly sexy trait, as he watched her with a sly grin.

"We're closing the lobby area for the night if you

wouldn't mind taking that scene to your room now," the desk clerk informed.

Londyn couldn't bear to look at him or respond. Her entire body was on fire after kissing Callum, and now even more so after being caught midembrace.

"Yes, of course. Miss Bellerose and I were just—" He moved to stand, then thought better and sat back down. "—uh, leaving."

"Very good, sir. Good night, Dr. Archer, Miss Bellerose." The man left, flicking off lights as he went.

Getting to her feet, she couldn't stop a giggle from escaping. "Oh my God. I haven't been caught like this since high school," she admitted.

Lounging on the couch, Callum rested his arms behind his head. "Yes, I usually have more self-control myself." He tugged on her hand, throwing her off-kilter and onto his lap once more. "You temptress, you," he teased, kissing the nape of her neck.

"Dr. Archer, *please*. I'd like to go to sleep as well," the lodge employee complained, his voice irritated that time.

Callum kissed her fast, then hauled them upright. "Yes, yes, we're going."

Hand latched with his, Londyn's loud laughter floated down the hall and into the elevator. When the door closed, Callum pressed her back against the steel wall and kissed her hard. Stars were among the celestial beings she saw as his lips locked with hers. Only when they reached their floor did he break his hold.

"As painfully as I want to lick every delectable inch of your delicious body tonight, I won't." His eyes dipped down her front. "You deserve so much more than a fast shag." He cupped her ass and pulled her against him; he was more than ready for action and obviously wanted her to feel it. "That fun can come later." Tucking her hair behind one ear, he nibbled on the lobe. "The first time, I want you writhing on my bed, wet and wanting all night long." The brown in his eyes turned a shade darker. "Only after you moan my name and come undone by my touch multiple times will I consider allowing you a break to sleep." His finger traced her lips, but he kept his mouth at bay.

Londyn had to force herself to swallow. Even breathing was a habit she had to kick-start.

He lowered his head and grazed her chin with his teeth. "But even then, I can't promise you'll get any rest. And then, my dear Londyn, I will never let you forget even a millisecond of our time together. That much I can promise you."

His provocative promises replayed in her mind the rest of the night. She wasn't sure how or when he'd walked her to her door or left her unattended with her thoughts. The only thing she knew was there was so much more to Callum than a stuck-up curator with a devilish tongue. He was the gasoline to the fire in her soul, and if she wasn't careful, he'd scorch her heart in the process.

CHAPTER ELEVEN

Fresh air. Londyn Bellerose was a breath of fresh air for Callum. It sounded cliché even to his cautious mind, but whenever she was around, it felt like breathing for the first time.

He checked his passport one last time and saw the stamp for Russia. It should've been a longer trip, according to the museum itinerary, but he skipped the last day of presentations in Moscow so he could make it back to Colorado before another day went by. Being apart from Londyn made him antsy. It didn't feel right at all. It was an odd and surreal sensation for the man who'd sworn to not cultivate feelings for her. That flew out the window almost as soon as he'd thought it.

He opened the front door to Archer House and inhaled. Londyn's cinnamon and chocolate essence somehow wafted throughout the house. It was eclectic.

Home. It feels like home.

Leaving his bags at the entry, he was glad he didn't tell Theodore he was coming back today. His old friend deserved some time with his boyfriend. *He should be engaged by now.* He knew Theodore had planned to propose during their short trip to New Mexico. Callum glanced at his watch. No doubt his friend would have a new story to tell when he returned.

"Callum? What're you doing back?" Londyn asked.

Turning toward the voice, he swore his heart skipped a beat. At the top of the dual staircase was Londyn in a sparkling black gown. His body instantly reacted to the sight of her. "I left early."

"That's great." She moved away from the railing and he relished the sight before him. "Do you want to come to the theater with us tonight? The girls are almost ready."

"I don't have a ticket." He swallowed as she carefully walked down the steps. Her train was long enough to trail behind her like a princess, and the tiny straps on the dress appeared thin enough to break with one tug. The neckline plunged into a deep V and came just shy of her belly button. In all, Londyn looked good enough to shag until he collapsed of exhaustion.

No, that's an everyday occurrence, he reminded himself.

"I bought you a ticket before I knew about your trip. Theodore was going to take your place, but he ran off too." She reached the bottom and smiled up at him.

"How was Russia?"

"Cold."

She gave him an unbelieving tilt of her head. "In the summer?"

He unbuttoned his suitcoat. "Yes, I dare say it's never balmy like here." Leaning over, he pressed a quick kiss to her cheek. "You look divine."

Crimson crossed her face. "Thanks."

Callum stood there simply staring into her blue-gray eyes. Her makeup was subtle but flawless. If he wasn't concerned of making it in time for the opening curtain, he'd cancel the reservations altogether and spend the evening with her alone. "I should change if we need to leave soon."

Londyn grabbed his watch and her eyes widened. "Yeah, hurry. We need to head out in fifteen minutes."

Jogging up the stairs, he heard her call out, "The girls should be ready. If not, please let me know and I'll get their butts in gear."

Sounds like a mum. He grinned at the thought of Londyn as Bailey and Bethany's mother, but the amusement quickly slipped off his face when he recalled that wasn't his plan. Moving down the hall, he cursed. He hadn't planned on opening his heart, but there he was doing exactly that.

Pulse racing when he reached his room, he tore off his clothes and grabbed a new suit set. *How can I have feelings? We haven't even slept together.*

Stopping himself there, Callum sat on the end of his bed. *It doesn't matter.*

That detail alone made his stomach jump. Just one kiss and he was hooked. If he ever moved their relationship to the bedroom, he couldn't be unbiased in his affections. His hand shook as he fastened the last button on his shirt.

Surely I don't love her. Checking his reflection, he noted the smile on his face. He hadn't even noticed it was there. All-around contentment didn't happen before Londyn. "Maybe I do."

"Maybe you do what?" Bethany asked from the doorway.

Clearing his throat, he grabbed a suit jacket. "Maybe we need to get going or we'll miss this play."

She hugged him tight. "I'm glad you're back."

"Me too, love." He ushered her out of the room and spotted Bailey by the stairs. Both girls wore blue dresses, though the shades differed. "What are we going to, anyhow? Londyn didn't tell me."

"Cats," Bethany informed him, then quickly walked down the stairs and hugged Londyn at the bottom. From his viewpoint, life couldn't get any better. A gorgeous woman who adored his girls and vice versa. In his mind, it was enough to be happy.

An hour later, the foursome sat in the theater box. Bethany and Bailey took over the front two seats, both leaning over the edge to see the stage.

"This is so cool," Bethany squealed, looking back

at them.

"Can we go to the theater again?" her sister asked.

Laughing, Callum swung his eyes up from the pamphlet. "The play hasn't even started. What if you don't like it?"

"We will," Bailey said with a confident grin.

Shaking his head, he tucked away the information about the play and turned toward Londyn. "Have you seen this one before?"

She rubbed her lips together. "Nope. My first time too."

"Something we have in common." His eyes dipped over her dress. There was a slit on the left side—his side—and it was tempting his fingers more than he could've imagined possible. Meeting her gaze, he asked, "What pulled you to the theater as a career?"

Londyn swiveled her body toward him, her knees brushing against his legs. "My parents took me to see *The Phantom of the Opera* when I was little." Her eyes took on a faraway gleam. "Watching the characters fall in love, hearing the swell of the orchestra that sent chills down my back, and seeing the other theatergoers created something in me that day. The magic of singing as a part of expressing life, plus the romance and intrigue…." She sighed whimsically. "I caught the theater bug that day, and it's never gone away."

Seeing her so animated about the theater made him smile. He could watch her all day and wouldn't mind one bit. "Sounds like it was meant to be." He nodded toward the girls. "They seem to be catching the same bug. It's quite contagious."

Londyn reached over and pulled his hand to her lap. "Let's hope you're not immune," she teased as the lights went down.

Lacing his fingers with hers, he whispered, "With you beside me, how could I be?"

***

If she'd thought Callum was charming before, Londyn had never been more wrong. The man was every inch a temptation, though he never did anything more than kiss her. In some respects, she found it admirable, but her body begged to differ.

Last week after the theater, she caught him humming "Memory," which of course made her tease him endlessly. They all enjoyed the theater despite the girls falling asleep toward the end, which didn't matter since Callum promised they'd go again.

"Looks like the theater isn't so bad after all," she'd joked after the girls were safely tucked in bed. Her sassiness earned her a long and steamy kiss outside her door. She would go for that any day of the week.

After his trip to Russia, she was grateful that he wouldn't be flying for some time. *Should he be traveling?* She smoothed her Colorado University T-shirt. *No, he wouldn't put his job on the back burner.* She bit her nail. *Would he?*

Bethany put the finishing touches on the fort in the living room while Bailey chatted with Gloria in the kitchen. If she could clone the two girls and keep them for herself, she would. Even though they had their own sass and flair, Londyn wouldn't have it any other way.

"All ready," Bethany proclaimed, waving her arms dramatically.

"Wait, I'm not there. Don't look, Londyn!" Bailey called, the pitter-patter of tiny feet coming down the hall.

Once both were in place, Londyn peeked into the tent-like structure made over the couches. It'd taken the girls over an hour to construct, and their efforts showed. "This is so much better than the forts I used to make." She stepped under the low clearance and inside. It was impressive no matter how she looked at it. Though it wasn't large enough to sit comfortably on the couches, the overabundance of pillows and blankets on the floor made up for the seating anomaly.

Bethany ducked in first and her sister followed. "Who made the forts with you when you were little? Did you have a sister too?"

Londyn got cozy under a blanket despite the warm weather outside the main house doors. "No, I wasn't blessed with a sibling. My mom helped mostly, but my dad also liked to join us." She smiled as memories surfaced. They'd had great times together up until the accident. Tears unexpectedly welled in her eyes and she cleared her throat, then glanced at Bailey. "What do you think, should we eat dinner in here?"

"Yes!" came their shouted reply.

"Then it's a good thing I already brought something," Callum's voice said from the fort opening.

Three sets of eyes swung to him. In one hand, he held a bag from their favorite Chinese restaurant and in the other was a movie. Londyn squinted to see the title. *Ever After. A chick flick.* A smile burst over her face at the offering. Whereas some men only heard her, Callum actually listened when she spoke of her favorite things. Today was proof of it too. Food and flicks. Maybe not every girl's fantasy, but it was hers. She'd mentioned her favorite Cinderella story over Skype while he was in Russia.

If he keeps this up, I'll fall way too hard for him.

"You mean it? We can eat on the floor in our fort?" Bailey asked, pulling him farther into the blanket and sheet contraption.

Callum smooshed in beside Bethany and handed her the bag. "Yes, but only if we watch a movie too."

Bailey snatched the DVD and hustled out of the tent toward the television. "Deal."

"Do you approve, Miss Bellerose?" he asked, unpacking the small white boxes. Bethany already had chopsticks in hand and was going to town on the lo mein.

Taking the offered sesame chicken and rice, Londyn nodded. "Heck yeah. You did well." She nodded to the TV where Bailey lingered. "Chinese and chick flicks?

Abi better watch out or I may replace her with you."

He grinned and focused on the appetizers. "Doesn't sound too bad to me." Leaning closer, he added, "But I want to do several things with you that I hope you haven't done with your roommate."

Gripping the box of chicken tighter, Londyn smirked and lowered her gaze. The temperature in the fort increased at his sexy invitation. She wouldn't turn down his advances, and she sure as hell had never kissed her best friend. *Except that one time when we were drunk....*

"Londyn, have you seen this movie?" Bethany asked, switching boxes with Bailey. "We watch it all the time.

"As it happens, I have." She shoveled in a bite of orange chicken. "It's one of my all-time favorites."

"Really? Why?" Bailey asked, a piece of rice on her chin.

The opening monologue started, and she tried not to say it word for word. It wasn't just one of her favorites—it *was* her favorite. "Well, it's basically a Cinderella story. I admire how Danielle never lets her evil stepmother and stepsister get her down." She scooped rice with the chopsticks. "Then, of course, there are all the books. I love books." She grinned at Bailey. "And we can't forget the prince. He's the epitome of perfect, in my opinion."

Bethany and Bailey cooed like girls at a slumber party. "Is it because of his accent? Or how he's a prince?"

Bailey asked.

"It's his hair, isn't it? I like his hair," Bethany added, slurping a noodle.

Chuckling, she finished chewing her food. After all their nights watching chick flicks, she was surprised the movie hadn't made an appearance until now. They appeared to love it.

Londyn's eyes swiveled over to Callum, who was surprisingly quiet throughout the conversation. Normally he added his own snarky quips, but that night he didn't. "All of those are reasons why he's gorgeous. But in my opinion, it's the prince's tenderness, passion, and ability to make Danielle feel like a princess that make him my favorite."

Bethany motioned for the fried rice. "Uh, sounds boring to me."

"Yeah," Bailey added, munching on an eggroll. "That stuff isn't romantic."

Callum chuckled and stuck his chopstick in his box. "Perhaps you need a new definition of romantic, then, girls. Everyday activities can be romantic."

Bailey rolled her eyes and both girls focused on the movie, but Londyn couldn't tear her gaze from him. If she didn't know better, she'd say the movie was among his favorites as well.

"Your chicken is getting cold," he pointed out with a nod.

"Oh, right." She lowered her eyes, embarrassed he'd caught her gawking.

"Did you mean that?" she asked after a few moments went by.

Setting aside the nearly empty carton of broccoli and beef, Callum subtly grabbed her free hand and tucked it in his lap. "Yes, I did. Romance doesn't have to be fancy or huge gestures. It can be simple things."

"Such as Chinese takeout and a chick flick?" She squeezed his hand, adoring the way his touch warmed her inside and out.

"Exactly." He winked, then moved closer until their legs were snugly intertwined.

With the low ceiling, Londyn could barely see the movie even when she leaned her head on Callum's shoulder, but it didn't matter. The girls lay on their stomachs, watching the film, and the adults sat cuddled together. It sounded like something a family would do on a Friday night.

Chinese and chick flicks. This is the life. She snuck a glance at him and worried her bottom lip. Somehow, Callum snuck into two more of her quick fixes when things went awry. Thinking about replicating it at home with Abi didn't sound cathartic anymore. Not when the person she really desired at her side was the man tracing circles on her palm.

Holy crap, he did it again. She met Callum's gaze, and he offered her a lethargic smile. Those brown eyes of his reminded her of drops of caramel.

Falling for him wasn't the plan. A summer fling was all she'd expected, yet the more time she spent with the intelligent Brit, the less she wanted their relationship to cease after the summer.

In less than two weeks, Londyn's three C's had been obliterated by this man. She gulped hard at the thought.

Do I honestly care?

The answer to that question caused her heart rate to double.

No.

CHAPTER TWELVE

Ten days later, Callum switched on the light in his study and grumbled at the stack of paperwork on his desk. Maddy warned him it'd be there upon his return, but he'd hoped she was pulling his leg.

"Not so much," he said, reviewing the mixture of envelopes and invoices. He'd tied up the loose ends for the next exhibit opening while in London over the last seven days. It'd snuck up on him before he noticed. Partly because of Londyn.

Callum sank into his chair and pulled off his tie. Talking to her over Skype when he was out of town wasn't the same as in person. *Not that we got to do much of it anyway.* Bailey and Bethany overtook the conversation whenever possible, leaving him happy to speak with them yet frustrated at the same time. Londyn sent him photos of their activities during his absence.

He rather wished he hadn't missed dune buggies and indoor skydiving. Where she came up with those ideas, he'd never know. He was just glad his girls were having fun and not missing him as much as he missed them.

Three car doors shut, summoning his attention to the driveway. Peering out the window, he spotted Londyn toss the keys to the Cadillac SUV—his SUV—to Theodore with a smile. Judging from the red tint to her skin, they'd been at a water park all day. Bethany and Bailey dragged their towels along the ground, both yawning. *Good, maybe they'll go to bed early.* He was sorely mistaken, however; once they saw him at the front door, they caught a second wind.

"Did you have fun today?" he asked, excited to hear their answers. He could honestly say that Londyn had changed his perspective with the girls. He cared more, if that was even possible.

"Yeah, we went on the lazy river like a million times. It was the best ever," Bailey replied, hugging him tight.

He kissed her cheek, the smell of chlorine prevalent on her skin. Her hair was still damp, as was her yellow and orange swimming suit. "Now that's my kind of day." He looked to Bethany. "And what did you like?"

Bethany dropped her beach towel and flopped to the divan in the entryway. "The surf rider. I did it most of the afternoon. My legs hurt. It's like surfing in the ocean except no sharks."

Callum stole the flip-flops off her feet and ticked

her toes. "My, that sounds tiring. I'll have to come next time so you can show off." He hugged her before she could escape.

"Oh don't worry, I took a video," Londyn added, setting down the multicolored beach bag. "I'll send it to you. She was amazing." She swiped through her phone, completely focused on her task. "There are some pictures too. I'll send those next."

Getting to his feet, Callum studied her face. She looked weary after all the sun. "Sounds good."

Alfred came into view and cleared his throat. "Sir, what should I tell Gloria to make for dinner?"

Callum scanned the faces of the three sun bunnies. "We'll order in." He eyed Londyn's red arms. They looked painful. While the girls weren't burnt at all, their nanny obviously forgot to reapply. "I think Italian is in order."

"Yay, pizza!" Bethany yelled.

"Good, because I'm starving," Bailey added.

Alfred nodded and then disappeared. He and his wife deserved a night off now and again. Callum made a note to discuss it with his mother when they returned to England. Since she was already there—and would stay at Archer Manor until their return—she could make the adjustment to the staff's schedules. It was one of the few things he didn't mind his mother controlling.

"Sounds perfect to me." Londyn pushed back the hair that had fallen from her once-perfect bun on the top of her head. He rather liked the ballerina look, especially when little curls rested on her neck. "You really read my mind."

"Glad to hear it." He pointed to her arms. "I'd hug you too, but your sunburn looks awfully painful." He nodded to the girls. "Go hop in the shower and get clean. By the time you're fresh as daisies, the food should be here."

The two redheads exchanged a look.

"Race you," Bailey said, starting down the hall

"Hey, no fair, you started early," Bethany complained, taking off after her.

Turning to Londyn, he said, "Now you do the same, but come back with aloe vera and I'll help you with the parts you can't reach." He carefully lifted the strap of her pink bikini off her neck. "It appears you think of others and forget yourself." Tenderly, he kissed her, the taste of coconut and cocoa butter on her lips. She nodded with a shrug, the act making her wince. "Well, not under my watch, love." He squeezed her ass, telling himself not to linger there, no matter how badly as he wanted to. "Hurry back."

Blushing an even deeper shade, Londyn rubbed her lips together. It seemed even those had a touch of sun. "I'm afraid I won't be much of a sparkplug for the upcoming nights. It hurts too much. I really should've put on more sunscreen." She studied her arms. "I don't know how this happened. I never burn."

"It's the altitude," he reminded. "We're much closer to the sun up here."

"Okay, yes, but I've been here two months and I feel bad because I—"

Callum placed his fingers over her mouth to stop her rampant thoughts. He loved hearing her talk, but touching her was even better. "Londyn, merely sitting on the same couch as you and holding your hand is enough for me," he advised, reading between the lines. He searched her gray eyes, the hue now his ultimate favorite. "I won't pretend that I haven't dreamed of kissing you deeply and endlessly since the moment I met you, but"—he hovered his lips above hers—"I'm in no rush. You're worth the wait, Londyn."

That time she groaned and wrapped her arms around his neck. "God, you're perfect." She pressed her lips to his, relinquishing any further discussion.

"If you don't go right this moment, your pizza won't ever get ordered," he warned, not sure what to do with his hands. He didn't want to cause further pain to her sunburn, and the temptation to run his fingers along her body increased each moment she stood in his embrace.

Her own fingers danced down the front of his chest and paused at his hips. "We can't have that, now can we?" She took three steps away, then asked, "Does this evening include any of my Cs? You know, chocolate and chick flicks."

Catching up with her, he caught her around the waist and dipped her in a kiss. She moaned as his tongue traced hers, and his desire to eat anything other than Londyn flew out the window. When he broke the kiss, he gazed at her heavy-lidded eyes. "If I had my way, you'd get *my* two Cs."

"And what're those?" she asked huskily. No doubt she already knew the answer, but wanted to hear the words come from his mouth. Well, he wouldn't give her such a pleasure. Not yet. Not tonight.

Righting her, he kissed her cheek. "Let's just say they both include me and leave it at that." He walked down the hall and added, "Feel free to use your imagination, Miss Bellerose."

The slight intake of her breath was worth walking away for. He wasn't sure how much longer he could resist the nanny when the simplest of her deeds made his world turn upside down.

*****

A night of breadsticks and cheese pizza was made better by Callum's gentle hands on her shoulders with the aloe vera. Naturally, Bethany and Bailey joined in to help, so the act was far from sensual, but it was something else entirely. It felt like a family. It felt like home.

Bailey wiggled on her lap, getting cozier, and Londyn kissed the top of her head. It was an act she grew more and more comfortable with each day. The girl was a snuggler, which helped her cause.

Glancing over at Callum, she saw Bethany cuddled up with him on the opposite side of the couch. Though they were close enough to touch, Londyn liked seeing them like this. It was homier than a Christmas card, the four of them together in the family room with *You've Got Mail* playing on the flat screen in front of them.

Other than the sunburn, she'd never felt better. The only thing missing was the old basset hound. If history was any indicator, Sherlock was snoring in his big bed beside Callum's desk. The most the dog did was chase squirrels, which looked more like a slow-motion action flick than anything else.

Halfway through the movie, Callum sought out her free hand and laced his fingers with hers. The scene, setting, and atmosphere filled her heart with serenity. She squeezed his hand and smiled above Bailey's head at him. He offered a similar response, but his grin was tired. He was recently in from London, and a movie night probably wasn't how he wanted to unwind. Though he appeared to be enjoying himself despite the yawns he hid behind his fist before resting his chin on Bethany's head and pressing a kiss to her temple.

Londyn tried to focus on one of her favorite movies but found she couldn't. The entire Kathleen Kelly and Joe Fox accidental romance always pulled her in for the duration of the film, but it wasn't working right then. Her mind was running a hundred miles an hour. The last weeks had been filled with activities, yet she was lonely. She knew it was because he'd been gone. She shook her head when Joe showed up with daisies at Kathleen's door.

Loneliness. That's exactly what it was, but she had

absolutely no reason for it. The Archer girls kept her busy from morning until night. Well, until they went to bed. That's when she felt the void of Callum the worst.

Shifting in her seat, she cringed at the chafing of sunburn and her wavering independence. Chatting over the airwaves didn't do much for their budding romance, especially when the girls usually interrupted them. She couldn't blame them for wanting his attention too. They adored him. Callum was a superior father, travel addict or no.

"Girls, what do you think about coming to the exhibit opening in two weeks?"

Bethany paused the movie and craned her neck at him. "Really? You mean it? We can come?"

Callum chuckled. "Why, of course. I think you're both old enough to enjoy the arts. What do you say, Bailey?"

The four-year-old stood and propped her hands on her hips. "What about Londyn? She should come too. She's old enough to enjoy the arts."

"Oh, honey, I—" she started.

"Londyn is coming too." Callum's eyes met hers with question. "Unless she doesn't want to, that is."

"Please, please, please come with us. It'll be so much fun." Bailey tugged on her arm.

"Yes, then we can show you our house in England," Bethany included, jumping to her feet.

Londyn laughed at their adorable antics. How could she say no to their incessant begging? "All right, all right." She poked Bailey's side and the girl giggled. "I'll tag along, but I don't have anything to wear to such a fancy and formal event. I doubt my old prom dress will fit," she pointed out.

"Oh, I know. You can wear one of our dress-up dresses," Bethany suggested.

"Well—"

"Um, no. That isn't happening," Callum interjected with a serious tone. His brown eyes skittered down her torso. "We'll have a dress made. End of discussion. I know a designer in London who can have it waiting when we arrive."

"You don't need to do that," she argued. "I'm sure I can find something at a store."

Callum toyed with the remote. "I know, but I want to. Something off the rack won't do you any justice." He tugged on Bethany's hair and she batted at his arm. "All my girls need a new gown for the gala. You leave it to me."

Suddenly feeling like Cinderella, Londyn grinned. "I guess I can live with a designer dress. When will we need to leave?"

"Next week," Bethany said assuredly with a snap of her fingers.

Callum tickled beneath his daughter's chin. "She's not wrong, but I could go for a lot less sass."

"As if," Bailey chimed in, surprising them all with a snarky attitude.

"I've lost all control," he laughed, and his girls toppled over him.

"Since we'll be there a few days before the museum

event, we can show you around London and our estate." He pushed Play on the movie and relaxed back on the couch.

"Sounds exciting to me. It's my first trip overseas." She reached out for his hand, but Bethany confiscated it instead. "I always hoped one of my plays would get picked up by a company overseas, so my passport goes everywhere with me."

Shrugging, she resolved that she couldn't ask for a better job. Though it started out as a summer job, it quickly became a gift she never wanted to return. *And wait until Abi hears where I'm going. She's going to die.*

Her smile waned when the reality of the gala coincided with the conclusion of her time with the Archers. She didn't want it to end, but their life was in England and hers was in New York.

All at once, chocolate became a necessity. She was in desperate need, despite the pull of Callum, her newfound fourth C.

"I'll be right back," she promised, moving Bailey to the couch. Callum nodded, whereas Bethany didn't pay any attention. The romance was getting to the good part, and clearly the girls loved the give-and-take of the characters. *And it only took watching chick flicks every night to get them addicted,* she thought with a grin.

It slowly fell from her face when she thought about the next few weeks once again. She'd leave them in England, no doubt, and travel home alone. *God, I'm going to miss them.* Despite their rowdy nature, endless energy, and sassy attitudes, Bailey and Bethany were angels.

Reaching the kitchen, she leaned her forehead against the freezer handle and closed her eyes. "What're you doing, Londyn? This is a job. You're getting too attached."

Opening the door, she stared at the row of pints of ice cream. Gloria bought them in bulk these days—a fact she'd also miss in New York. She grabbed the flavor with fudge in the middle and fished out a spoon.

Taking a big bite, Londyn noticed tears welling in her eyes. The summer was coming to a close, and she felt even more lost than when she'd arrived. The goal was to take a break from the theater and enjoy life, and she'd done plenty of both, but now she didn't desire the mundane coffee shop and endless rejections of her plays. She wanted a family like the one who'd all but adopted her.

But this isn't your family. This is Callum's family.

A piece of mail on the counter caught her attention. It was addressed to Callum alone, and the handwriting was flowery and smooth. The return address only had the name J. Turner.

Oh my God. Is it from Jessica? Her stomach dropped at the notion. He'd mentioned his ex-girlfriend tried to contact him, but she assumed the attempts were in the past. She picked it up but set it back down again, sweeping away a tear she hadn't noticed on her cheek.

Spooning another chunk of chocolate to her mouth, she went back and forth until she finally ripped it open. She wiped the back of her hand on her face. *Why the hell am I crying? Callum and I are nothing. No, we're less than nothing. We're two people who kissed a few times. I shouldn't be getting upset over the possibility that his ex wrote him.*

Her eyes widened as she read the neatly written letter. Sure enough, it was from Jessica. Her heart thudded wildly. Jessica wanted to see the girls, but also him. She wanted him.

Londyn gasped when she read the last line: **I still love you, Cal. I always have. I was wrong. I want you back.**

The letter floated to the floor as the words registered. Londyn felt a stabbing sensation in her heart. When she rubbed a fist over her chest, she was disappointed when she didn't find a knife. It would've made it easier. Surely Callum had contacted Jessica. Why else would she write such earnest words and beg for a second chance?

Another thought crossed her mind and instantly chilled her. *Maybe they met up in London.*

The chocolate ice cream long forgotten, Londyn returned to the family room. Bethany was braiding Bailey's red hair as Callum watched the two with a content expression. Looking up when she entered, he patted the spot beside him.

She couldn't. It was too much. "I'm sorry, but I'm

really tired. I think I'll call it a night," she said with a wave to the girls. They both hopped up and hugged her. The instant they left her side, Londyn hastily left the room. Callum called after her, but she didn't stop until she was in her room with the door locked. She leaned her back against the solid oak and let the tears flow freely.

"Londyn, love, are you all right? Was it something I said?" Callum's soft questions through the door sounded too perfect. "Or didn't say?"

"I'm fine," she replied.

"Londyn?"

"Truly. Just tired." She pressed her hands over her mouth, hoping he couldn't hear her muted sobs. She'd never even cried over her last breakup, just got drunk and ate chocolate.

And this isn't a breakup, she reminded herself, closing her eyes. *It's so much worse.*

He knocked gently. "I don't believe you. Tell me what's wrong. Please."

"Nothing. I just need time to myself. Please, Callum." She sank to the floor when he sighed. Even that was sexy. And it ripped out a piece of her heart.

"All right. If you want to talk at any time, you know where I am."

Londyn wiped her eyes and listened as he walked down the hall. *You need to get it together. Even if his ex is in love with him, he said he wasn't in love with her.* Uncertainty clawed into her mind and the sunburn suddenly fell to second place for which part of her body ached the most. No amount of Chinese, chocolate, or chick flicks could save her either. A conundrum she'd never thought possible until Callum.

***

After putting the girls to bed, Callum rubbed the back of his neck and walked into the kitchen. He'd had to carry Bailey since she fell asleep near the end of the movie. Bethany was almost in the same boat, so he turned off the romance flick a few minutes before the conclusion. *They can watch it another time*, he decided. They were too tired to appreciate the wonderfully written script anyhow.

Turning on the light, he frowned at the sight of Londyn's ice cream tub on the counter. Not putting things away wasn't like her at all; she kept the girls' room spotless and never left even a dish out of place.

After putting the chocolate ice cream away, his eyes caught something on the floor. Stooping down, he picked up the paper and saw it was a letter. To him. From Jessica.

Bloody hell.

He scanned the contents and crumpled the note. It was just like every other time she'd contacted him. *She must be in rehab,* he thought, his pulse racing. The pieces fell together, and he cursed under his breath. *Londyn read the letter when she came to the kitchen.*

He instantly craved a large tumbler of bourbon. *And then she left.* Closing his eyes, he shook his head. That was why she practically ran from him and wouldn't open the door.

She thinks I still love Jessica.

He stuffed the waste of a tree into his pocket. Somehow he needed to show her that Jessica meant nothing to him. Londyn, on the other hand, meant more to him each day he knew her, which made him hesitate. He'd known her only a couple months, but he already wished she'd never leave. Not at the end of the summer. Not ever.

Well, he wasn't one to sit idly by and let her stew. He knew it wouldn't end well.

Hustling through the house, he pounded on her door. "Londyn, open the door straight away." He probably should've been quieter or even tried the handle first, but he couldn't wait. He needed to see her and explain.

Fumbling around from within echoed until the door swung open and she grumpily looked at him. Her eyes were swollen and red.

"You've been crying."

She didn't answer, simply crossed her arms over her chest. "What do you want, Callum? I was trying to sleep. I actually just fell asleep when—"

"I don't love her."

"Um, okay." She rubbed her lips together. "It's really none of my business."

He clenched and unclenched his hands. "But it is

your business." He took in her appearance of messy hair, green Victoria's Secret shorts that barely covered her fine arse, and a pink tank with nothing underneath.

"Why?"

Taking a cue from one of the movies she deemed her favorite, Callum stepped into the room and shut the door. Backing her up against it, he let his eyes adjust to the darkness before speaking. She looked ravishing no matter the light. A fact he'd never forget.

"Because I love someone else," he confessed.

Londyn inhaled sharply, her chest moving up and down swiftly as she registered his words. "Oh? Who?"

Callum tipped her chin up with his fingers, then traced her neck. "You. I love you."

Her blue eyes flicked to his face. "You do? But what about—"

Frustrated with her lack of response, he captured her lips beneath his and pressed his body against hers. It felt soft, smooth, and so many levels of perfect. Careful not to hurt her sunburn, he secured her wrists above her head with one hand and slid his tongue between her teeth.

"Yes, I love you, Londyn. I don't give a shit about some letter." He pulled back just enough to look into her desire-glazed eyes. "I love the way you light up a room when you walk into it. I love that you sometimes slip up and say your thoughts out loud. I love how you always see the good in life and don't give up on your dreams. I love how you think chocolate, Chinese, and chick flicks can cure everything." He kissed her neck and she arched her back. "I love how you care for my girls as if they're your own. I love your heart, your body, your height, your eyes." He cupped her face and kissed her jaw. "I love who I am when I'm with you, because it's the best version of myself. But most importantly, I love that you're gorgeous and you don't even know it. It may sound crazy because I haven't known you long, but I love you, Londyn."

Tears slipped from her eyes and onto his fingers. She opened her mouth to speak, but no words escaped her plump lips. He wiped away the tears with his thumbs and searched her face.

"Please say something. I can't keep holding my breath."

Londyn cleared her throat. "Have you been drinking?"

Chuckling, he shook his head. "The only thing I'm drunk on is you, Londyn Bellerose, and I don't want to be sober ever again."

That was all it took for Londyn to lean forward. Their lips colliding, she wriggled free of his hold and laced her fingers through his hair, tugging him closer until he swore he'd slide under her skin.

"Does this mean—"

"I love you too, Callum Archer," she interrupted, nibbling his top lip. Her hands drifted over his shoulders and dipped to his arse. "And not just because you have a rocking body for a curator."

He smirked and nuzzled her nose. "Oh yeah? Then why?"

Reversing their roles, she shoved him against the back of the door. The force in her act only turned him on more. He would have way too much fun with this girl, and he couldn't wait.

"I love how passionate you are about your job. I've never seen anyone come alive while discussing archaeological digs. I love that you get jealous and think I don't notice." She licked the side of his neck, his shivers trailing her act. "I love how independent you are even when you don't have to be. I love how you love those girls of yours so much that you'd do anything for them." Her hands snaked beneath his shirt and traced his abs. "I love how I could listen to you talk and never get sick of it." She blushed. "Even when you're pissed, it's sexy as hell." Lightly kissing his lips, she finished, "But mostly I love how you make me feel loved, wanted, and a part of your family."

Callum's heart swelled at her statements. He'd only fallen in love once, but it seemed juvenile compared to the way his emotions flared around the beautiful woman who had him wedged between a door and her luscious body.

He gripped her waist and saw her face flash pain. "The sunburn." He cursed in Italian and she laughed.

"I'm sorry. I didn't plan this, I swear." She slightly pulled away. "Will you sleep with me?" His brows shot up and she laughed. "Just sleeping, Dr. Archer."

She grabbed his hand and led him to the bed. "I don't want to be apart from you even if I can't touch you in all the ways I've wanted to ever since the first day I saw you."

Kicking off his shoes, Callum tore off his shirt and pants. "You wanted me when we met?" he asked, now in boxers alone.

Londyn eased into the bed, agony on her brow. Only when she let out a breath of relief at being situated comfortably did he slide in the spot next to her. "Yes, of course." She switched to her shoulder to face him. "It was the accent initially. What can I say? It's hot."

Running a hand over her hair, he sighed. "Hmm, maybe we shouldn't go to England. There is a plethora of accented men there to steal you away."

She softly patted his cheek. "Not happening. Nobody could steal me away from you."

He kissed the tip of her nose, inhaling her scrumptious chocolate scent. "I'll hold you to that."

Yawning, Londyn nudged closer to him on the pillow. "Just don't leave me for some short chick, okay? If you do, I'll kick her ass and then yours."

"I wouldn't dream of it." Sleep crowding his body, he nodded but wouldn't let his eyelids droop. He wanted to stay there until he passed out from exhaustion. He thought even just looking at her was the best remedy to any ailment, and he planned to put it to the test.

After she turned on her shoulder away from him, her breathing evened out. He could watch her all night, every night. Pulling a sheet over her first, he wrapped an arm around her waist, careful not to disturb her newly found slumber.

"Callum?"

"Yeah, Londyn?"

"Stop staring at me. I can't sleep when you do that." She hugged his arm. "It's creepy, and you're anything but creepy."

Laughing softly, he kissed the nape of her neck. "As you wish."

"Don't go all *Princess Bride* on me," she warned, lacing their fingers together and snuggling them against her breast. "I know all the chick flicks, so I expect some originality from my British lover."

"Anything for you, love." He grinned in the darkness. Sure, his accent was sexy to most women, but hearing *his* woman tell him how much she loved it made it ten times better.

It took every ounce of self-control not to explore her, but he knew he'd have plenty of time later. For the time being, he'd simply enjoy the cinnamon lingering on her skin along with chlorine, chocolate, and him.

"Or I could say them in a foreign language and you'd never know," he added, palming her arse.

His rebellious reply resulted in Londyn pressing her arse fully against his groin. He was already hard, but her blatant act made it much worse.

"You're slowly killing me," he warned in her ear.

She kissed his hand. "Don't worry, I know CPR.

Unlike some people."

Drifting off to sleep with Londyn in his arms and a smile on his face was the best thing he'd ever done. And he had more firsts to enjoy with her. The most important being curing her sunburn so he could show her exactly how much she turned him on.

He wasn't letting her go. Not when being around her made his soul feel alive for the first time in years.

CHAPTER THIRTEEN

The next week flew by for Londyn. Between the girls' piano recitals, packing all her belongings, and preparing for the trip across the pond, she scarcely had any downtime. Now, as she sat in first class—for the first time ever—she watched Callum help Bethany with a crossword puzzle. He was incredible. While she'd suffered with the aftereffects of her failure to apply sunscreen, he was a complete gentleman. Painstakingly so. Not that she expected anything different from the man who'd waited nearly two months to kiss her.

Bailey shifted on the seat beside her after falling asleep following takeoff. Callum chuckled at something Bethany said, summoning Londyn's attention. Not once did he try to hurry along their physical relationship. It was torturous every night he held her tenderly, not groping or complaining one bit while she begged him to do something—anything. But he'd merely kiss her slowly until she couldn't feel her limbs, then tuck her in his arms. They'd fallen asleep like that almost every night since.

She loved his thoughtfulness, but she was thoroughly done with it. Her sunburn was healed, and she had a nice deep tan for him to devour. *He'd better do it soon too.*

The plane touched down later that night, the flight longer than any she'd ever taken before. Since Theodore tagged along as well, he made sure they had a car waiting upon arrival. The tall man easily tucked their baggage away in the trunk of the SUV, then climbed in the passenger seat.

Londyn was fascinated by the banter between Theodore and the driver. It was as if they were speaking a dialect all their own.

And here I thought we spoke the same language.

"We'll show you the sights tomorrow," Callum promised when he caught her pressing her nose against the car window. The darkness enveloped the majority of the tourist attractions, but they were glorious with the night's lights.

She grinned at him. "Will you be my personal tour guide?"

"If you'd like, yes," he chuckled. "But don't expect me to make a peep at Buckingham Palace. Those guards won't move, so don't even try."

"Damn. That was my next question." Londyn

checked over her shoulder and saw the girls asleep in the second row of seats. Leaning over, she asked, "And will I get the private tour of your bedroom too?"

His brown eyes languidly slid over her face. "I think that can be arranged," he said in a hushed tone.

By the time they reached the castle-like house, Londyn could scarcely keep her eyes open, but even through the dark night, the place was magnificent in every possible way. She was shown to an enormous bedroom and promptly face-planted. There'd be time to explore later. The gala wasn't for two days, enough time to catch up on sleep and prepare for the best night of her life.

Snuggling under the covers, Londyn heard Callum's sexy accent from down the hallway. She doubted he'd visit her that night. A thirteen-hour flight was tiring no matter how many times he made the trip. They all deserved a restful night.

Still, when the other side of the bed sank an hour later, she smiled sleepily. She'd gotten used to him being beside her more than she'd dreamed possible.

"I don't think I can bear even one night without you next to me anymore," Callum whispered, pulling her into his arms. His earthy cologne clung to his neck, the scent comforting her. The heat from his shirtless torso seeped into her clothes and to her flesh.

Nothing felt better than this. She was 100 percent positive.

His statement made sleep elude her. Over the last

week, she packed her limited belongings and left them to be shipped to New York. He hadn't said anything. For as much as she knew, he'd be fine with her going home directly after the exhibit opening.

Turning over, Londyn saw he was already asleep. She lightly traced the side of his face and pushed back his hair. Even sleeping, Callum was every inch a prince.

Her heart seized the longer she watched him. Unless he told her otherwise, she'd do exactly what she'd set out to do. Exchanged words of love didn't change the plan. In three days, she'd be back home.

She snuggled closer. The problem was her home lay beside her, and it was going to break her heart to leave.

***

The next day, Callum watched Londyn as she took in the sights he rarely gave a second glance. It was her childlike consumption of all London had to offer that made him review the bustling city with fresh eyes. Bethany and Bailey pointed out their favorite spots, told her the best places to eat, and took way too many photos with her throughout the day. Despite the camera's flash, the tourist traps, and the ridiculous souvenirs, he enjoyed himself more than he'd admit.

As Londyn and the girls took a whirl on the famous London Eye, his phone rang, distracting him for the moment. "Yes?"

"Sir, was I to direct all of Miss Bellerose's items to

the country house or did you wish for some to remain here?" Alfred inquired.

"Um." Callum paused at the question that forced him to think rationally. Of course he'd seen her pack— she wasn't coy about it—and yes, he'd noticed her subtle hints about leaving. He wasn't blind, but now he wished he were. Instead of directing the butler to ship her items to New York, Callum had asked Alfred to wait until after the museum gala. His hope was to ask her to stay.

Glancing up at the wheel, he waved at the trio. They looked to be having a fantastic time while he stayed safely on solid ground. It was odd that he could fly without problem, but amusement park rides set his fear of heights into action.

"Callum?"

He shook his head to clear his mind. "Yes, sorry. Please hold off for the time being."

"Ah, so you haven't discussed it with her?"

Callum gritted his teeth. The old man sounded more like a father than an employee. "Not yet, no. It's on the agenda for tonight."

"Hmm."

"It is," he argued. The aged Brit probably wore an ostentatious smirk with one brow raised if Callum knew him. And he did. "I wanted to wait for the right moment."

"Of course." Alfred cleared his throat. "Well, get on with it so we can close the house. I suspect you and the girls will be staying in England afterward as summer is nigh over?"

Londyn, Bailey, and Bethany hopped off the giant Ferris wheel. "That's correct. I'll touch base with you later. Cheerio."

"Who was that?" Londyn asked, looping her arm through his. She wore the most ridiculous hat with the Union Jack flag stamped all over it. Despite her tourist look, she was beautiful. She was always beautiful.

"Alfred was checking in. They're closing up the house until our next visit and will be on a plane following that."

"Oh, sure. Makes sense." Her eyes matched the gray clouds overhead and he wished it were the right moment. But it wasn't.

"Come on, love. I believe we missed Big Ben, and that won't do."

She squealed with delight as they walked down the sidewalk.

After dinner, he promised, kissing her temple. *After the girls are in bed and it's just us.*

***

"And this, my lady, is my bedroom," Callum stated, pushing the heavy door wide.

Londyn peeked in with a shy grin. "Oh, is it? This is where you take all the ladies, eh?"

Catching her in his arms, he guided her backward

into the room. "Not all. Just the special ones."

"Hmm, then I take it I'm special in some way?" She ran her fingers over his navy tie. He looked much too put together for what she wanted from him.

Callum's hands traveled up her back and cupped the base of her neck. His brown eyes intimately swept over her face. "That's putting it lightly, love."

Melting at the sound of his words combined with the kisses he spread along her neck, Londyn sighed in contentment. *This is how it should've always been.*

An abrupt bell chime disrupted the moment. Easing back, Callum fished his phone from his breast pocket and scanned the screen. "Sorry, it's the museum." He kissed her lips quickly. "I need to take this. Be five minutes." He nodded to the bed. "Feel free to make yourself comfortable."

Disappointed at the interruption, Londyn glanced around the room after he left. The soft glow from the lamp in the corner cast a romantic hue over the masculine room. The Victorian paneled walls were painted a dark shade of gray, the color abounding in the high-ceilinged room. An antique chair and writing desk sat off to a corner of the expansive room while a thick Persian rug lay under the king-sized bed. It was obvious an interior designer put the room together; it was highly unlikely Callum picked out the pile of gray and olive-colored pillows on the pillowtop.

Londyn sat on the end of the elevated bed and ran her fingers along the dark cream down comforter.

Without a doubt, the thread count on the sheets would be orgasmic.

Speaking of, she thought, hearing Callum's voice outside the door.

She slid off her light sweater, a red lace bra the only item remaining on her torso. Creeping to the door, she peeked out and saw Callum pace as he spoke. She didn't know what museum disaster he was handling, but he looked fantastic doing it.

"Maddy, I'll be in tomorrow morning. Just make sure the interns don't move anything until I get there," he said, stuffing his free hand into the pocket of his tan slacks. The man didn't know how to dress down, a fact she grew to love more each day. Still, she couldn't help but tease him when the opportunity presented itself.

"Cal, do you have a moment?" His mother's voice met her before the woman appeared. Caught off guard, Londyn gripped the doorframe and hid behind the thick wood. Mrs. Archer had seen more than enough of her; the woman definitely didn't need to see her half naked again.

Callum finished his call, then nodded. "Yes, but only a moment. I have other pressing matters to attend to." His attitude changed as if to guard himself. It was a sad reality about his mother, one Londyn wished remedied as soon as humanly possible.

Mary folded her hands together in front of her professional-looking green dress. "I hear you have become quite fond of the nanny."

Callum took a slow breath in. "I'm not merely fond of her, Mother. I love her."

The Archer matriarch scoffed. "Seriously, Cal? Love? You do recall what happened the last time you caught feelings for an American girl, don't you?"

His hand tightened around the cell phone. "Yes, I am more than aware, thank you."

"The nanny? Of all people." She shook her head in irritation. "I should've set you up with Lady Stern's daughter years ago. She'd do much better for you than the two women you profess to love. Why, I—"

"Stop," he jumped in, the vein in his neck bulging. "Just stop. You're a part of my life and my daughters' lives, but you don't run them." He turned on his heel. "So please stop trying."

Londyn rushed from her hiding spot as he approached. Her peeping Tom abilities probably weren't high on the list of admirable qualities for his mother.

"And for fuck's sake, stop calling me Cal. I am *not* my father, nor will I be called by his name any longer," he added before steering into the bedroom and slamming the door.

The echo of heels disappeared down the hall.

In bated silence, Londyn watched him from her spot beside the desk. His shoulders slumped forward, and she instantly wanted to console him. He inhaled slowly as if trying to calm down, his eyes fixed on the refurbished wood floors.

"She never stops. I'm sorry you had to hear that," he said softly after a minute passed.

Taking a step toward him, Londyn shook her head. "I'm not. It takes guts to stand up for yourself. Believe me, I know."

Finally he looked up, then closed the distance between them. "You aren't like many women, are you, Londyn?"

She squeezed his hand. "I sure hope not. I already had T-shirts made with just my name on them. I only give them out to my very important friends."

He smirked. "I'd like to say you're joking, but it sounds like something you'd do."

She held out her wrists. "Guilty as charged, though I haven't confirmed the order yet."

As if realizing her state of undress just then, he slid his eyes over her torso. "Why, Miss Bellerose, you seem to have lost a piece of clothing in my absence."

She leaned in and untucked his shirt. "Want to join me?" She leisurely unbuttoned the soft fabric. "Clothes are optional."

His heart thudded beneath her hands as she moved up his chest. Feeling the initial excitement swell beneath her touch encouraged her to tug his tie free from his neck. The useless fabric fell at her feet as she peeled off his shirt.

"I may be so inclined to join." He unzipped her jean shorts and shoved them from her hips, then slipped his fingers beneath her red lace underwear. "Do you have any incentives?"

Catching sight of his black boxers, she traced his package over his pants that suddenly seemed quite a bit smaller. "I'm double-jointed," she informed him with a sly smile.

"Is that so?" He cupped her ass and pulled her to him. She swore the hue to his eyes turned as deep as chocolate, a color she adored almost as much as the man in her grasp.

Nipping his bottom lip, she nodded. "Yep."

Callum picked her up by the hips and carefully settled her on the edge of the bed. "I wouldn't mind exploring your special talent." He knelt in front of her and unhurriedly rid her of the lacy bikini bottoms.

Londyn's body reacted to his low voice and even lower head as he kissed her inner thigh. Gently pushing her flat on the covers, he kept a hand on her chest when he traced her other thigh with his lips. The softness of his smooth jaw sent shivers up Londyn's body, straight to the apex between her legs.

"Tell me, Miss Bellerose, do you want to scream my name?" he asked, not looking up from the center of her tightening core.

"Yes."

Callum traced the springy curls first with his fingers, then his mouth. "And do you want to wake the neighbors when I'm inside you?" One finger slid between the curls and disappeared into the wet depths. When she didn't immediately answer, he added a second finger and deliberately pumped his hand to replicate a more intrusive, primal act.

"Yes," she panted and arched her back when his cool tongue slid between her thighs. He pressed her back to the bed at the rebellion.

When he returned to the business at hand, she reacted the same. His low growl only further enticed her to wriggle at the foreign yet encouraged kiss. "Oh no, you're not getting away now, Londyn." His tongue flicked hard and she gasped, clinging to the bedsheets. "You're mine, and you're staying mine."

Digging his fingers into her hips, Callum pulled her down the bed and onto his waiting mouth. The possessiveness of his stroking fingers and swirling tongue sent her stomach into a mass of butterflies. Grasping his short hair, she felt her pulse quicken. Never did she imagine the proper Callum to turn into a sex-craved demigod behind closed doors.

Shit, I hope he locked it.

Then her mind blanked when he adjusted his position, giving his tongue better entry. Loud moaning drifted through the room, and it took her a moment to realize it was her making the sounds in unison with his skilled mouth.

Londyn's vision blurred and her body felt weightless as she crested a wave of ecstasy. Calling out his name, she rode out the orgasm as Callum engulfed it, never once moving from his position.

Legs trembling from the most powerful jolt she'd

ever experienced, she looked down at Callum and saw a satisfied grin on his lips. He licked the fingers once inside her one by one, his gaze never moving from hers.

Holy damn. It was enough to fill her with desire once more. No other man could make the act more sensual—though that list wasn't long, as Callum was the single man to make her come unglued so quickly. It was as though her body had been waiting for him to dish out that coveted award.

Her breathing still erratic, Londyn leaned up and caught his lips with her own. His tongue tangled with hers, the taste of herself never to be forgotten in combination with him.

Callum moved from the floor and broke their kiss long enough to hoist her up the bed. "I don't think you were loud enough," he teased, unfastening her bra. The red apparatus fell to the bed, and he flung it to the floor. His pupils dilated as he took in the swell of her breasts. Carefully cupping them, he murmured, "You really should burn anything that obscures these from me." His mouth fastened to her right nipple, and she gasped at the sensation.

Tremors ran down Londyn's back the longer he caressed one breast and then the other, never satisfied until her copper nipples were hard, wet, and wanting more from him.

Seeing his pants still in place, she slipped her hand down the front of his boxers. She mewed when he caught her nipple between his teeth and pulled ever so slightly.

"Someone's getting impatient," he chuckled.

She offered him a determined grin. "I can't help that I want you."

Hopping off the bed, he shed his remaining clothes and returned with a condom fully enclosing his manhood.

Londyn could've wept at the sight of him standing in front of her in all his glory. She tilted her head to the left and let out a low whistle. "Damn."

He laughed and climbed on the bed. "Once you go Brit, you lose your wit."

Smirking deviously, she gripped the jutting length between them. "Is that your attempt at a joke, Dr. Archer?" She slowly stroked, kissing down his neck and swirling her tongue at his collarbone.

"Perhaps." He tugged her chin up and passionately captured her lips. "I want to go slow with you, but you're making it very difficult."

Londyn pushed his chest until he lay on his back. "Then I'll make it easy for you," she said, climbing on top of him.

Hands steady on her hips, Callum guided her until he was fully sheathed. She closed her eyes momentarily, adjusting to his girth. Finally one with him, she rocked her hips, the intense sensation rubbing the bud at the front of her folds. Palms pressed to his chest, she ran her tongue along his neck, nibbling and biting as she rode him. When she tried to slow her tempo and grind her hips sensually into him, Callum's low moan spurred her action faster. Being anywhere near the man was sexy, but her current position was the best in the house.

Seemingly done with her teasing, Callum rolled them over and swung one of her legs to his shoulder, the other tucked beneath his muscled body.

"Do you want me, Londyn?" he asked, hovering at her entrance. She lifted her hips, but he wouldn't allow any penetration.

Throat dry, she stared into his desire-filled eyes. "Yes."

"What do you want, Londyn?" His hand traced down her leg and squeezed her breast.

He was absolutely breathtaking. A single command from her would break the self-control of his strained muscles. He'd stay there all night if she asked, but she wanted the complete opposite. She wanted nothing between them. Ever.

"Say the words," he urged.

"Love me. I want you to love me, Callum," she pleaded.

He sighed. "I believe I can help with that." His face relaxed as he slammed into her at the last syllable.

Biting her bottom lip to keep from screaming, she lifted her hips, greedily accepting every solid inch of him. If she died during the first thrust, it'd be well worth it.

He pulled back and pushed deep, not once looking anywhere but her face. Each thrust further coiled her, summoning her body's obedience. She had no control anymore, not from the moment he'd fully possessed her. Their bodies matched in rhythm, each one creating a vortex of nerves between Londyn's legs.

I can't. Not again. Not so soon.

Callum's tempo increased, her hips wildly matching him, needing to be closer than they already were. A muscle in his forehead jerked as he rocked her harder, faster. Unable to sway even an ounce of her body, Londyn came down hard again. His name passed her lips in a muted moan when his mouth crashed on hers.

"You've no idea what you do to me, Londyn Bellerose," he confessed, his body collapsing against hers with a shudder of delight.

They lay there spent, each trying to catch their breath. Callum leaned his forehead to hers and gently lowered her leg from its perch. Longing surged throughout her body, the residual effects from Callum's innermost touch, prompting the orgasmic sensation to continue.

Kissing his chin, she forced his eyes to her. "I think you're right."

"About what?" he asked, smoothing back her hair.

"You really did make me lose my wits. I'm witless for you." She wrapped her legs around his waist. "I don't think I can go back to anyone other than you."

Smirking, he rolled her onto him and kissed her hard. "Good, because neither can I."

Londyn ran her fingers through his hair, marveling at the unearthed riches this man had to offer. He wasn't like all the rest. He hadn't simply screwed her—that much she saw in his cognac eyes. He'd made love to her just like she'd asked. She thought she knew what it meant, but tracing his biceps with her lips, she smiled. She'd been wrong, and she'd gladly admit it to anyone who asked.

Her eyes watered at the notion that it'd taken twenty-eight years to find a love like the one Callum offered. *Better late than never.*

"Stay with me." His normally clear voice held a hint of gravel.

Focusing on the man beneath her, she furrowed her brow. "What?"

Callum sat up, catching her on his lap. "Stay in England with me, Londyn." His hand dipped to her ass and he lifted her until she was level to his lips. "Please."

"But what about—"

"Do it here. You can continue to write your plays here and submit them to Broadway or the London theater or Beijing if you want." He kissed the side of her neck, spreading goose bumps over her skin. "I love you, Londyn, and I never want you out of my sight, out of my bed, or out of my life ever."

The veracity in his brown gaze caused her heart to beat double time. It wasn't a proposal, but it was as close as she'd get. For a while, anyhow.

Kissing his waiting lips, she nodded. "All right, I'll stay."

"Good." He pulled her to the bed and tucked her in his arms. "Otherwise, I'd have to overnight your bags from the UK. And that's not cheap, my dear."

Sitting up, she playfully swatted his chest. "You already had them sent here?" His lopsided grin made her giddy. *How was that even possible?* She didn't care.

"I had a hunch you'd see reason one way or another," he said, kissing her again.

Londyn giggled when he nipped her throat. "Oh really? And did you seduce me into your bed to show me your reason?"

He sat back and grinned. "It may have crossed my mind a time or two."

Her brows rose in shock, and she bit one of his nipples. "Suddenly so sassy. What ever will I do with you?" she teased, prompting him to settle her under his body. The weight of his naked flesh was almost as delicious as the view.

Pinning her wrists above her head with one hand, Callum gazed down at her. His heated manhood pressed awkwardly into her belly button, surprising her. "I can think of a few things."

"Such as?"

"For one, I don't believe you woke the neighbors." He sucked on her breast, his free hand trailing down her body. "And secondly, you better grab the tie you so carelessly discarded. I have a special use for it."

Buying time, she traced the lines of his abs. "Ready

so soon, Dr. Archer?"

Callum enclosed her lips with his. "I'm always ready for you, love.

Without a doubt in her mind, Londyn knew it was the truth. There wasn't anything about the man she couldn't believe. As long as it stayed that way, so would she.

CHAPTER FOURTEEN

After straightening the golden cat idol for the third time, Callum gave the room one final pass. Crowds of people already milled about the Egyptian exhibition. Everywhere he looked, ancient artifacts stared back at him. That was why he loved history so much, the intrigue of finding lost civilizations and unearthing thousands of years of lost time. It'd make anyone with a sour demeanor think twice about frowning while in the presence of the discoveries.

The archaeologists who dug up the priceless pieces of history stood near the largest find, the sarcophagus of Queen Nefertiti's mummified remains. He'd preen like a peacock too had he found the influential ruler. Naturally, reporters peppered the scientists with questions and cameras flashed, but it was the queen herself who the men and women cared about. The impressive items found in the tomb caught international attention even before the museum hauled them back to London. Why, even the ruler's name meant 'the beautiful one has arrived.' By anyone's standards, the powerful queen would attract hordes on the legends alone.

Leaning over the balcony railing, he surveyed the crowd. Not one person appeared out of place, everyone wearing black tie apparel from head to toe. He ran a hand over his suitcoat, his heart beating excitedly underneath the crisply dry-cleaned duds.

A string quartet quietly played near the dance floor, though thus far, the guests were more concerned with the open bar than the waltz. It happened more often than not at these gatherings. While he wasn't a fan of endless champagne, the booze often loosened purse strings. A fact the museum needed to exploit to continue their digs for additional Egyptian pharaohs.

His phone vibrated from his pocket. Checking the message, he shifted his weight. It was Maddy, informing him the board members had arrived at last. They were never early, presumably for appearance's sake. One last adjustment to his black bow tie and Callum set off down the stairs.

The short meeting with the rich and influential members went smoothly, a few pats on the back and handshakes before he lost them to the throng of art lovers. They were impressed and raved about the exhibit. *As they should.*

He moved toward the outskirts of the throng, not

eager to rub elbows unless duty called. A waft of chocolate brûlée greeted him, and his mind immediately returned to the night before with Londyn. She was gorgeous, not that he'd expected anything opposite. He let out a breath and fidgeted with his phone. Never had he experienced anything close to last night. A quick shag it was not—more along the lines of a combining of souls. He couldn't think of one woman who came close to the connection he shared with Londyn. She knew what he wanted even before he asked.

An image of her slender wrists tied together flashed through his mind. That had been around three in the morning. Sleep wasn't a commodity when Londyn lay beside him. His body wouldn't stop longing for her, and he was pleased that she mirrored his endless hunger. Oh, what fun he'd have with her. Every inch of Londyn's body deserved to be kissed, and he was more than ready to take up that challenge.

Maybe tonight we'll—

"Has your lady friend shown up yet?" Maddy asked, appearing at his side.

He coughed away the thoughts of the bedsheet tango not twelve hours earlier and the countless ways he wanted to claim Londyn. *Professional. Keep it professional.*

Eyeing her, he smiled. She didn't resemble a scientist tonight, with a flowing red gown and her hair all done up.

"Not yet. With three ladies attending, it'll take three

times longer, I assume." He took a glass of champagne from a passing waiter. "I'll be sure to introduce you, though, when she arrives. She's bringing the girls. A first for all of them."

Maddy took a sip from her fluted glass and choked on the bubbles. When she caught her breath, Callum saw the reason behind her esophageal malfunction. He was positive it was catching, since more throats sputtered on booze around them.

Standing at the top of the staircase was Londyn, even more beautiful than usual, if that was possible.

"Whoa," his coworker muttered. "Who's she?"

A smile spread over his face, and he handed his glass to her. "Londyn. She is Londyn." He set his feet moving before another word could be uttered. The urge to rub it in every man's face was obvious when he confidently strutted toward her. Not one person in the room was blind to the fact that Londyn was his.

Callum swore his heart stopped beating when he reached the base of the long stairwell. Dressed in a royal blue strapless work of art was Londyn Bellerose. On her left was Bethany in an emerald green designer number, Bailey in a light pink dress on her right.

"You all look absolutely gorgeous," he complimented, taking his daughters' hands and kissing them first before finishing with Londyn.

Bethany grinned while Bailey twirled her poofy skirts. "Look, Daddy, I'm wearing kitten heels. How fun are these? Just the name is fun." Bailey lifted her hem enough to prove her point. "Meow. I'm a kitten."

"Darling, those are fabulous," Callum said, winking at her. He was certain it was the first of many times that heels would be the focus of a conversation with the diva-in-training.

"Where's the food? I'm starving," Bethany asked, scanning the room skeptically. "You said there'd be food."

Callum chuckled and pointed to the waiters. "And there is. Anywhere you look, sweetheart."

"Oh, yum!" Bethany's blue eyes lit up, and she grabbed her sister's hand.

"Try not to break anything, *please*," he called after them, though neither looked back to heed his warning.

"You're very handsome tonight," Londyn noted, taking his hand. It was pure satin, just like the rest of her body. His chest puffed with pride at the beautiful woman on his arm. She drew glances left and right but didn't seem to notice. It was part of her allure and why she was perfect for him. She didn't strut around and look for attention; Londyn captured it by simply being herself.

There's nothing better.

"And what about every other night?" he teased.

She leaned over and lightly kissed his cheek. "Well, if I'm going off last night…." She let the rest linger, then added, "But honestly, you're handsome each night *and* day, so I think that answers your question."

He encircled her waist with his arm and pulled her close. "It does. And might I add, you're the loveliest lady here tonight." Her chocolate and cinnamon scent mingled with whatever hairspray the stylist used. If they had time to sneak off, he knew an office more than ready to christen. "But I can tell you more later," he said as Maddy approached. "Londyn, this is my colleague and chum, Madeline Jones."

Shaking the offered hand, Londyn smiled politely. "So nice to meet you. Have you worked with Callum long?"

The assistant curator nodded. "Longer than most."

"You've enjoyed it, don't lie." As he spoke, a buzzing sound met his ears. He patted his chest, but it wasn't him. "Love, is that your phone?"

Gripping the small purse he hadn't even noticed, Londyn blushed. It perfectly matched the red shade of her lips. "Oh, it's Abi. I need to take this." She apologized, then made a beeline for the corridor outside.

Watching her walk away was just as impressive. Her small heels clicked quietly, and the sway of her hips pulled several male heads in her direction. He wasn't one for fashion, but the way the gown hugged every delightful curve of her body should've been a sin.

"She's quite pretty," Maddy remarked, pulling his gaze from Londyn's plump behind.

He nodded in agreement. "Yes, and she's brilliant as well."

Maddy snorted and mumbled under her breath before making an excuse and leaving him.

During Londyn's absence, Callum managed to shake a few hands, charm potential donors, and check on his daughters. They'd found a small group of children and were getting along famously.

When twenty minutes passed, his stomach balled into a giant knot, so he went in search of his missing date. When he stepped out into the warm evening, he immediately saw her. She paced slowly, the phone clutched to her ear.If he wasn't worried about what had caught her attention so thoroughly, he'd simply stay there and watch the gently sway of the gown and listen to the rustle of the wind through the leaves.

"Okay, well tell them I'll give them an answer tomorrow," she said.

His heart plunged into his stomach as he took in her animated eyes and giddy smile. Already he wished she hadn't taken the call. Whatever spell he hoped the night would create broke the instant she'd answered it.

"Good news?" he asked after she hung up.

Londyn twirled around, the hem swishing softly. She resembled a modern Cinderella in the masterpiece, and her hair was too perfect to be real. But it was. Everything about Londyn was real. Including the joy on her face.

"As it turns out, yes." She clasped his hands. "Broadway accepted my play. I mean, it's Off-Broadway at first to see how it goes, but it's Broadway nevertheless!"

A sack of rocks might as well have landed on his gut. He couldn't breathe. "Oh?"

"I can't believe it. Talk about a dream come true. Broadway, Off-Broadway, I don't care. It's incredible. Oh my God, how amazing is this? The director actually went to my apartment, but obviously I wasn't there. I need to call them in the morning to discuss everything." She sighed happily and swiped a thumb across her phone. "But that means I'll need to go to New York to help out the directors and actors…"

She kept going, but he wasn't listening anymore. Her cheerfulness would soon be his demise.

"That's fantastic news," he congratulated when she finished. "I'm so proud of you." He wished it was more lively, but he couldn't stomach it. Not when his mind fast-forwarded to what it meant for him. For them.

She squeezed his hands, compelling him to look up from her dress. "I won't have to leave for a while yet."

He nodded, though the act felt more robotic than smooth. "But when you do, it'll be for months at a time."

As the reality sank in, her smile faded. "I suppose so, but I can fly back on weekends and such. The flight won't be as long from New York."

"Mmhmm." He untangled his hands and took a step backward. "You need to do what's best for your career and for you. I completely understand." He cleared his throat. "It's going to make things here more difficult."

"Why? The girls are used to you traveling the world for work." Her eyes narrowed. "And you'd expect me to be all right with your continued flouncing, so what's the difference? I'd be home when I could, same as you."

Callum's palms began to sweat. Nightmares from the last time a woman went off and chased her dreams dredged up the longer Londyn spoke. "This is a lot to process."

"Yes, but I'm not turning down Broadway." She moved until his eyes clashed with hers. "Broadway, Callum. As in the best place for any writer to be. If you had the chance to study under the best artists in the world, you'd do it without argument. That's what I'm doing."

More apparitions circled his mind, a panic attack threatening to surface. He needed to get away for a minute and clear his head. "I, uh… I need to head back in there. Busy night for schmoozing new donors."

Once she dipped her head, he practically raced inside. The moment he entered the spirited room, he mentally kicked himself. This was Londyn's career break, and he was raining on it by feeling sorry for how it'd affect his life.

I'm being stupid. She deserves this. He swallowed his pride and inhaled. *Apologize. I need to apologize.*

Turning around, he realized his mistake too late when she was no longer on the veranda.

Dammit, man, now you've done it.

He did his best not to panic, but with his heart and mind racing, it was a losing battle. *She's not Jessica. She won't run.* Navigating the crowd, he didn't bother returning the greetings from his fellow museum pals. He was on a mission to find a woman.

Breaking through the horde, he audibly gasped at the sight before his eyes and his shoes glued to the floor.

She was not the woman he was searching for.

***

The day had started out perfectly. Callum had tenderly kissed her until she woke with a smile on her face. That was how she wanted each morning to begin and each day to end. With Callum. After avoiding responsibilities for as long as possible, he'd left her, but not before thoroughly reminding her of his adoration. Multiple times, in fact. From there, how could a woman not be in a good mood? A night full of steamy and sweet sex followed by a morning of more of the same. It was perfect.

Too perfect, it seemed.

Now, hours later, emotions sifted through Londyn's mind more than the filters in a model's selfies. Stomping up the stairwell, she winced when her ankle turned. "Damn heels. This is why I don't wear you," she grumbled.

The new Egyptian collection loomed ahead, and since she didn't want to face Callum or his friends quite yet, she decided to take a stroll into history. Hieroglyphs met her gaze upon approach, the unique combination of pictures and symbols making her think of the artwork Bailey painted last week. The girl had talent and her life was only beginning.

A frown clouded her face. *Damn, I'm going to miss her.*

She moved around an elderly couple debating the techniques used to excavate the site. A large vase with a doglike head stood out from behind thick glass. It was stunning, as were all the pieces scattered tastefully along the exhibit room. *He did this.* It was one thing for Callum to speak animatedly about his work, but seeing it was a whole different matter. *He really is amazing.*

Peering at a gold ring with a green gem on top, she regretted running off. It was immature, and what his ex-girlfriend did years ago; her heart ached at the thought. It was his worst fear, and she'd given him a reminder of the pain because she was pissed at how he reacted.

Damn, Londyn, you screwed up.

She checked her phone, then stuffed it away when no message from Callum shone back at her.

Circling a glass column with a cat statue inside, she bit the inside of her cheek. "I should be excited, right? This is huge. He just doesn't get it," she said to the artifact, then scoffed. "I'm talking to a piece of art."

Laughter floated from the party the floor below. Others steered around the exhibits, admiring the art long lost to the desert. A couple butted in front of her to ogle an oversized bowl etched in symbols. In that moment, she missed Callum's comforting presence and light aura. He'd be showing off his knowledge about the piece if he was beside her. This was his life, even if she didn't get excited about it. *Maybe I'm being too hard on him.*

The blue gown she wore now ideally matched her mood. It'd been enough to make her jaw drop when she saw it earlier in the day. It appeared Callum knew fashion as well as art—the designer gown was top-of-the-line and fit her to perfection. *Just like him.*

She brushed at the loose curls from where they were bunched on her left shoulder. Enough was enough. She needed to talk to him, to talk out their situation instead of letting it fester and boil to destroy them both.

The main exhibit from the dig was the last she reviewed. Queen Nefertiti was stunning if the bust of her held true to her form. A short description of the pharaoh's wife sat nearby, and she scanned the contents. It was exactly as Callum said: the woman was strong, bold, and possessed fearless beauty no matter her foe. The underlying love story of the queen and her husband, King Akhenaten, made her smile. They'd shared a deep and inseparable love, according to Dr. Archer. It was exactly what she wanted from life.

And Callum is it. I need to go to him.

Londyn swallowed hard. She needed to find him in order to reiterate precisely what she wanted. *Who* she wanted.

She left the room and peered down at the happy

mass below. Bethany danced with a curly haired boy while Bailey stuck her tongue out and pretended to gag. No matter what happened, she'd miss the two redheads when she returned to New York. *But I'll be back*, she promised, moving to the back stairwell.

Arguing between a couple became louder the closer she got to the bottom. From the sounds of it, an American woman and a British man bickering about children. Londyn tried to silence her heels in order to avoid the duo engrossed in heated conversation. As she took the last step, two bodies came into view and her legs froze.

"Callum, I love you and our girls. Please don't do this," she pleaded. "Not again."

"No, Jessica. You had your chance and you royally fucked it up for everyone. You mean nothing to me or the girls. Your rights were terminated. I've moved on, and so should you."

Jessica laughed and tossed a lock of straight red hair over her bony shoulder. The black gown fit her like a seductive glove. Londyn understood now why Callum described her as an adult version of the girls. The redhead was petite like them and barely tall enough to ride a roller coaster. *She's gorgeous. And short.* A combination she'd seen before when it came to the men in her life and their exes who swooped in like vultures.

"Have you, Cal?" Jessica asked.

"Yes, actually. I'm happy," he argued, his face red with frustration. "And you should know I've already called for security."

Silently, Londyn cheered him on. So far he was every inch the gentleman she knew and loved.

"Fine. You think you're happy, but does she awaken every naughty desire you have?" Jessica's voice lowered to a sultry tone, and alarm bells went off in Londyn's mind. Her hands snaked up his torso, her body all but hugging his. "Does she kiss you like this?"

Londyn should've moved, screamed, yelled even, but all she could do was stare while another woman passionately kissed her man.

Her heart veered to the closest cliff and nosedived. She could hear the explosion rattle her heart loose from her rib cage when Jessica clasped the back of his head and kissed him hard. From her spot, it didn't look like he fought the hold either.

Fuck my life. History repeated in front of her eyes. This time around, the knife went clean through. Londyn's mouth dropped open, and she was worried her eyes would bulge out of their sockets. *He has to have some feelings leftover for her. He's too perfect otherwise.*

Her hands quaked as she took the final step to the floor. Watching them ripped out her heart and put it through a blender, but she couldn't look away. She needed this betrayal forever ingrained in her mind when she was weak and missing him. She'd think of this moment when Chinese food was cold, the chocolate box empty, and the chick flick blared on the television.

"Son of a bitch." She didn't realize she'd said the words aloud until Callum broke free, his face red.

"What the hell, Jessica? You can't go around kissing people. Especially ones who don't want it." He glowered at the redhead, but she only smiled. The scene would've been better if his lips weren't smeared with pink lipstick. Then and there, Londyn she swore to never wear that horrid shade ever again.

His gaze shifted to her and his face went from angry to embarrassed. "Londyn." He pushed Jessica's hand away. "It's not what it looks like. I can explain."

"Her? This is the jolly blue giant who stole you from me?" Jessica jeered with a bitchy glare. "She looks like she's fresh off a farm."

"Call me all the names you want, but you should look at yourself first." Swallowing her resentment for Callum, Londyn stepped up to the redhead and scowled down her nose at her. The height difference really brought it home for her. "You're the world's worst mom. I wish we could ban you from the United States, because we're better than what you did to those beautiful girls. You don't deserve an iota of happiness after what you put them through." Jessica's eyes flashed rage, so Londyn kept going before she lost her nerve. "Stay the hell away from all three of them, or I'll show you just how much of a badass farm girl I can truly be."

Finished with her hollow threat, Londyn offered Jessica an equally bitchy smirk, then turned on her toes.

Callum stood to the side, his eyes forlorn and guilty, yet a smidgen of pride shone through. Jessica fled as if burned, leaving them alone. Forever, if she knew what was good for her.

"Londyn—"

She held up her hand and shook her head in disgust. She didn't want to be right about him, but she was. "Don't. I can't believe I listened to you. You obviously have some kind of feelings for her. I mean, why else would she show up here? Tonight." Tears pricked her eyes. "I was a fool to fall for you." She moved a foot, but his hand on her arm stopped her.

"Please, wait," he begged. "It didn't mean anything."

Londyn glared at him. "That's not what it looked like from my point of view."

Callum's hands swept through his hair. "I know. I know."

It wasn't the time or place, but she needed to air her concerns. "You don't want me to go to New York, do you?"

"Well no, but—"

"I knew it." A tear broke free from her dam and trickled down her cheek. "I can't trust you. In one moment you say you love me, and the next you freak out about my play being on Broadway." She motioned to his mouth. It still held remnants of pink lipstick. "And then you kiss your ex-girlfriend. Your very attractive ex."

"I didn't kiss—" Callum wiped his lips with the

back of his hand. "I'm not going to make excuses here because we're both adults and I don't love her—"

"So you're okay if other women kiss you just because they can?" she scoffed. "Great. That's not what I want in a man."

Callum gripped her shoulders and forced her to look into his eyes. It hurt to meet the sincere brown depths. "You're putting words in my mouth."

"Oh, I'm sorry. Did you want someone else's tongue instead?" She couldn't stop the bitchiness if she tried, and she really didn't want to. Her heart was in millions of tiny pieces thanks to him. She jutted her chin toward a nearby blonde. "Maybe the cute waitress over there will suit your fancy."

"Dammit, Londyn, stop. Just stop." He gently shook her. "I love you. Not Jessica, not anyone else. And you're who I want to be with. To kiss every day. To love. I don't want anyone else." His eyes searched hers with sincerity. "You have to believe me."

"Do I?"

He sighed and his brows furrowed. "No. I guess not." His shoulders sagged in defeat. "But it'll break my heart if you don't."

Londyn steadied her breathing, on the cusp of falling apart. "Then maybe you'll know how I feel right now." The instant the words escaped, she hated them. She broke free from his hold. "Goodbye, Dr. Archer. I wish you all the best."

His brown eyes slid shut and he held still for a

moment before opening them again. The eyes she once couldn't go a day without seeing held unshed tears.

It was all too much for her, so she escaped to the swarm of socialites. She was running. Yes, running again. It was what she did best. She ran from Iowa, she ran from New York, and now she was running from Callum. It made sense to her brain, but not her heart. A fact she wanted to dissuade, yet wouldn't allow herself to do.

A broken heart to end the summer. Just my luck.

CHAPTER FIFTEEN

The constant tick of the wall clock echoed in the room, meticulously wearing at Callum's resolve to get anything done that day. Each time the hand moved, it signified another second Londyn was out of his life for good.

Thus far, two months had passed since she'd disappeared in the middle of the night, wearing a dress befitting a fairy-tale princess. The irony was not lost to him. At least Londyn had the better sense to leave Bethany and Bailey a recorded video message about why she left—minus the adult issues—and how much she'd miss them. Not once did she reference him or her feelings toward him, but she did invite the girls to her Off-Broadway production. The girls, not him. That wasn't lost in translation either. It was blatant and yet another sword to his soul.

The New York newspaper to his left sat unread and mocking him. Theodore had brought in the section of upcoming theater shows. Evidently *Rampant Thoughts* by Londyn Bellerose was one "not to be missed," as his old friend put it. The play opened in less than a week, and nary a word had been heard from the woman who'd penned it. The same could be said from him as well. He didn't try to make contact despite Theodore insisting. He'd said his piece and she'd ignored him. A second round of rejection would be unfathomable to his feeble heart.

The full agenda of tasks for the next day stared at him from the computer screen, the desire to do any of it sorely lacking. It had been ever since she left. He'd taken on longer and more trips to cope, but none of the work dented the pain. It only made it worse when he came home and smelled the light scent of chocolate and cinnamon on his pillow. He couldn't bring himself to have it washed; having a sliver of Londyn was better than none, even if his judgment told him otherwise.

The old basset hound at his feet stretched and yawned, then went back to sleep on his plush dog bed. If Callum could be half as satisfied as Sherlock, he'd gladly trade lives.

Bethany was currently slaughtering "Canon in D" on the piano down the hall in the music room. Had he the motivation, he'd get up and close the door to appease his bleeding ears. Paying hundreds of dollars to the instructor and still having a daughter who lacked was appalling, but he didn't give a shit. His mother was the one who demanded the girls learn musical instruments. He'd rather them paint.

Sherlock's ears perked up when Bailey appeared in his door. "Daddy, are we going to Londyn's play?" she asked with a sweet smile. Climbing on the leather seat across from his desk, she spread out a letter.

He let out a sigh. "Um, no, my dear, we're not."

She scrunched her little nose and shoved the paper at him. "But she misses us. She says so herself."

That got his attention. "She wrote to you?" He snatched the neatly penned note. "Is this the first one?"

"Nope. She sends one to Bethany and me every week." The girl grabbed the paperweight off his desk and gazed into the frozen bubbles. "Doesn't she write to you?"

"No." Callum skimmed the contents of the letter. He hadn't expected Londyn to keep in contact, but then again, she was always doing her own thing. It was an admirable quality, even if it drove him batty.

"Oh, well do you write to her?" she asked.

"No again." He wasn't fond of the constant questions when they dealt with a woman he already couldn't get out of his mind.

Bailey's bottom lip quivered. "Don't you love her?"

The innocent question made him look up into his daughter's concerned blue eyes. Somehow she'd climbed on his desk and sat in front of him all while he'd read Londyn's words.

"I'm afraid it's not as simple as that, Bailey." He handed her the letter. "Things between Londyn and me are complicated."

Bailey twisted her hair around her pinky finger. "But you love her, right? I saw the two of you kiss."

Callum held up a hand to correct the faulty association of love and kissing, but she kept going.

"Plus I heard her talk to Abi about you." The little girl giggled. "She didn't think I could hear, but I did. She should've whispered."

"What? When?" While he didn't condone eavesdropping, he needed to hear something positive about Londyn.

Bailey shrugged and wrapped his red tie around her small hand as if it were a bandage. "I don't know. It was like last week when we Skyped."

Callum pushed aside the fact that his girls somehow got their grimy paws on a phone to video chat with her. *Theodore, no doubt.* He focused on the girl now nearly choking him by accident with the tie. "What did they say?"

"I don't remember." She nodded to the dog nearby. "I was playing with Sherlock during that part, but she said your name."

He did his best not to let his face fall, but disappointment doused him. "Oh."

"Her friend asked Londyn if she loved you," Bethany stated, joining them. Apparently she was through with her rehearsing for the day.

Callum tried to keep calm. For all he knew, the stunning playwright cursed his name. "And her response?"

Bethany sat cross-legged on a chair. "Londyn said you drove her mad, but somehow she loved you anyway."

A rush of adrenaline coursed through his veins. Though this was secondhand, there had to be some truth to it. "Really?"

"Yep." Bethany tapped her chin. "And there was something about you being the Atkin to her Nefritie" Her brows knit in puzzlement. "What's that mean?"

She remembered the story I told her. He licked his lips, heart already lighter. It was a legend, but the most romantic one he knew. He'd told her months before, but somehow she didn't forget. Any of it.

Well, neither did he.

Feeling a new burst of hope, he stood. "It's Akhenaten and Nefertiti." He kissed Bailey's head, then hugged Bethany. Both wore puzzled expressions, so he explained, "It means she still thinks about me and hasn't given up." He grabbed his jacket from the coatrack. "At least I hope so."

"What're you going to do?" Bailey asked, now standing by her sister.

Callum dialed a number on his cell phone, his stomach rolling with excited nervousness. "I'm going to do precisely what I promised her I'd do."

He wasn't sure if it was the worst misuse of airline

miles or the best waste of time. He'd figure it out once his feet hit New York pavement.

***

Whoever told her there was no business like show business had a knuckle sandwich coming their way. Londyn fell onto the pillowtop and stared at the ceiling. Ever since her arrival from England, it'd been nonstop theater productions. She'd met with the Off-Broadway executives and firmed up her deal. That was before auditions squeaked out and rewrites to the script were done the very same week. It was a whirlwind of activity, and she almost loved every minute of it.

In honesty, she felt bad for not being around as much. She came home and was immediately engulfed in all things theater. Still, the highlight of her return was tossing a flyer for the play at Blake. Her ex's face blanched, and no words bubbled up from the usually chatty Italian playboy. It was catty, immature, and vile, but she deserved the satisfaction after what he'd done to her and the play she'd helped write.

Oreo meowed loudly and jumped on her belly. She patted his head while he walked in a circle until he deemed her stomach comfy enough to lie down on. Thanks to her lucrative summer job, she'd quit the coffee shop for good and been running on fumes for the last two months.

Londyn stopped her fingers under Oreo's chin.

"Wow. Two months already. Crazy, right, Oreo?" The cat bit her finger in protest to her words and not actions.

The little downtime she had was spent amid chocolate wrappers, Chinese takeout boxes, and never-ending chick flicks. Despite her efforts, not one of them helped ease the ache caused by leaving Callum. In fact, her go-to Cs made her think of him that much more. *He really did destroy my fixes*, she mourned. The truth made her repeat them until she was numb. Nothing helped, nothing soothed. Nothing was Callum.

"Hey, I thought I heard you. You're in late," Abi said from the bathroom. She sank into the spot beside Londyn and the pair eyed the ceiling speckled with water damage. "How was rehearsal?"

"Good. Great, actually. I think we'll be ready for the opening in a couple days." Londyn sighed and closed her eyes. "The director is fabulous, and the leads are really jiving." She turned her head and flicked her gaze to Abi. "You're still coming on Thursday night, aren't you?"

"Opening night? Yep. Already got my ticket." She stole Oreo from her roommate's stomach. "I tried to get this dick one too, but I guess you're too classy for animal fans now," she teased. "If we were in Queens, they would've sold me one."

Londyn laughed. "Hey, I'm all for whatever sells tickets."

"Are you nervous?" Abi asked.

"Hell yes. It's nerve-racking. What if it flops?

What if the critics hate it and my name is tainted forever by this catastrophe?" Her gut rolled at all the different ways her life could change depending on how the play was received. There were pros, but also plenty of cons to worry over until the reviews were read.

"Damn, girl, calm down. You have a few days to tweak the play." Abi yawned. "Plus, you knew being Off-Broadway was a risk. If you do well, there's the possibility of Broadway. And if you suck, there's still Off-Off-Broadway before you even have to consider returning to Queens."

She snorted. "Yeah, that's not happening ever again."

"There's always London," her friend reminded her softly. "I hear they have a nice theater."

Londyn opted out of replying to the sly remark. The thought had crossed her mind more than once since arriving back in New York.

A train whizzed by the window, pausing their conversation until it'd passed.

"Did you finish those curtains for the last scene? The props manager asked about them," Londyn asked when she could compose her thoughts again.

Abi bobbed her head. "Had them sent over by courier an hour ago." She grinned. "Thanks for getting me the gig. I'm really meshing with the wardrobe director. I think it could be a full-time thing if it goes well."

Londyn squeezed her friend's hand. She deserved it, and when the opportunity came up, Abi was the first and only person she'd recommended for the job. "Happy to help. After all you've done for me, it's the least I can do."

Oreo sneezed and then promptly jumped to his cat tower. They watched his fat body teeter at the top. "One of these days he's going to break it," she noted, and they both giggled.

"Look, I know you said you didn't want to talk to him, but have you?" Abi asked quietly.

Taking a slow breath, she kept her eyes glued to the ceiling. "No." Thinking back to the night of the gala, Londyn's pulse quickened. It was all going swimmingly until she answered the phone call. The scene on the patio and then inside solidified it for her. Hell, Theodore even drove her back to Archer Manor and helped her pack.

The hastily put-together bag was interesting to unpack. Every article of clothing was wrinkled and smelled like Callum. A horrible combination for her distraught mind. She'd never admit it, but somehow one of his shirts made it home with her. Currently, it was under her pillow for those times when smelling his cologne was the single way to fall asleep.

Tucking her secret away, Londyn focused on that night. She couldn't leave without saying goodbye. At least not to the girls. Theodore recorded her short video and promised to show them in the morning. She swore to never be like their mother, but her words paled to what she wanted to say. History repeated itself that night for her, but she didn't let it happen for Bailey and Bethany. They deserved better than even her video message.

The pain on Callum's face flooded her memory. Her heart hurt just recalling the anguish scrawled across his handsome features. That alone made her almost take back her words and fling herself into his arms. Almost.

I should've left him a note. His ex-girlfriend did the kind courtesy, but she couldn't. Instead, she'd shoved down her feelings and caught the next flight to New York. Showing up at the break of dawn sure gave Abi a scare, but at least she'd had the good sense to bring chocolate donuts.

"Earth to Londyn."

She blinked rapidly, freeing her brain of the past. "Sorry. What'd you say?"

"Well, I asked if you still thought about Callum, but your far-off eyes answered the question." She propped up on her elbow and poked her friend's arm. "Why didn't you call him? Skype, maybe? Hell, I bet he'd take an email or text."

"I'm sure he would, but it's not in the cards. He's probably with his pretty ex-girlfriend who's all wrong for him." She punched her fluffy pillow when the visual of Callum kissing Jessica resurfaced. "I don't need him. I have my play."

"Hmm, you're right. You don't need him." Abi tilted her neck to the left, almond-colored eyes curious. "But you want him, and I don't mean in bed." She fanned herself dramatically. "From the little you told me, I want him too. I mean, I saw those pics. He's a fine piece of—"

"Okay, I'm—" Londyn started to get up, but her roommate pulled her back down to the bed.

"But you want him in the 'let's settle down and have stupidly gorgeous kids' type of way," Abi pointed out with a smile.

"It's not happening, Abs. Leave it be."

Abi moped and tossed a pillow at her. "Hell no, I won't leave it be. You're acting like a cotton-headed ninny muggins." Londyn tried not to smile at the movie reference, so she matched her friend's glower as she kept speaking. "Yeah, he was a dumbass and kissed his ex. Guys are morons sometimes, but what'd he do right after that? Huh, Londyn? What'd he say?"

Londyn attempted to swallow back the memory but it rushed forward with a vengeance. Her eyes misted when the words tumbled free. "That he didn't want anyone but me."

"And?"

"And that he loved me." She cast her eyes to the worn carpet. "Damn. Saying it out loud makes me seem like a complete immature bitch." Snatching a pillow, she hugged it. "Shit, I'm the worst. I can't believe I said that stuff to him. I'm the very definition of a lost cause. I just threw him away like he didn't mean anything." Her eyes widened and she ran her hands through her hair. "Oh my God. How could I do that? He's perfect.

Callum is literally the most perfect guy out there. For me, at least."

Abi giggled. "Praise Jesus! You aren't as blonde as I thought."

"But it's been two months. Sixty long days." She crossed her arms over her chest, despair trickling into her cheery disposition. "No. It's too late. Plus I have to stay here and make sure the play doesn't implode. I can't just fly to England and beg him to forgive me for being a bitch."

Abi grabbed Londyn's phone and handed it to her. "Call him. If he doesn't answer, leave a message. And if his voice mail is full, text that big, beautiful, blond Brit."

Londyn's stomach jolted in fear as she gnawed on her bottom lip. "Are you sure?"

Abi touched the screen. "Dial, girlfriend."

Taking a deep breath, Londyn hit Callum's number from the list of contacts. "Straight to voice mail." She listened another moment. "And it's not set up, of course."

"Text him," Abi prodded.

"Calm down, I'll get there."

"Yeah, when I'm fifty."

Londyn ignored the jab and typed a short text.

Londyn: Can we talk?

She held it up for her friend to examine. "See? Message sent. Now can I go to bed? I'm beat."

Abi's grin widened and she crawled into her bed

five feet away. "Yay! And yes, you've earned some rest. Send him a nude and I'll even throw in a gourmet breakfast."

Rolling her eyes, Londyn flicked off the light and climbed under the covers. However Callum took the text, she'd have to face reality.

Either he'll want to talk, or he'll ignore me.

She deserved the latter, but her heart prayed she wasn't wiped from his memory. He sure as hell wasn't gone from hers.

***

Londyn stuffed the last bite of chocolate croissant into her mouth and walked to the stage with an energy drink in hand. The orchestra was already in place and played a warm-up ditty. If Saturday night was anything like Thursday and Friday, she was in store for another happy crowd.

The makeup artists waved as she weaved through the obstacles of backstage. No matter how many days she was there, it felt like the first time every night. The theater had always been part of her life, and now she was just as much its heartbeat. Props rolled here and there, readying for the opening curtain.

The initial reviews were in and raved of her brilliance. Her aunt was due to visit next week to celebrate the preliminary highs while Abi popped the first corkscrew Thursday night. She tentatively rejoiced in the reviews, but they weren't who she wanted to hear from when it came to her play. She wouldn't admit it out loud, but she craved Callum's thoughts on the production.

Checking behind the curtain, she frowned. The lack of bodies in the audience disturbed her. On the other nights, people trickled in slowly and not all at once. Catching sight of the woman in charge of tickets, she flagged her down.

"Hey, are we starting at a different time tonight?" she asked.

The woman typing on her phone didn't even glance up. "Nope. Same time."

Londyn glanced around the room, worry gnawing her gut. "Then why isn't anyone here yet?"

"Oh, that. I forgot to tell you." A whoosh sound signified a sent message and she met Londyn's gaze. "The theater is sold out."

"Sold out? What do you mean?" Her heart thudded at the words every playwright wanted to hear.

"I mean somebody bought every open ticket for their viewing pleasure." She swiped her thumb across the iPhone screen. "Probably a celebrity of some kind. They like their privacy, you know?"

No matter how many times she thought the words, Londyn couldn't digest them. "Seriously? Is it common for Off-Broadway shows?"

The brunette nodded. "When the play's good, yeah. Way to go, Miss Bellerose. Let's keep it going, and you'll be on Broadway's big stage before spring."

Left alone again, Londyn racked her mind. She couldn't think of any major or minor celebrity in New York who might be interested in her work.

Shrugging it off, she checked her phone. No response from Callum yet. Her resilience waned as more days went by without contact.

As tempting as reaching out again was, the option was quickly vetoed by Abi. "He could be overseas or in a meeting. Give him time" was what her best friend had said.

If he wanted to talk, he'd make the next move.

She shoved the phone into her back pocket. *Well, he better hurry up.*

Deciding to check in with Abi, she navigated the maze of doors and hallways. She'd sit out the first two acts with her friend, then watch the last part of the third act with the director. Being present for the entire play only made her anxious, so after the first night, she changed up the routine. "Abs, guess what?"

The dark-haired beauty whipped up her head from the stitch in her hands. "What?"

"Somebody bought out the theater," she said excitedly.

"What? No way." Abi raised her brows in question. "You're pulling my leg, aren't you?"

Londyn straddled a folding chair and sat on it backward. "Not at all. The PR chick just told me. How exciting, right? It's probably some movie star."

Abi snorted. "Or a rich perv who likes sexy love stories."

She shook her head. "I don't know, Abi. I've got a great feeling about tonight." She popped a piece of chocolate in her mouth and rubbed her belly. "Right here."

"Yeah, that's a symptom of too much sugar. When I left this morning, your face was covered in cocoa powder from your cereal. Did you snort the stuff?" Abi stood and hung up the newly fixed shirt. "Have you eaten anything healthy today? Or any day, for that matter? Chinese and chocolate is all I've seen you eat since you got back from England."

Londyn tapped her index fingers together. "Hmm, I had chocolate puffs for first breakfast, a chocolate croissant for second breakfast, a chocolate bar, a hot dog from the stand outside—"

Abi shook her head in disappointment. "Dear Lord, how are you even alive after all that junk?"

She tapped her chin. "Oh, and a coffee about ten minutes ago."

"Double-shot espresso?" her friend guessed.

"How'd you know?"

Abi laughed. "Just a hunch. You get all jittery and shit after too many sweets and caffeine." She pointed to the energy drink. "Plus there's that. You really need to cut down or you'll go into a sugar coma. Have you been to the gym lately? Because after all that junk food, you're going to regret not going."

Londyn shrugged. She couldn't focus on eating healthy or exercising. The play was her obsession, and whatever food she ate—or didn't—had nothing to do with Callum. *I think.* She pushed aside the wayward thought.

"C'mon, let's do something with your hair while we wait on this mystery guest," Abi suggested, holding up a brush.

Three hours later, Londyn peeked out from behind the red curtain as the last scene unfolded. Fear initially seized her during intermission when she couldn't spot anyone in the audience. The theater maintained the dark atmosphere, making her squinting ridiculous. Her nerves jumped here and there as the sugar tapered out of her system. She needed a refill of something to maintain the buzz.

"And you're sure somebody's watching and we're not performing to empty seats?" she asked for the third time.

The public relations director nodded. "I'm sure. He checked in up front. Calm down. The guy's probably back a few rows so the actors can't see who it is." She waved as she walked away. "It isn't uncommon for famous people. See you tomorrow."

Londyn's worry didn't disappear at the reassuring words, her fingers fretfully rubbing together. She'd have to go out there and bow. It's what the director told her when he'd found out the place was sold out by one person. She still wasn't confident about it. Sure, it was her work of art, but coming face-to-face with the man she now dubbed her biggest fan tattered her nerves.

The swell of the last note rang clear, and she held her breath. She'd never felt like throwing up on stage before right then. The theater had been her sacred ground since high school, but that night it felt more like a haunted forest.

God, I hope it's not a pervy guy like Abi said.

Smoothing her jeans and shirt, she waited until the cast bowed before she emerged from backstage. Walking into the bright spotlights, she squinted. Once her eyes adjusted to the beams, she caught sight of flowers in front of the orchestra. *Were they there before?* She couldn't remember.

After a quick bow, she held up her hand to shield her gaze. Another pot of sunflowers was near the steps, more popping into view as she followed the line of cheery yellow buds.

What the hell?

She scanned the expanse frantically. No one was sitting in the red theater seats.

Heart racing at the possibilities circling her mind, she stepped to the end of the stage. Either she had a stalker who knew her favorite flower—which was impossible because she rarely told anyone—or… she couldn't dare to hope the alternative.

The tech guys in the back let the lights fade around her until a floodlight hit her fast and a shaky voice met her ears from the left. "Londyn."

Timidly, she turned toward the British lilt that

repeated in her head every night. Surely this wasn't real. "Callum, what're—" He held up a hand. "God, he looks perfect," she thought, then groaned when she realized she'd said it out loud. Her tongue had no filter around him. It never did.

He bit back a smile at her slip. "Let me get this out, please."

Londyn slammed her mouth shut and pinched her arm to make certain she wasn't hallucinating. She had consumed an enormous amount of sweets and caffeine that day, after all. *Ouch.* No, he was real. Very real in his denim jeans, green button-up shirt, and dark khaki suitcoat. She held in a smirk at his green and gold tie. He looked too good to be true. Professor vibe and all.

"I had this long, flowery speech I wrote on the plane, but when I got to New York, it didn't seem like enough." He waved his arms to the sunflowers. "So I went with actual flowers instead." He inched toward her, his speed wary yet confident. "Each one of these is for every moment I thought about you since you left." He chuckled and scratched his neck. "And if you can't tell already, it happened quite a lot." He stopped three feet from her. "A whole hell of a lot."

Gazing around the theater, she spotted flowers lining every aisle and each chair. If that wasn't enough, the balcony was filled with yellow dots. They even sat on the steps up to the stage. Already she was overwhelmed, and he'd only started talking. Thinking back, she was impressed that he remembered her favorite flower. It'd been a passing statement, one she didn't expect him to ever care to remember.

Breathing shallowly, Londyn realized what he'd done that night, and she fought back the ugliest of cries. He'd kept his word and bought out her show just like he'd said—despite the words being sarcastic when originally uttered.

"I may have bought out a few stores in the process, but it's worth it." His brown eyes met hers, and she tried to hold the tears at bay when she saw the emotions filling them. But it was no use. They flowed like a leaky hose. "You're worth all this and so much more."

Londyn saw bodies from the corner of her eyes and her face heated. They were the main attraction now, and the impromptu encore held as much mystery as the man now beside her. The same man she'd doubted she'd ever see again.

"I'm sorry," she whispered, suddenly hoarse. "I shouldn't have left like that. It was stupid."

Callum nodded, a smile playing on those kissable lips. "No, you shouldn't have, but you're forgiven." He captured her hand with his warm one. "And I hope I am too."

"Callum, I—"

"Hush, woman, I'm trying to be romantic here," he said, and an eruption of chuckles resounded around them.

She pressed her free hand against her mouth to keep from breaking his concentration once more.

"I'm sorry, Londyn. I'm sorry for thinking about myself instead of you. It's something I aim to correct immediately." His gaze shifted to her hand. "I hope you'll give me the opportunity, because I'm so in love with every part of you that I'm afraid I'll wake up and realize this was all a dream." His hands were suddenly on either side of her cheeks, nose nearly touching hers. "That you are the best dream I could ever conjure, and it was all in my imagination."

Tears slid down her cheeks, and he tenderly wiped them away as he searched her face. "But as I stand here, smelling your addictive chocolate and cinnamon essence, and touching you, I know it's not. Because if it were a dream, I'd have already kissed you. And you'd swear to never leave me again."

Sniffles echoed through the onlooking thespians, mirroring the epic shattering of her resolve. She parted her lips to speak, but he chose that moment to drop to one knee.

"Marry me, Londyn." He squeezed her hand. "I promise I'll do everything possible to show you on a daily basis how much you mean to me."

Shivers ran up and down her spine when he finished, his light brown eyes studying her hopefully. A pin could've dropped in the back of the giant theater and been heard perfectly from their position.

Heart thudding against her ribs, Londyn gasped when a ring appeared in his outstretched fingers. It was worthy of a royal, but she didn't care about any of the pomp. What she did care about was the man kneeling in front of her. The man she couldn't imagine living another day without.

"Oh my God, say something or I will," Abi yelled frantically.

Laughing, Londyn winked at her friend and then nodded. "Yes. Yes, I'll marry you."

Callum swooped her off her feet at the last word. Shoes flinging to the stage, she pressed her lips against his once the world stopped spinning. Cheers rang out from the company as Callum slipped the ring on her finger.

It fit perfectly. Just like him.

CHAPTER SIXTEEN

Two Years Later

Nothing could dampen the day. The sun was shining, birds twittered outside the windows, and nary a cloud lined the blue skies.

"He's missing," Abi announced, eyes wide.

Except that.

Londyn paused the cherry lipstick from connecting with her lips. "What? He's missing? How is he missing?" She stood and paced the marble floor of the Corinthia Hotel in London.

Abi caught her breath. "I really need to start working out again." She patted her chest, eyes sliding over to the champagne. "This should help."

"Abs, where is Callum?" She propped her hands against the lace on her hips. The Caroline Castigliano gown was one-of-a-kind. She was reminded of that whenever her skin touched the silk overlaid with floral lace.

"Theodore said Callum was with him one minute and gone the next." She glanced to the mirror and smoothed her disheveled hair. "I mean, damn. I'd think his best man would know his whereabouts, but evidently not."

Running her palms against the lace, Londyn peered out the window. This wasn't like Callum, but if Abi was already three drinks in, Theodore probably was too. Their track record of miscommunicating during the last month in England was now legendary. Most likely, her fiancé wasn't missing, but had told his best man exactly where he was going and it fell on deaf ears.

She shook a finger. "He better get his ass here or—"

"Or what? You'll finally tell him about—" Abi jumped in.

"About what? Do you have a secret?" Bethany asked, entering the suite. Her little sister followed hot on her heels.

"Nothing," Londyn and Abi said simultaneously.

Bailey gasped when her eyes ran over Londyn's gown. She rushed over to the woman who'd soon be her mother and gave her a giant hug. "Whoa, you look so pretty," she cooed, delicately tracing the lace.

Londyn leaned down and kissed her cheek. "Thanks, sweetie. You look very beautiful too." She glanced to Bethany, who wore a matching charcoal-gray dress.

"You both do."

"Have either of you seen your dad lately?" Abi asked, sipping straight from the champagne bottle now.

"Not since this morning," Bethany replied, playing on her phone. The whole growing up thing was still difficult for Londyn to accept for the eight-year-old.

Panic began to filter through Londyn's body. Stabilizing herself against a chair, she took a deep, slow breath. *Surely he isn't doing this. He isn't standing me up, right?* Holding her stomach, she closed her eyes.

"Great news, I found him," Theodore shouted, bursting into the room. Bethany and Bailey shrieked at the loud intrusion, and he grinned sheepishly. "Oops, sorry." He wrapped an arm around the girls' shoulders. "He was outside this whole time. Man, I swear he did it on purpose."

Londyn opened her eyes and shot blue-gray daggers at the man she saw more as a brother.

"Seriously?" Abi said, punching his arm lightly. "She was starting to freak out."

"Shit, I'm sorry, Londyn." Theodore swept a hand over the back of his neck. "He slipped outside when I wasn't looking."

"I'm fine. Don't worry about it," she replied with a small smile.

Theodore and Abi went round and round arguing before they left the room with the girls in tow. If they didn't both prefer men, they'd make a cute couple.

Relaxing at the knowledge that her fiancé was

actually getting a breath of air instead of hightailing it to Scotland, Londyn let out a shaky exhale. The last two years were full of ups and downs. Though her play failed to catch Broadway's love, the Queen's Theater in London captured *Rampant Thoughts* instead.

Standing on her tiptoes, she caught sight of the top of the theater she called home. Since then, two more of her plays had debuted on the polished stage. It appeared her scripts were a better hit with Brits than Americans. Much like her luck with men.

I always knew I was in the wrong country.

Sliding her silver heels on, Londyn took one last look around the room. She'd leave it single and come back married. "About damn time."

Despite the adjustment to living with a man full-time, she wouldn't trade her time with Callum, Bethany, and Bailey for Broadway. They were her world now, and leaving wasn't an option. *Ever.* Even if Callum tended to snore during the springtime.

She smirked at the thought. They sparred like an old married couple but made up like lovestruck teenagers. Each day that passed, she grew more infatuated with her British lover. No, he wouldn't leave her today— their wedding day—or any other day. Her moment of doubt was shameful, and she blamed it entirely on the recent lack of sleep, stress, and hormones.

Mary Archer's voice drifted from down the hall, but Londyn didn't bother to let it worry her. Her soon-to-be mother-in-law had gone through a metamorphosis over the last two years. Though the new man in her life may have had something to do with the drastic change. Sure, the woman still lived in part of Archer Manor, but she was more of a grandmother these days than a strict manipulator of all things fun.

Every now and then, Londyn would help out at the Archer Chocolatery in London. She was positive her attention to the factory helped build the bridge to Mary as well. It wasn't like she ever wanted to run out of chocolate. Especially free chocolate.

Her phone dinged, and she checked the message. Aunt Glenda and Uncle Stew were downstairs waiting impatiently for the ceremony to begin. It came as no surprise to Londyn when her aunt told her the good news. Glenda deserved all the happiness in the world. By sheer luck, they'd both found it the same summer. It was a short three months neither woman would ever forget.

"Londyn, darling, can I come in?"

Her stomach jumped at the sound of her fiancé's voice. "Callum?"

"Yeah, it's me." He cracked open the door and peeked inside.

Londyn hustled behind a tall chair so only her hair and eyes were visible. "What're you doing? You know the superstition—"

Callum kept his gaze steady with hers. "Sod superstition. Can I come in?"

"Fine, but don't look at me. It's supposed to be a surprise." She held in a giggle. Honestly she didn't give a damn, but she'd spent a wad of cash on the gown, and she wanted to see his reaction in front of their entire family.

His tone softened. "I heard Theodore and Abi gave you a scare. I wanted to make sure you're all right." He stepped into the room with a hand over his eyes. It was adorable as he blindly batted at his surroundings with his other arm.

He was adorable. *And he's all mine.*

"I'm perfect now." She walked over and pressed a kiss to his lips.

"I really want to open my eyes and see you," he murmured between kisses. "Because if you look as good as you smell, we'll be late to our own wedding."

Londyn kissed the side of his neck, his scent sending tingles down to her perfectly manicured toes. She'd missed him. His job having taken him around the globe for the last month, all she wanted to do was kiss him all night long when he'd arrived two days ago. "Whose idea was it to sleep in separate bedrooms again?"

Callum caught her bottom lip between his teeth, not once opening his eyes. "Yours."

Tracing his smooth jaw with her index finger, she kissed him again. "Damn, that was a stupid idea."

He chuckled. "I don't know. I rather liked it when you suggested it. Though I can assure you it's not happening again." He nuzzled her neck. "You're mine, Londyn Bellerose, and I'm never letting you go."

Londyn studied his face. Even without seeing his

eyes, she was positive they were sincere beneath his long lashes. "Good, because neither am I."

"Hey, Londyn, we need to head—" Abi walked into the room and paused. "Geez, I leave for two minutes and you're making out."

"Give me another minute, and then I'm all yours."

Once her maid of honor left, Londyn grabbed Callum's hands. "I have a confession."

"Oh?"

She nodded. "I'm afraid you're going to have to share me."

"With whom?" he asked, face curious.

She placed his hands on her stomach. Instantly his eyelids snapped open and caramel-colored eyes searched her face.

"I have a confession too," he whispered.

Her eyebrows rose. "Oh, do you?"

"Yes." He gently rubbed her still-flat stomach. "I knew, and I couldn't be more thrilled."

Londyn laughed. "What? You knew? How? When?"

Callum looked down at her waist, a grin playing his handsome face. "My dear, when you turned down seconds on your favorite chocolate tart, I knew something was wrong." He kissed her temple. "If there's one thing I've learned, you and your chocolate addiction aren't to be trifled with unless there's good reason."

Pressing her forehead against his, she sighed. No man understood her like him. No man supported her dreams like this Brit. No other man was perfect for her. No other man was Callum.

"I love you, Callum Archer."

His lips lightly met hers. "And I love you, Londyn soon-to-be Archer." His eyes glanced over her dress hungrily. "Will you marry me now so I can kiss every inch of what's under that gorgeous gown?"

Blushing, she nodded. "I'll marry you any day of the week."

Callum opened the door and blew her a kiss. "Today will do just fine, Londyn. I'll use the other days to make you fall even more in love with me."

She leaned against the handle. "I look forward to it, Dr. Archer."

His eyes darkened and he looked longingly over her exquisite form. "The next time I see you, Miss Bellerose, you're going to take my breath away— just like the first time I met you—so if I can't speak, you'll know why." He kissed the top of her hand, then disappeared down the hall.

Londyn pressed her lips together, watching him retreat. He was the guy every girl dreamed of. Looks, brains, and a heart of solid gold. The British accent didn't hurt things either. She never thought her summer in Colorado would lead to her falling for her very own Prince Charming.

She didn't need her three Cs anymore. She had something better: a family.

Then again, maybe I do have three Cs. Callum,

children, and chocolate. She grinned. *You can't take chocolate from a girl.*

Touching her curls, she nodded. Nothing was better than Callum and chocolate, but that was another story entirely.

Checking her reflection, she touched up her lipstick that had smeared during the five minutes with her fiancé. She'd lost her heart during her summer abroad, and like in a fairytale, Londyn was positive they'd live the happiest of ever afters.

Just like in those chick flicks Callum replaced.

Thanks for reading *Hearts Abroad*. I do hope you enjoyed Londyn and Callum's story. I appreciate your help in spreading the word, including telling a friend. Before you go, it would mean so much to me if you would take a few minutes to write a review and share how you feel about my story so others may find my work. Reviews really do help readers find books. Please leave a review on your favorite book site.

Don't miss out on New Releases, Exclusive Giveaways and much more!

Join my newsletter:
WWW.SKYEMCNEIL.COM

Like me on Facebook:
WWW.FACEBOOK.COM/SKYESTHELIMITWRITING

Join my reader group:
WWW.FACEBOOK.COM/GROUPS/287389708375366

Follow me on Twitter:
WWW.TWITTER.COM/Skye_McNeil7

Follow me on Pinterest:
WWW.PINTEREST.COM/SKYEMCNEIL

Follow me on Goodreads:
WWW.GOODREADS.COM/SKYEMCNEIL

Follow me on Instagram:
WWW.INSTAGRAM.COM/MCNEILSKYE

Visit my website for my current booklist:
WWW.SKYEMCNEIL.COM

I love to hear from you directly, too. Please feel free to email me at SKYESTHELIMITMCNEIL@GMAIL.COM or check out my website WWW.SKYEMCNEIL.COM for updates.

ACKNOWLEDGMENTS

I can't say thank you enough to my incredible publisher, Hot Tree Publishing, and the editors, beta readers, cover designers, and support team who make each story a work of art.

Thank you National Novel Writing Month (NaNoWriMo) for making me write a novel in a month. Starbucks also thanks you for my purchases.

ABOUT THE PUBLISHER

Hot Tree Publishing opened its doors in 2015 with an aspiration to bring quality fiction to the world of readers. With the initial focus on romance and a wide spread of romance subgenres, we have since opened Tangled Tree Publishing, our crime, thriller, and suspense imprint.

Firmly seated in the industry as a leading editing provider to independent authors and small publishing houses, Hot Tree Publishing is the sister company to Hot Tree Editing, founded in 2012. Having established in-house editing and promotions, plus having a well-respected market presence, Hot Tree Publishing endeavors to be a leader in bringing quality stories to the world of readers.

Interested in discovering more amazing reads brought to you by Hot Tree Publishing? Head over to the website for information:

WWW.HOTTREEPUBLISHING.COM

www.ingramcontent.com/pod-product-compliance
Lightning Source LLC
Chambersburg PA
CBHW051631180726
48284CB00006B/1690